RELATIVELY NORMA

NORMA

by
Anna Livia

Published by Onlywomen Press Ltd.
38 Mount Pleasant, London WC1X 0AP

Cover design by Cath Jackson

Typesetting by Dark Moon, 114 Coldharbour Lane, London
SE5 9PZ.
Cover printed in Great Britain by Chromocraft Ltd., Shep-
perton, Middx.
Printed in Great Britain by Redwood Burn Ltd., Trowbridge,
and bound by Pegasus Bookbinding, Melksham.

ISBN 0 906500 10 9

For me, Trista and Qwerty

Acknowledgements

Thanks to Carley and Moira for their help with the first draft, to my Writers' Group for reading it through and to Elaine and Cath for their work as editors.

Anna Livia was born in Dublin in 1955 and spent her childhood in Africa. She went to seven different schools including a boys' boarding school in the Swazi mountains and studied French and Italian at university. She has taught French and English at the University of Avignon, conducted the 41 bus from Tottenham Hale to Archway and dressed cabaret artistes at The Talk of the Town. She is currently an unemployed lesbian feminist and lives in a communal house in Stockwell with four bathrooms. She spends her time writing or biting her nails and has frequent dinner engagements to discuss humour with her Women and Language group. She has chosen not to have a cat, is not fond of plants and has never been to the States.

CONTENTS

It's quite a thrill for me
Being here with you
It's such a trip for me
So this is reality
I've been studying every movement
I've even talked to a Spart
Now I want you to be natural
Just relax and be as you are
For the sake of Marx and the revolution

I'm moving in with Norma
I'm going to make her a star
So I'm chucking away Das Kapital
And I'll shop in Bankstown Square
For the sake of Marx and the revolution
And the ordinary woman

I'm making observations
Character simulations
I'll mix with her friends and relations
And she'll be a part of me
I'm moving in with Norma
To get background for my book
I'm immortalising her life
I'm eating her onions and tripe
For the sake of Marx and the revolution
And the ordinary woman
I'm going to bed with the ordinary woman

The things I've done for the movement
The things I've done for Marx
I'll make these sacrifices
And take it like a star
For the sake of Marx and the revolution
And the ordinary woman

(first heard at a feminist conference in Sydney and recorded
from the oral tradition.)

Chapter 1
Brixton to Balga

When Minnie opened her eyes and took her hands down from her face, she found herself sitting hunched up at the bottom of the wardrobe, arms hugging her knees. The phone was still ringing. Ting, ting. Ting, ting.

— Oh no, not again! she thought. Why was it that every time the phone rang, rather than simply answer it like normal people, or disguise her voice and say,

— No, I'm afraid I'm not here, she immediately leapt for the cupboard?

Sighing heavily, she creaked to her feet. The ringing had stopped. She went back to her paperwork. The sheet in front of her read so far:—

— I am not a man
— I am not a mother
— I am not very big
— I am not Australian

It was no good, try as she might, she could not get any further. She could not think of any other categories into which she might but failed to fit. In desperation she leafed through the odd assortment of concert tickets, school exercise books and bad passionate poems stashed away in her nostalgia box. She laid her very own "Loser's Guide to Successful Suicide" on the table in front of her.

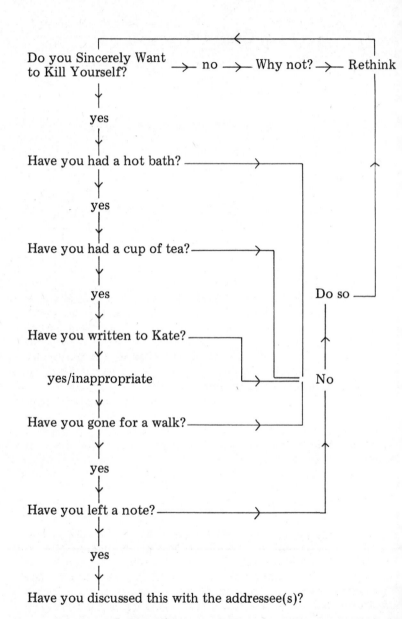

Do you Sincerely Want to Kill Yourself? → no → Why not? → Rethink

↓ yes

Have you had a hot bath? →

↓ yes

Have you had a cup of tea? →

↓ yes

Have you written to Kate?

yes/inappropriate →

Have you gone for a walk? →

↓ yes

Have you left a note? →

↓ yes

Have you discussed this with the addressee(s)?

Do so →

No

She had only ever got as far as discussing her potential suicide with the potential addressee of a potential suicide note.

— Look, if you want to cop out, Minnie, you can, Kate had said, but don't lay it on me.

What made the guide so successful was that if you did manage to reach the end of the diagram still feeling you wanted to eat worms, then you were probably right to go ahead. Minnie's problem was that she was never quite sure who the "you" in the question was addressed to. She could tell from their behaviour that other people recognised themselves as this "you" who spoke and ate and had opinions, but hard though she tried, she could never quite coincide with the "I" she held at arms length and who claimed to be her. After years of searching she had given up on the "real her" and called this other "Milly". They could have been made for each other. Milly was adept at being whoever anyone else wanted her to be. Minnie would draw people out and get them talking about themselves, their jobs, their preferences, and Milly would obligingly correspond with their vision of the world. Inevitably the speaker would suggest that Minnie too would make an admirable Sunday school teacher, midwife or even, hesitantly as the young woman's sex was something of a stumbling block, a bricklayer.

— My little Minnie's a bullet-headed fury, her mother used to say, and Minnie was awash with a feeling of boiled egg fullness. She always knew who she was with her mother.

— Now, I want all the girls to line up on my left and the boys on my right, Miss Nomer had said on Min's first day at school.

— Minnie, dear, come away from the fish pond, you'll get your pretty dress wet.

Minnie had felt mortified and confused. Whoever heard of a bullet wearing a dress? As she grew older, the contradictions got worse. Her mother would write her sick notes saying,

— I'm sorry Minnie wasn't at school today, but she was feeling green and weepy.

Minnie would turn up the next day doing her best to look convalescent, still a little grassy round the gills, but the teacher would ask,

— What exactly was wrong with you?

9

— Ting, ting. Ting, ting.

Like a trained rat, Minnie jumped for the wardrobe. The phone gave no visual clues to tell you who to be or how to answer.

— Minnie, Pho o one . . .

— I know it's the blasted phone, swore Minnie through clenched teeth (her knees were pulled up under her jaw, rendering speech difficult). Why does Kate think I'm sitting here in the dark?

— It's the travel agent. He says all flights are booked out till January. You can't go.

Minnie's plan to see her mother in Australia for a life-giving draught of "who she really was" had been watered down through her indecision between Christmas on the beach with her family and an anti-festive nut roast at home with the others. However, the agent's resounding negative goaded her into action. She could hear his slimey smile. She flew down the stairs and ten minutes later had booked a flight on a complicated but successful mixture of Thai, Malaysian and Garuda. Her cool mastery of the dreaded telephone, now that she was on the dialling end, surprised her, but she put it down to Milly's hidden talents. Finally she phoned the agent and told him to confirm her booking as he had her money. He said he'd phone back. As she thought about this smug slug, the trip began to feel like an exercise in mind over matter. The crunch came on the return call.

— Oh, hello, Miss Débar? Yes, well we've cancelled your booking, dear. You would have had to pay in Australian dollars, you know and that would have cost £10 more.

Minnie paused to draw breath; now that she was actually engaged in battle with this infernal machine, it didn't seem nearly so frightening. Milly would have been confused between pathetic helplessness and middle class arrogance, for Minnie something hit the roof.

— Listen to me you stupid bastard. I am going to Australia, I am leaving next Tuesday and I am staying one month. If I am still in London on the seventh, something very nasty is going to happen to your balls.

It was the first time she had yelled this last word over the telephone, but she hoped malignantly that it wouldn't be the last.

And thus it was that she found herself on a plane bound

for Perth. Beryl was her mother, and no-one but no-one but her own apathy was going to stand between them. Perhaps her early clash with the travel agent should have warned her that Australia wasn't meant to be easy. As it was, she felt guilty at being a feminist with enough money to fly half way round the world. It took four days to reach Perth, not a miracle of speed even in these inflationary times. She spent the day in Bangkok, rather surprised that it could be so hot and light in one part of the world, when she happened to know it was cold and damp in another. In K.L.* she tele-grammed her mother to meet her at the airport, confident that maternal delight would more than compensate Beryl for any inconvenience, and in Perth she stepped down from the plane exclaiming, like other first time Australians, at the warmth of the night. Then she tore across the runway, shoved her way through passport control, grabbed her rucksack before anyone else and charged, first through the gates.

— There's my little Minnie, said her mother's voice, sound-ing surprised, though she must have been waiting an hour, eyes trained for the first glimpse.

— Mum, mum, yelled Minnie, and people smiled sympa-thetically as she hurled herself forward, knocking them over with her rucksack, and threw herself round her mother's neck.

Her sisters were delighted with her and, though dubious about her short hair and pasty skin, were willing to attribute both to the British climate.

— Gosh, my first impressions of Australia, thought Minnie, trying to concentrate, but the girls kept jabbering about hairdressing and boyfriends and Beryl kept turning round in the front seat to look at her daughter and make sure she was really there.

— This is the Causeway, said John from the driver's seat, that's the Swan Brewery over there with the lights, and that's King's Park.

Minnie realised with a start that all these places were perfectly familiar to her mother, that this was in fact her mother's home.

— Beautiful downtown Balga, the girls sang out as the taxi drew up the drive. They danced all over the house (which mum assured her was quite uncharacteristic now they were

11

so grown up), showing her the laundry room, the colour television and the outdoor swimming pool, tokens of the new Australian affluence. In London Mum had had two gas rings and no hot water so Min didn't care what anyone said, Australia was a good place to be.

— Ingrid, Laura, bed, her mother said firmly, when they had eaten all the soda cake they could fit in their mouths. Ingrid malingered over another slice to take to bed with her. Beryl turned to her,

— Stand not upon the order of your going.

— But go at once, Minnie finished, eyes moist with memories.

Beryl smiled,

— Coming for a swim?

So Minnie and her mother slipped naked into the pool at 5 o'clock in the morning. As she swished about in the warm darkness Minnie felt the weight of the rucksack she had carted round K.L.* leave her shoulders along with other more metaphysical worries. Next day she slept blissfully, and awoke to the exotic demands of jet lag and culture shock. She became curious as to where the darkness had cast her up and ventured outside to look at the brick-red new home units only recently reclaimed from the bush. On one side were great black boys and banksia and an old weather board house with veranda and rain barrel, just like her mother's pictures. On the other was a new concrete open-plan shopping centre where you went to the chemist for stamps and cheques and the deli people had the key to the tennis courts on the reserve. Minnie still felt like an outsider observing objects of sociological interest.

In the evening of this strange new day, where even the light lasted longer than in England, Ingrid's boyfriend, John, came round in his panel van. This was where he and Ingrid slept if he was staying over.

— The two of them went "parking" one night in the conventional way, Beryl explained, her eyes sparkling indulgent complicity, but the police moved them on three times so they ended up ignominiously in the front yard.

Ingrid wasn't sure how she felt about this open discussion of her sex life and changed the subject,

— Now John's here, let's go see "My Brilliant Career" at the Windsor.

12

* Kuala Lumpur (Ed.)

The new wealth did not yet stretch to a car and the outer suburbs were notoriously bereft of public transport. Sandra, Mrs-over-the-road, had offered to sell them her Kingswood (her most prized possession) due to the curious poverty of the new home owner, but for the moment the whole family relied on the girls' boyfriends for mobility.

It was a jolly party that set out; sensing that they would not appreciate each others' thoughts, they kept companionable silence as so many families do. Ingrid was wondering what her big sister thought of her boyfriend, caught between pleasure that they seemed to get on so well — Minnie would always show an interest in an engine and could sound quite knowledgeable about fibre glass — and a vague sense of jealousy that her sister saw more in her boyfriend than she herself did. He was a dear sweet thing, always willing to do anything for anyone, but wasn't he just a little boring? She sneaked a look at big sister, but Min was lying on the mattress in the back, droning along to Joan Armatrading's "Me, Myself, I". Laura lay next to her, grateful for the breathing space ill afforded by her tight shiny black jeans. She was adding up how many more wage cheques she would need from Coles before she could buy her own car and musing that her foster mother had put much more effort into getting Ingrid her apprenticeship than she ever had into Laura, otherwise she'd be working in a kindy now, instead of bloody garden corner. Beryl, oblivious of the hunch of resentment stoked up next to her, was thinking how nice it was to have little Minnie home again and why didn't she stay in Perth and marry a tame Aussie. Perhaps if she introduced her to lovely John from work ... She had resented the telegram from Malaysia and the consequent flurry and panic. Why Minnie could not have phoned from London instead of all this laborious spontaneity ... Beryl was rather afraid of her eldest daughter's tongue (but then, she found all three of them a bit of a strain) and avoided argument as she had always done with her first husband, by drifting off into her favourite thought, which began "I have made a garden where things grow ... " She saw herself back in Balham, staring out over the steaming sink, into the little flower bed beyond, and comforting herself with the thought that he could not violate this part of her, because he didn't know it existed. The little poem, if that's what it was, made more sense in

Australia where she had transplanted her youngest daughter to give her the carefree warmth and expanding economy she now wished for the elder. She did not wonder what would have become of Laura if they had not come to Perth, as such questions were out of line with her determinism. She had come, she had had to come, and Laura had come to live with them. Now she need only put a little pressure on Min, and she would stay as well. Children needed a push in the right direction, nothing too obvious or they would opinionate and that was tedious. Take Ingrid's friend, Wendy, for example; nothing personal, but Beryl hadn't liked her choice in boyfriends. She was sure they took heroin and stole cars, (she was probably right), and had gently persuaded her daughter that Wendy just wasn't very interesting.

The film was sentimental, but like a true family film, it had something in it for everyone. John Boyfriend cried because Sybilla would not marry the handsome Englishman. She looked so like Ingrid, didn't they agree? Ingrid was thinking that she could act like that too if she could be bothered, and reached for another Opal Fruit. Laura reckoned that if other chicks could make a film, she bloody well could, and anyway it would be better than working at Coles. Beryl felt the more first rate films that came out of her country of adoption the better, because it would prove her right. She was a very patriotic migrant; the government could find no fault with her if it tried. At the back of her mind was always the fear that this irrational, masculine institution might one day send her back to her husband. It was like an unfathomable god which must continually be appeased by offerings of gratitude. Minnie was still looking around slightly dazed, beaming at everyone and everything. She had slotted cheerfully back into her old place as Beryl's daughter and Ingrid's sister, putting the intervening six years and London expectations on ice.

When she heard her sister was coming out, Ingrid, nine years her junior, had become silent and watchful. In the old days, Minnie had shared her room and, when offering the same facility again, Ingrid worried lest her sister treat her batik paintings in the same cavalier fashion she had treated her old pre-raphaelite posters. Minnie had breezed in and covered them (not bothering to take them down) with political stuff in ugly colours and unsubtle form. But Ingrid

14

loved her elder sister and wrote to her religiously of every change of boyfriend. Left to herself, Ingrid would sit on a beach towel, eat, and have nice thoughts. Men would think about her late at night when in bed with other women. Her women friends were attracted by her serene confidence that the world needed her and would do its best to look after her. Minnie was not serene, she was small, square and angry. Sometimes Ingrid admired her for being so clever but mostly she was content to let her big sister make her laugh and paint pictures of impossible men who would not yield in their own interest, and of women more furious even than big sister Min.

For Laura, Minnie was more of a problem. Try as she would, she could not quite get the idea out of her head that Minnie would supplant her in Beryl's affections, or that Minnie would be jealous that she had supplanted her. She watched apprehensively as Min hurtled through the airport gates, cheered that she was not at all pretty but worried as to what her friends would make of her new sister's hair cut. Years of being parcelled around from one children's home to another had given her an unholy fear of any change whatever. When Beryl had moved out to the suburbs, Laura had been as edgy as a cat and insisted on decorating her room just as it was in the old place. During the actual drive in solemn procession behind the removal van, she had kept her head tucked tightly beneath her paws and had been so useless and miserable at stowing crockery that Beryl packed her off to a friend's for the weekend. And now they were asking her to welcome this newcomer into the house, like a long lost sister. But Laura was not all dread, a lot of her was curious to see how Min would turn out and even hopeful that she might cause some excitement that Laura could watch from a place of safety.

Beryl, unequivocally, wanted Min to settle down but knew, at the same time, that it was safe to want this because Min never would. Beryl would joke with her terror of London, saying she would go back for Min's wedding (as the most unlikely event she could think of). Min would joke with her own legendary stinginess and add that in that case she would pay her mother's fare. Beryl felt her big daughter was really on her own two feet now and looked forward to the time when the younger ones went their own way too, so that she could get on and explore this new country of which she had so far seen no more than a tantalising morsel. She could feel herself greedy for discovery, wanting to go to all the places that made even dinky di Aussies shudder in horror at the heat: Marble Bar, Lake Woods, Cooktown. Not Sydney or Melbourne, hadn't she lived too long in London to inhabit its satellite suburbs? Of course, John would come too, because this was his country, his most valuable wedding present to her, and he would be delighted at the opportunity to explore it with her.

It wasn't until the third day, then, that Minnie began to realise that her position in the world could not be entirely determined by her mother. She had been rushed around the city sights and country zones, her mind was laden with Australian place names: Gnangara, Herdsman, Floreat, but now they had come to rest in front of the telly in the family room. Ingrid was getting changed to go out and Beryl was absently putting Laura's Abba records back into their covers with half an ear on the teeve. The programme was Countdown, Australian for "Top of the Pops", and Minnie was groaning at the inanity of the d.j.

— But Min, said Beryl, wondering if "double album" meant you had two record sleeves to look for, it's John Muzak, Perth's number one self-confessed poofta, your protected species. You can't attack him.

— Poofta is he? asked John Boyfriend, this was his speciality, if you like we could go for a cruise round town, there's a toilet near the uni where you can watch the pooftas going in and out.

— Oh, leave them alone, Minnie sighed, the nearest she could get to liberal boredom.

Once started, however, there was a constant stream to remind her that there were certain positions which she did not wish to occupy. At the library next day, she and her mother wandered contentedly round the shelves occasionally muttering,

— Middlemarch, oh marvellous marvellous, or

— Mum, haven't you read that already?

— Yes, but you know how I love a Victorian murderess. Until they reached Anthologies and Beryl pointed to The Lesbian Reader.

— Get that, Minnie, just your sort of thing.

— It's ok, I can get it at home. They both knew "I've already read it" would have been nearer the mark, but Minnie suspected her mother of wanting a filial confession so that she could choose from her list of reactions. Would it be:

— Oh, Minnie, I'm SO sorry, or

— But you promised, or simply

— Well, you'll have separate beds in my house, thank you very much.

Things might have continued unchanged as Minnie got into the role of daughter with something to hide but who hides it very well and her family accepted her as an honorary heterosexual, still asking questions like what she did about birth control, if it hadn't been for Laura's little sister, Moira. Moira was just who Laura would have been if Beryl hadn't saved her from the Home Front. Beryl's determinism obviously deterred her from really thinking this, just as her socialism forbade her the use of the word "save" in this context. There existed, nevertheless, a confusion of the two girls into one, due to the similarity in their names, and they looked so alike that only the oppressive glint of Moira's steel tooth brace prevented a serious faux pas. There were four such little girls, seriated in age and size, whom Irene, their mother, alternately looked after lavishly and dumped in the nearest Home. They were originally from Scotland, which meant there were now no relatives to take the girls in when Irene couldn't cope. When still a believer, the League of Catholic Women would come round to help her out, afterwards there was the social services, but neither could get on with their job without patronising questions about the state of her soul or her "sense of maternal responsibility"; the former were simply shorter winded. Laura could remember a period of bliss which must have lasted about five years when her mother had a boyfriend who was into kids and they had an "uncle" who loved them and earned good money. All Laura's childhood stories, Beryl noticed, of being rushed to Perth with the flying doctor service, or family picnics on the front lawn because the car had broken down, seemed to date from that time.

Now Laura would look into the grasses on long walks with Beryl and ask were they going to pick some for the difficult weeks, knowing it was alright really, these people had three

17

square meals a day, every single day. Food had always been a problem. She didn't eat meat, which had been awkward in many of the Homes she had been in and caused countless rows with her mother. One Christmas Irene had spent all the welfare money on a gigantic ham, which was all they had to eat for weeks on end. Another time there had been no money for shoes for the girls (although Brisbane and Perth were officially hot enough for children to attend school barefoot, the social stigma remained) but Mum had spent the weekend at the Pavlova Hotel with a friend. The final straw seemed to have been Laura's atheism. The only Home left, to which the girls had not already been sent in their long career, was Catholic. Irene had been prepared to pretend, for the sake of having her home to herself again, to a religious sentiment she no longer felt. She had been furious to receive a phone call that very Sunday to the effect that "they" were very sorry, they were unable to keep dear Laura with them. She had refused to go to church and they were afraid for her influence on the younger children. Laura's mother collected her from the Home, threw her raggedy bags in the back of the car, and refused to speak to her all the way home. Laura was doing this to spite her; couldn't her daughter see that she just wanted to borrow her life back for a while, the way she longed for the long slim body that had been hers before she had had children? Let Laura wait till she was a mother, then she'd know. As they walked in the front door, Laura looked at Irene, trying to give voice to the speech which had formed itself in her mind, but all she could say was:—

— I'm not going to church, and I'm not going to eat meat.

That night she moved her things into the shed at the bottom of the garden where there was electricity and a hole in the door for her cat to climb through. When Beryl had gone round there, two years ago now, to collect Laura's things, she remarked,

— Laura's mother talks about her as if she was the lodger, complaining that she eats too much and keeps odd hours. What Irene thought about it all, Beryl never found out. Moira was still in the Home, eating meat and going to church, but had been spared the worst of her mother's excesses by asking to be made a Ward of the State. She asked to come to Beryl's on Christmas Day as all the aunties went home to

18

their own families and it wasn't right for a child to spend Christmas by herself. She might get into mischief or run away to Queensland and get arrested for hitch-hiking.

Moira arrived early in the morning, wearing very tight pink jeans, looking rather overwhelmed that everyone in the family had a present for her.

— But I don't know all these people, she whispered to Laura.

— It's alright, they're just into cosy Christmases.

Laura was the only chick in the world with any guts according to Moira, but why was she pissing around with these pommies? They'd dropped their own mother like a hot fucking brick, bloody liability she was. Still, while she was there, Moira felt she might as well root out any talent. Possibility of some action from the direction of Ingrid's boyfriend. Moira knew she was skinnier than her sister, if only she didn't have that bloody brace, made her feel like something out of Star Wars.

It seemed to Minnie that Moira punctuated everything she said with a little nervous giggle. Her movements were obscenely provocative, as though she felt sex was her only asset and no one could possibly be interested in her for anything else. The only time Minnie had seen her really enjoy herself was when they were in the pool together, racing each other, seeing how long they could stand on their hands or sit on the bottom. Beryl had found Moira having a little weep on Laura's bed and made sure to fill her full of brandivino. It made her much worse; she giggled and giggled and would not leave poor John alone. She was beginning to give Laura the woops.

The girls had bubble mixture in their stockings. Ingrid appeared with the bottles and they all jumped into the water while Stepfather blew bubbles for them to chase. Moira was at first reluctant.

— That man's still here. (She wasn't used to a man who lived in, the uncles mostly having come and gone as they pleased).

Everyone laughed.

— I'm not sure what to make of my husband being called "that man", Beryl smiled.

The afternoon waxed light and easy. Beryl got on with the washing up, once convinced that all her dependants were playing nicely together. Step grandma, unceremoniously referred to by everyone save Milly as Steppo, fell peacefully asleep. As she fished bits of greasy turkey and peas from the bottom of the sink, Beryl watched John blow an enormous bubble which Ingrid caught neatly on the end of a lolly stick.

— She's not usually so graceful, Beryl mused, perhaps it's because no-one's watching. Beryl felt almost like a disinterested observer watching a scene from family life. Moira had picked up another bottle of mixture. While the others were still shrieking with laughter and jumping up to burst bubbles, she clambered out of the pool and made her way over to Steppo's deck chair, a stream of buoyant sputtering rainbows following in her wake. The devastatingly naughty idea of holding the bubble stick over Steppo's mouth visited Moira and Beryl simultaneously, but Beryl felt paralysed to intervene. The older woman looked on powerlessly as Moira stretched out her arm and placed the stick gently in front of the snoring grandmother. The result was electric. Everyone froze as yes, very slowly Steppo exhaled, propelling a gigantic, beautifully formed bubble as she did so. And then Moira giggled. Beryl could have hit her, she was so annoyed by her own complicity as well as Moira's lack of self control. Of course, Steppo woke up with a start, trying to pretend she hadn't dozed off, and there was Moira standing over her with her dreadful metallic grin.

— Moira, dear, please let Winnie have her sleep in peace, said Beryl crisply, not above humiliating her mother-in-law to make her pay for her own embarassment.

— I wasn't asleep, just resting my eyes for a few seconds, muttered Winnie petulantly.

— Let's put the telly on, was Ingrid's bright suggestion, and we can all have another lump of christmas cake.

And that was how they came to be watching D.H. Lawrence's The Fox, on Christmas evening 198-, where two women fall in love under the pressure of close confinement and frozen wastes. When the women began to kiss each other, Moira, feeling herself still under reproach for her enormity, and anxious to show Boyfriend her orthodoxy in other areas, shrieked,

— Oh it's horrible, it's disgustin'! Two women kissing, I can't bear to look, and she hid her face in much the same way as Laura had in the car on Removal Day.

Minnie hadn't seen it coming. She had been lulled into a false sense of security by a full stomach, a wine fumed brain and the great gales of laughter that she, Laura and Ingrid had let off in the bedroom at the sight of Steppo's surprised face spattered by the enormous soap bubble. As the two women in the film turned towards each other, another scene forced its way in on her with naked insistence: Gerry's skin, very pale and soft as she kissed her for the last time. Moira's repulsion seemed to address itself to her directly, as though Moira too had seen that long neck, infinitely vulnerable as it turned away from her.

— No it's not disgusting, Minnie stormed, forgetting whcre she was, and probably waking Winnie a second time in a desperate attempt to protect other women: women kissing furtively in doorways or openly at the Sols Arms. She was trembling with fury and glared at Moira as if to scorch her. Moira still had her face in her hands and the others were glued to the box. Most of them did not mistake Minnie's tone but none wished to comment.

Presently Stepfather called a taxi, being too pissed to drive his own that night, and Moira was bundled off home again. In her pocket was a piece of cake for later that Ingrid had given her and in a bag beside her were all the presents she'd amassed. She still wasn't quite sober and knew she would be late getting in; to make the aunties feel sorry for her and to forget about the time, she burst into tears as soon as she arrived. They put it down to excess emotion and tucked her up in bed with a cup of cocoa (water not milk). Later she crept out again to be sick and tear her photo of Laura into shreds.

Chapter 2
Hay Street Mall And Freemantle

Minnie now felt like a leper, waiting for her disease to show so that her family would throw her out, not wanting to do the decent thing herself. Milly was of no use to her: she had not travelled half way round the world to lie to her mother. She had reached the point where she would not mention women friends by name, in case her mother thought "that's the one". Letters from Kate actually became a source of embarassment (instead of the humorous comfort they used to be: Kate bumbled her way from one crisis to the next), lest her mother realise how often she wrote. She was torn between reading bits out to show how harmless they were, and keeping the fact of their arrival a secret. Her head was a turmoil of yearning and fantasy about impossible women, while her speech became more and more reticent and neutered. She would speak of "the people I live with" or "someone from work", however innocent the association. As her mind was already filled with feminist alterations, replacing "girl" with "woman", the effort to replace "woman" with "person" reduced her to a stuttering wreck. It felt as though all the thoughts she was trying vainly to confine to her own mind must needs spill out and have their wicked way.

She would wander around Hay Street Mall in the centre of town, hungry for crowds, and wonder could they tell just by looking at her that she was a lesbian who hadn't told her mother. She sat so long on a bench in the Mall while a hippy played a didgeridoo that the tips of her ears got sunburnt. She gazed at the women passing by and, if they had short hair and dungarees, she liked to imagine they too were lesbians (they probably were, see police identikit). Then the Mall would empty and the women would sit around naked playing guitars and smoking dope, like in the old hippy days but without the swagger. Or else everything would continue as normal, women would be drinking tea or drifting in and

22

out of shops, but there wouldn't be any men around. She couldn't decide which image she preferred. She stared at a group of ocker tribesmen with their thongs, khaki shorts and tins of Swan, complete with pot bellies and hands on hips. They were shouting and yelling at each other but stopped to wolf whistle two women walking past; they grinned a lecherous grin from the sides of their mouth with a slurp of their tongue and a wink from the corner of their eye, followed up by a guffaw to each other. It was then that they noticed her staring at them. Menacingly they advanced in her direction, but as they approached, sneering and snarling, they vanished without trace, one after the other ... In their place were four women selling Rouge, while others were flocking to get their copy before it ran out.

— I'd like an extra copy for my neighbour, she's eighty-four and bed-ridden and can still remember the bad old days when men ran everything by electing themselves to committees and "lesbian" was a dirty word.

— Must ave been awful in them days, said a refugee from Bermondsey, bad enough when the Tories started the tiered womanhood system. You know, blacks and socially deprived women as breeders (sheltered workshop they called it) and the graduate girls as token men. That's when I come over ere.

— Is this the issue on twentieth century penetration myths?

— Yeah. Rather controversial, some people say it's carping on. Reminding men of what they've lost.

— Or suggesting they try and get it back.

— Have you read the article on artificial menstruation among adolescent boys? Apparently some of them actually die of it: cut themselves open once a month so they can bleed like normal people.

— That's dreadful. They shouldn't be ashamed of their bodies, poor things, men have their own unique contribution to make.

One of the sellers moved forward to where Minnie sat watching, enchanted.

— Would you like to make a contribution?

— What? she stammered, as the sunlight turned greyer, she began to feel the dry, tight itch of sunburn on her shoulders, and the noisy strutting presence of men reasserted itself in the Mall. It was like being invaded by small insects who insisted on ruling the world.

— To Rouge, you mean? Yes, yes, here you are. She glanced furtively around, realising the men had been there all the time but had not had to compensate for being men.

— Oh dear, she laughed at herself, let me give you my vision. I could have been Margaret Thatcher.

— Actually, I'll um have ten copies.

— That's more than I've sold all morning. You're not lining a carpet with them are you?

— No, Minnie grinned, I want to take some back with me to London. She was slowly regaining her composure and becoming the enterprising intercontinental traveller. Milly was impressed.

— How many have you sold?

— Fourteen, but ten of those are yours and we don't really count England in our sales figures.

— That's not very good.

— No, especially as it's New Year's Eve tomorrow and the streets are packed with people. Are you really from London? You must know Isis.

Minnie felt amused at the other woman's small-worldism; did she really imagine that two people would necessarily know one another just because both lived in London? It wasn't like the back of Woop-Woop. However, embarassingly enough, Minnie had to admit that actually she DID know Isis, perhaps this said something about the smallness of the international feminist scene.

— She's the one with the T shirt saying "Soc Femme" on one side, and "Soc Butch" on the other.

— Wow, do you mean that she's from W.A.?

— Yis, what's wrong with you women from London? I've heard there's a magazine for every ebb and flow of the movement, but you don't ever talk to each other.

— Come on Linda, we're going to Freo, should be easier to get rid of them down there. Much trendier; guilt pays.

— Where are you going? Wanna lift?

Now Minnie had heard of Freo as a close-knit, hairy place selling red henna and muesli, so when offered a lift she replied stoutly,

— It's a remarkable coincidence, but that's just where I was heading.

She trotted off behind them and slipped into the back of a very beat up Morris whose back door (the one that opened) she had to hold shut to prevent it swinging in the road. On her lap was a large pile of unsold Rouges, and her feet were propped up on a box of feminist literature. She began to feel at home.

— So, you're a friend of Isis, are you? Is she having lots of relationships?

Minnie did not quite know how to explain that you could "know" any number of women in London, without being a friend of any of them. She acknowledged the acquaintance, but regretted her knowledge was too slight to furnish the required details. Linda smiled to herself.

— Are you a lesbian? was the next question.

Minnie sighed, thinking back to a very pleasant evening she had spent with Laura, watching Star Wars II. Before the film they had strolled around town in the twilight hours between the shops closing and the cinemas opening, which West Australians use profitably by hanging around in the Mall watching each other walk up and down, rather like an Italian Sunday. It can be a very educational two hours when the intricacies of the latest fashions are exchanged between darting eyes and backward looks. It was here that Minnie was first introduced to the delights of banana smoothie. After the film, and missing the credits, they had rushed for the bus, worrying lest it stop short and leave them to walk along the bush road so late at night. In fact the bus had gone all the way to the terminus which was but a few hundred metres from where they lived. As they stepped down from the bus, a gang of grey shadows appeared, oozing out of the bush. The women leapt away and ran up the road. Perhaps they would have done wiser to play it cool, but patriarchy is not a well known nerve restorer. The young men noted Minnie's cropped hair, boiler suit and zipped jacket; Laura's peroxide blonde hair, high heels and strapless dress. One of the likely lads dashed across the road brandishing his stick and jeered,

— Are you a lesbian?

-- Yes, I am, Minnie answered shortly, only the last person to ask me that was a bloke with a stick in his hand.

— Stupid little sod, you should have told him to get knotted.

Minnie wasn't sure if she or the bloke was the "little sod"

being referred to, but then she was paranoid about anything to do with sexuality, especially hers. She remembered Laura's tense, frightened face, and how she hadn't dared hold her hand to calm her down for fear of provoking actual violence. They had walked slowly (almost respectfully) past the young man, the stick seemed to lend him dignity, he had his opinion and was entitled to ram it down anyone else's throat. Laura gripped her front door key in her hand, pathetic defence against attack. The policewoman who had lectured on rape at Hollywood High had recommended this method as more effective means might be taken for offensive weapons.

— You've flown from London to Perth for five weeks, the questioning continued, are you very rich?

Another sensitive spot, the woman couldn't have found it more unerringly if she'd been an acupuncturist.

— Not really, Minnie replied, but what I have I spend travelling.

It was an excuse like any other, but had at least the woman of the world mystique about it. By the time Minnie got out of the car to catch the bus back again, she had scored four addresses and an invitation to a New Year's party. As she reviewed the conversation she had just had in the car, she was dragged back to Manchester and her first meeting with Gerry: the same tension in the air, the same direct, hostile questions. But Minnie hadn't been convinced by the hostility, and had been excited by the directness. It had seemed they were playing a game of keeping each other interested.

— Pink boots! Flash git aren't you? S'pose you're from London come up to impress us.

Despite the disparaging tone, Minnie could not help feeling that Gerry *was* impressed.

— Why are you wearing black springs in your ears?

— If you're a lesbian feminist, what are you doing in a straight gay club?

Minnie adopted a veneer of sophistication she would have been hard put to back up, seeing as this was the first club she had been to in her life, but she was sure Gerry would not have believed her because Brixton spelt lesbian ghetto.

— How long have you been a lesbian?

— About the last five minutes.

— What happened then?

— I met you.

26

-- I'm the town heavy, you know.

— Thought Manchester was a city, still, if you say so.

Slowly the snooker table, the women with the billiard cues, faces flashing blue, green and red in the strobe lighting, the disco music and the rowdy gang of feminists trying to get members to sign them in faded from her eyes. She jumped on the bus, looked up from paying the driver and spotted Ingrid in the third seat back, staring vacantly out of the window. What on earth was her sister doing as far south as Freo, and why wasn't she already home?

That morning Beryl woke her at 7 am, as she did every morning. Ingrid reached for some water, careful not to wake her sister. Then she clambered over the sleeping hulk and put a pair of knickers on; she always put her knickers on before taking her nightie off, it seemed more decent that way. They were white, her knickers, they had to be white, that was the colour of her uniform and anything else would show through.

— The customers don't want to know what colour panties you're wearing; only that you've got some on, Johnny François would say, with a play of lewd innuendo.

— Don't know why he bothers, the scornful Simone would snide, everyone knows he's as queer as a coot.

Ingrid went out to the line to get her uniform, placidly ironing out the wrinkles and buttoning it up, starched collar and all. Every evening she or Beryl put it through the washing machine and let it dry overnight. It was in her contract. Johnny's was a good place to work, hundred per cent union shop, and at least she had a contract for God's sake, but he was french and very fussy. Constitutional, some said, couldn't help it. The girls weren't allowed to wear surgical gloves, looked too clinical, make the customers think there were poisons around; instead they had great ugly washing up types that you had to take off to do any fiddly things involving chemicals. Ingrid didn't object to the other rules particularly, like shaving her legs, using deodorant and showering once a day, but she did wonder why these things had to be so rigorously regulated if, as Johnny said,

— They're all just things you'd do anyway.

She'd had her hair done on the firm. They liked you to have it done there so that if customers admired it there was extra publicity for the shop, and of course it was a free hair cut for the girls. The wages were good, more than Laura earned at Coles and she'd have a trade at the end of four years, if she hadn't got bored and had babies by then. For the moment there were no signs of boredom: she got on fine with the others and the old ladies doted on her. Already some of them asked for her by name and they were always offering her their grandsons. So Ingrid trotted off to work more happy than not, most days.

— Perm waiting for you, Ingrid.

Ingrid glanced across as she took off her gloves. It was the Presbyterian lady. She sighed. The first time she had blue-rinsed the Presbyterian lady had been during her first few weeks when she was still very new and smiled at everyone all the time until her face ached and she wondered what to do with her mouth. She had been smiling away while briskly and efficiently preparing for the rinse, when the lady said,

— Stop grinning to yourself, dear, and listen. They have to do me backwards.

Ingrid gaped and protested,

— You have to do it forwards, otherwise you can't get at the hair at the nape of the neck.

— Ah yes, the old woman nodded wisely, but then I shall faint.

— Oh no, you might drown! yelped Ingrid in terror.

The lady stared at her indignantly.

— My dear young girl, I was the lady's champion three years running in Brisbane in the thirties and my grand-daughter was the only woman life saver during the great rip at Bondi. I do not intend to end my days blowing bubbles in two inches of soapy water at the hair-dresser's.

She sat bolt upright in the chair and was looking impressively majestic when unfortunately she glanced at herself in the mirror. The image of an elderly woman trying to look dignified with a plastic frill round her neck and a panic-stricken young girl twisting her wrists with eyebrows in deep despair, struck her as so impossibly amusing that she burst into helpless giggles. For Ingrid the strain of her enforced smile and effort to understand incomprehensible old ladies was just too much, she held onto the lady's chair and cacked herself laughing.

— Hah hah hah, splutter, you'd have to hold my head under water . . .

— Wheeze, groan, high-pitched squeak, hairdresser's

apprentice drowns swimming ace.

— Just sharing a joke with a customer, are we, Ingrid? snarled Johnny as he surveyed the two quaking lumps. Ingrid became aware, as she wiped the tears from her eyes, that everyone in the shop was watching the scene with the greatest interest. The lady, still doubled over in her chair, slowly sat up as straight as the slight hump in her back would allow, wiped her eyes with Ingrid's hanky, and said,

— I was just reminiscing about my youth, Mr François, and the dear girl was kind enough to find an old lady's stories amusing.

— Quite so, quite so, hissed Johnny through tautened lips, one does one's best to please the customers.

So the lady told Ingrid all about Bondi and the rip which had launched life saving clubs in the national imagination. How during that now mythical competition all the volunteers had been swept out to sea by the most enormous rip and within half an hour all one hundred and fifty of them had been rescued. Ingrid, as she deftly took the curlers out of the lady's hair, and brushed the wiry waves, described Steppo's soap bubble on Christmas Day. She and the lady had parted the best of friends and the next time the lady asked for Ingrid by name. As soon as Ingrid saw her walk into the salon, she had begun to grin, knowing that the lady would ask for her specially and anticipating a lightening of the day's burden. The lady sat down and worked herself into a comfortable position, making exaggerated little grimaces with her face while setting her mobile wrinkles to best effect. Ingrid's heart warmed to her, as she wondered how they would get back into their previous complicity.

— Which church do you go to? the lady asked. Ingrid felt utterly dismayed; church wasn't something you joked about. You were either serious or you ignored it. Only lapsed Catholics bothered to torture up jokes. Until the age of 11 or 12, Ingrid had thought of churches as simply the places where jumble sales happened. (She was the product of a strict liberal upbringing).

— Er, we don't know yet, we've only just moved in.

It was difficult to tell how far Ingrid's ignorance of matters religious was disingenuous and how far frank naivety. At fifteen years old she had almost certainly heard of God, but whether she had heard of his mysterious ways was a moot point. It is certain, however, that when people spoke of the church, she thought of harvest festival and having to bring tins of tomato soup for school assembly.

The lady looked at her a little quizzically, but continued,
— We're all Presbyterian in my family.

Something about the way she pronounced the word "presbyterian" reminded Ingrid of Laura's mother, whereas the lady normally talked like a rather refined Eastern Stater.
— Are you Scottish? she asked obligingly. Laura's mother was Scottish.
— Yes, my dear, said the lady, delighted, you obviously know your Calvin. My grandfather was from St. Andrews.

Ingrid wondered why the nicest people had to do pompous things to their souls on Sunday and, worse still, tell everyone else about it. She reflected gloomily that the lady was sure to check up on her and she would have to invent a non-contributory, all souls barred church to go to.

Anyway, all this had been over a week ago, and she had a perm to do now.
— Hello, Mrs Bovis, she said cheerily.
— My dear Ingrid, I've brought my water wings with me just in case. Ingrid winced. A joke was a joke, not a bloody institution, but there was worse to come.
— I've arranged for someone to pick you up next Sunday, and of course any of your brothers and sisters who want to go. It's an old friend of the family.
— I knew it, thought Ingrid, those sorts of families shouldn't be allowed.
— And she assures me it will be no inconvenience as she passes through Balga anyway. Now, would you like an English toffee? I've just bought them at the Olde English Sweet Shoppe in Murray Street.

This was the moment, if ever, to produce the Long-distance Church of the Latter Day Representatives: going on her brief trade union experience, anything "representative" meant that Ingrid wasn't meant to go. But she was struck dumb. She didn't want Mrs Bovis to know about her own private altar, and then there was the toffee problem. There was nothing in the world that Ingrid wanted more. On bad days in the salon, she would count the minutes till 10.30 when she would be able to crunch through a biscuit, or two if she was clever enough to catch Simone's eye and make tea for the seniors. This was the only rule to which she seriously objected; "no eating in front of the customers" had forced her to discontinue her normal placid habit of chumbling her way through the most difficult day with the help of a packet of chocolate Wheeton biscuits. She had tried asking to be made a special exception: she was a very good biscuit eater, her face remained immaculate and practice had restrained her from sucking molten chocolate from her finger tips (though this was arguably the best bit), but no; the one exception to this draconian measure was sweets or titbits offered by the customers themselves. In that case you were allowed to accompany them in their habit. Johnny did not like food and was said to owe his thin, nervous irritability to his diet of black coffee and citrus fruit. He did not like women much either and somehow associated them with eating.

When Mrs Bovis offered her a toffee, it threw Ingrid onto the horns of the most awful dilemma. On the one hand, she always accepted sweets from Mrs Bovis, not to do so now would be pure self-sacrifice. On the other, wasn't taking a toffee equivalent to approving of the proposal? Could she last out till lunch time without the tempting titbit? Mrs Bovis passed the packet over to her, and almost without thinking, she plunged her hand in, hoping that the well loved chewing motion would soothe her into a decision.

— Oh take two.

As well hung for a sheep as a lamb; Ingrid took two. Perhaps church would be alright once she got there. A lot of people swore by it. But, even as she thought this, a vision of old ladies elbowing each other for worn green jumpers while the vicar smiled beatifically in the doorway, a cup of tea in his hands, came into her mind. She frowned.

— And you will be ready by 8 o'clock?

Mrs Bovis sounded like Johnny, any moment Ingrid was expecting to be told what to wear, but the older woman, sure of her prey, was more tactful. Ingrid stuffed the toffee in her mouth before she could repent and set about the perm, now convinced that Mrs Bovis creased up with laughter was a sight she was never likely to see again. It must have been an exceptional moment in a tight-lipped bullying life of religious piety and Family duties. Ingrid wondered what on earth she was going to do when the car pulled up in front of the house. She could be ill, she supposed, but that entailed explaining

31

her friendship with Mrs Bovis to her mother and she wasn't sure she could do that. Beryl expressed the same contempt for all old ladies as she did for her mother-in-law. They were "old bats" to her and she wished her daughter was working somewhere a bit more with it. Ingrid had not forgotten the pressure her mother had put on her to end her friendship with Wendy.

— She's so terribly sweet, Beryl had said, and things had not been the same. Ingrid had not been able to help watching her friend for signs of advancing insipidity. She did not wish to hear Mrs Bovis called an "old bat". She was sure that in her starchy way, by taking her to church, the old woman was offering her the best thing she had, and Ingrid was possessed of enormous loyalty to former giggling partners. Perhaps she would just have to explain to the old family friend that her own religion had the thickness of warm treacle and consisted in a devout belief that everyone loved her and that men were put on this earth to adore her. She hated to give offence, and was sure the women's breadmaking and knitting club was the greatest fun, but her own beliefs were elsewhere. She could imagine it would be fun to learn to bake thick knotty loaves of bread and smell the yeast, or combine rich colours in warm wools, but maybe it wasn't really like that. Something about Mrs Bovis' navy blue suit suggested an air of puritanism that not even the wayward curls of her perm could quite dispel.

She decided to leave it to the spur of the moment; the car would draw up and an idea would come. Either she would get into the car or she wouldn't, but either way something would happen. This state of irresolution left her in a very bad frame of mind, so that when her next customer came she felt thoroughly disagreeable and cross that such a pleasant world could be made so complicated. Other people were such a problem. She dawdled over the next shampoo and set, still sucking her toffee and mumbled rather incoherently,

— Would you like me to bring you any tea or coffee?

The woman did not appear to hear, and Ingrid realised with a groan that she must be deaf. Usually she was fascinated and welcomed the signs of old age; old people seemed to have a poetic licence for any degree of personal quirkiness and idiosyncrasy. When Ingrid had first discovered the word "idiosyncrasy" in a school reading test and gone home to look it up, she had been rapt by it as a kind of acceptable idiocy. This time, however, she just felt cross and punished the woman for being deaf by scrubbing her head instead of the gentle massage laid down in the manual.

— Be careful, dearie, I have a large wart on the back of my head, the woman said very gently but loudly because she could not pitch it right. Of course Johnny eagle-ears heard.

— Ingrid, this sort of thing just will not do. You must make allowances for the customers' disabilities. They can't help it you know. Now are you going to finish this one off or must I give it to someone else?

Ingrid winced with embarrassment, more for the deaf woman who couldn't hear herself called "it" than for her own hurt pride. She shut up and finished off the shampoo through a web of tears and when she came to the wart she felt almost protective towards it. She stared at it; it really was very large and impressively ugly. It stood out from the woman's head, whitey grey, with smaller lumps on it and a tuft of hairs at the very end. It was so innocent that she had a sudden urge to pick it, like wanting to push her forefinger into the soft bit of a baby's brain, before the bone had grown together, because it was the thing you absolutely musn't do. However she found that once she let herself think this, she no longer wanted to do it. She simply washed the deaf woman's head with an air of long familiarity.

By five o'clock she had had a thoroughly rotten day. The seniors had ordered her all over the place. She had had to leave a perm to go and clean up a basin and been told off afterwards because the perm was more important than the basin and she should have known better than to leave a customer dangling with curlers in her hair. By chance the roster let her and Simone off at the same time.

— Poor little Ingrid, you look shat off, though I suppose I shouldn't call you Ingrid anymore.

— Why not? Ingrid snapped. It's my name.

— Oh haven't you heard? Johnny says Ingrid is a German name and some of the customers lost husbands in the last war. He says we'll have to call you Fran.

— Fran? Bloody Fran? I won't answer, why can't he call me Thingy if he wants a nickname?

— Will Miss Thingy please come to reception? Can't see it somehow. Look, come for a drink with me and calm down.

— A drink? What, now? Just us? Mum doesn't let me go into pubs alone.

— You won't be alone, you'll be with me.

— No. I mean without a man, silly.

Ingrid was however easily persuaded that this counted as a New Year's drink with the girls, especially as she had the next day off. They went to the Ocker Pig in Fremantle on Simone's recommendation, and sat in the lounge where children and therefore women were allowed. The public bar resembled nothing so much as a gigantic urinal lined with green tiles, where men stood pouring it in one end and pissing it out the other, the whole lot being hosed out at 11 o'clock: men, tiles and piss.

— Johnny fancies himself as a dictator, remarked Simone casually, only he can't make it in the real world, so he bosses us girls around. Tells us what to eat, what to wear, where to live and (with a wink at Ingrid) what to call ourselves. Salon'd be alright if it wasn't for him.

— Oh, I hate men, they're so petty, Ingrid burst out, surprised at herself, but instantly reassured once she realised it was easy to say because she didn't mean it.

— Didn't think I'd hear you say that, Ing, but you can set your mind at rest; Johnny's not a bloke, he's a poofta.

Ingrid breathed in.

— Haven't you seen those keys dangling from his levis? It's a sure sign.

— I thought that was because his jeans were too tight for them to fit in his pockets.

— Well, exactly.

Put like that, of course, it was irrefutable.

— See those two guys over there? I reckon they've got the hots for us. You on?

— But what would Boyfriend say?

— Doesn't have to know, does he?

— Look, I thought we were going to have a drink together, alone, I mean just the two of us.

— What, two chicks? You kinky or something?

— No, don't be stupid, it's just that, well, my boyfriend wouldn't like it. That wasn't really why, but Ingrid didn't feel like explaining she was quite happy chatting to Simone about work or whatever and would probably have found Boyfriend a crowd right then.

— Well, if that's how you feel, piss off home to him then.

At that moment two young women clicked in on high heels and wobbled over to the men Simone had pointed out. One of the men stood up and went over to the bar for a round, as he passed their table he winked at Simone and whispered,

— Too bad, Sheila, got company this evening. Still, maybe next time, you never know your luck, and he lurched off.

— See, said Simone triumphantly, they did fancy a bit.

Ingrid felt she had been taken out by a senior and fluffed her big moment by a stupid attachment to a bloke she didn't even like. Simone was embarrassed, though she'd never admit it, that her sex appeal had failed in front of an apprentice. They finished their martinis and left.

Which is how Ingrid came to be on the same bus, three seats from the front, as Minnie was to catch on her way back from Freo.

— Ingrid! How come you're not home already?

— Oh, they asked me to work late because of the New Year rush, and they're giving me tomorrow off so we can go to Rotto.

Minnie was not to be sidetracked, she didn't like her sister having secrets from her.

— But you work in Hay Street.

— So? What's with the Inquisition, big sister? Guilty conscience? I've been at the Fremantle shop because one of the girls was off sick today. Anyway, I could ask you the same question.

Ingrid would have liked to discuss Simone with Minnie, but she wasn't going to spill her beans unless her sister did likewise.

— Oh, I went down to look at the market.

And both sisters slipped off into the silent reverie which filled their minds when not actively engaged in conversation. Minnie liked having her sister with her as she felt less vulnerable than when she was alone and men did not hassle her nearly as much. She was always surprised to see that men looked at her in exactly the same way they did other women, although she was not the slightest bit interested in them. Ingrid continued to gaze mutely out of the window. It seems that unprobing silence is the bedrock of family life, and it's a wonder children ever learn to speak.

Minnie was wondering if she would actually dare to go to this party on New Year's Eve. She would know no one except the women who had invited her and who she was rather afraid of. She would turn up not knowing if dresses had hit the Perth feminist scene yet. Of course clothes didn't matter at all, except that they did enormously, especially when everyone would be seeing her for the first time and judging her accordingly. Perhaps later on, when they knew her better, they might revise their first impressions but first she had to get to know them at all. If she turned up in her pink and black socks with lurex jacket to match and they were still in uniform khaki they would say she had stepped out of an S & M male fantasy world. If she wore overalls and a T shirt and they were into baggy trousers and leather jackets they would think she was giving in to stereotypes of butch horse-riding lesbians. Maybe she'd wear the overalls but offset them with earrings; in which case she'd lose either way. However, having made contact with the Perth feminists, she was determined to bring in the New Year with Women Only.

Ingrid, once she'd put the church question on ice, was true to her resolve. Instead, she thought about Johnny. She summoned him before her eyes and examined him closely. Nicely cropped and waved hair, but then, he did own a chain of hair dressing salons.

— Exactly, Simone would say, but I mean, really, you could go on saying that indefinitely. He wore tight jeans and brightly coloured Hawaian shirts, always beautifully washed and ironed. Did he press them himself every morning like she had to, or did he have a boyfriend at home to do it?

— Oh, she thought, I suppose he must be camp, because it certainly never occurred to me that he might have a girlfriend at home to do it. Perhaps it was his mother. She was sure now that at any rate he didn't do it himself or he wouldn't be so lousy to her. That might not follow logically, but somehow she just knew that if you had to clean up after yourself, you did not terrorise employees who got to work late or force them to wear tights and scrub floors on their knees. Any conclusion she came to was along the lines of: she knew Boyfriend couldn't stick pooftas, but then she had to admit he was pretty narrow minded about these things (it was only a few years ago that his mother had stopped going to the

36

shops in white gloves), but she, Ingrid, didn't give a shit who her boss was fucking (so long as it wasn't her) if he was half way decent to the salon girls. Which he wasn't.

Minnie wondered how she would get out of the house, whichever way she chose to dress, without Ingrid's boyfriend offering her a lift. She was not going to arrive at a women's party and clamber ignominiously out from the back of her sister's boyfriend's panel van or let Boyfriend see that there were only women there and refer this information to Ingrid. She went back to her theme tune, how do you tell someone you're homosexual?

— How do you tell someone's homosexual? There, it was out, Ingrid had let her private world invade the linear present.

It shot through the linear present and landed slap bang in the middle of Minnie's private world, where she was as startled to find it as if she'd been Steppo, awakening to find her face dripping with bubble mixture.

— You don't; they tell you, otherwise they aren't.

This made absolute sense to Ingrid and put her mind at rest. As long as no one actually told her they were a poofta she could go on reacting to them as people. The danger wasn't very great: who would voluntarily tell someone they were a pervert?

Chapter 3
In The Office

The day before New Year's Eve Beryl was hard at work typing statements that one or other of her dynamic young bosses had left on the dictaphone before he went to dinner with an important client. The two young men were very careful not to make Beryl do anything degrading that they could perfectly well do themselves, like making coffee or ordering sandwiches, and when they had installed the dictaphone it had of course been done with Beryl's approval. She had to agree that it left her at liberty to do the typing when she chose, which fitted in with her flexible work schedule, but she found that actually she was spending almost all her time typing as the young men could talk much more quickly than they could write or dictate. They did a lot of injunctions in the ordinary way, but over Christmas it was astronomical. Husbands seemed to treat the festive season as an excuse to hit the bottle and their wives at the same time; there was always a build up of domestic violence cases, starting as a slow trickle in early December when he heard his bonus had been stopped for bad time keeping, to a veritable torrent when the kids' holidays started and they were underfoot all day. Ironically, Christmas was about the worst time to apply for an injunction as all the younger, sympathetic judges went East on holiday and only the almost bedridden, gouty remnants stuck around. Beryl kept the tissue box permanently on hand as one by one women queued up to tell their stories of kicks and bruises and fear that he would hit the kids next. She marvelled at their resilience; how could they suffer this continuous battering and still care about someone else? It seemed that the only way to make them angry was through their children. Her first husband hadn't beaten her, but she'd divorced him for mental cruelty and since then she no longer put the kids first. They had a whole army of social workers to look out for them and make sure her husband's ill treatment wasn't making her a bad mother.

— Mrs Bolt, here blow your nose, love, I know he blacks your eyes if you let him near the place, so why do you keep having him back? Promise me you'll actually go through with the divorce this time.

— Oh, Mrs T. I don't know what to do. It all seems so simple sitting here in your nice office with the rubber plant there looking like it hasn't a care in the world; I know it's best for me just to divorce the bastard and admit that the whole thing was a failure, but then I start thinking, well what does that say about me? All I've ever done in my life is get married and have a kid, not that I regret it, I wouldn't want to change a minute of it. It wasn't all cuts and harsh words, otherwise how do you think Sadie got born? Got to look on the bright side, hey?

Beryl shuddered.

— Now she's left home though, I don't have anyone else. When he's actually there, I know he's a brutal man, but when he goes away I keep thinking he'll change. I mean, you shouldn't give up on people, should you? He can't help himself. He's promised to try Alcoholics Anonymous and with this new job he's got in the Solomon Islands, he'll be away months at a time and he says he'll send me money every week.

— He won't do it, you know he won't, and we can't enforce maintenance up there. He'll be back on your doorstep before the bruises have time to heal.

— No, you're right. I know you're right really. He's here at the moment and he's told my brother he'll be round to see me on the weekend. I'm that scared.

— Oh dear, you really should have come in earlier, dear, if he was making these threats. I know the police aren't much good, but why don't you hire a security firm, like M.S.S. for example, to patrol the premises? They'll put up a big sign saying "These premises are under surveillance" and send a car to check up every so often. You know you can afford it.

— I couldn't do that; he'd go wild if he thought I was spending his money keeping him out of his own house. Perhaps I should try for a reconciliation?

Beryl continued the conversation, but knew it was going round and round in circles. She simply did not understand what on earth Mrs Bolt was clinging to. She took refuge in the conclusion, much against her better judgement, that some women, oh only a tiny percentage, must actually ask to be beaten. She did not, of course, ask Mrs. Bolt.

Mrs Bolt, for her part, found the other woman sympathetic, but there was something in her manner that was vaguely patronising. It was quite simple; she was scared to leave home. She had grown dumb under the hail of bruises which left no room to plan further ahead than dodging the next blow. It had gone on too long and she was too old to start standing up for herself now. If sympathy was all she could get from other women, then she would be grateful for sympathy. The tissues came in handy too. She had got married very young, and Mr Bolt and her daughter were the only job she had ever known. He was a mechanic and earned good wages; everyone had been proud of her match. If she left him, what would she do? The very act of renting a flat on her own spelt fear and possible rape; certainly this was what Mr Bolt scared her with if ever she spoke of leaving him, and he made a point of reading aloud all rape articles in the papers.

Beryl might have understood some of this, were she not desperately trying to convince herself that her new found land did not have the same problems as the old and that she had indeed found a safe haven. She herself had married at eighteen, and gave birth to a daughter almost immediately. Just as this daughter was turning eight, and she was thinking of going out to work, she had had a second child. Her husband did not object to her working, but when she finally started a job four years later, he simply stopped her housekeeping. The family of five (another child, a boy, had been born in the intervening years) had lived off what she earned as a typist. She hadn't known she could do anything about this, and would not have dared if she had.

Minnie's father was a psychiatrist with a private accountant to look after his money, yet Minnie bought her uniform second hand from the parent teacher jumble sale. No one knew, of course, the school was very discreet, and when the time had come for university interviews, her headmistress had paid out of her own pocket. If anything, her father's salary was a hindrance: had it not existed, she would have been eligible for free school meals, clothing vouchers and a bus pass. Perhaps they weren't on the poverty line, but if a

40

woman gets her class from her husband, I wonder where that left Beryl? Her father was a stockbroker, and her husband a psychiatrist, but every Friday night after work she would struggle home from Sainsbury's, Ingrid in tow and Minnie helping with the heavy bags. Some weeks she would send the kids to glean in Hildreth Road, sure these were the actions of a "bad mother" but afraid the stall keepers would be angry if a middle-aged lady picked over their mushy tomatoes.

On the way home she would drop in on her sister and she could be sure that if she stayed too long or her husband got hungry, he would come over and get her rather than fix a bite to eat for himself. Sometimes he would go away to conferences in Stockholm and they would eat what they liked. When he was home he insisted on meat, though on her salary they could scarcely afford cheese, even in those days. She would try buying Protoveg and disguising that in stew, but he didn't like the taste and would taunt her with her awful cooking. So when he went away, the family banqueted on as much beans on toast as they could eat, and no one went to bed hungry. Mary down the laundrette would always ask after him, and if he was away from home again, she would kindly assume that, like so many men in the area, he was back inside, and she would refuse payment for Beryl's service wash so Minnie didn't have to be late for school.

One evening, when Beryl's asthma was so bad that every breath was a torture to her, she had begged her husband to go to the all-night chemist and get her some pills on her repeat prescription. Her voice was an awful racking whisper but he replied,

— Nonsense, darling, it's all psychosomatic. You know these things only work if you believe in them. Read my recent paper on the subject. Why don't you take some Hermeseetas if you want a sugar pill? And then he had laughed, as if he had made a joke.

Minnie, biting her nails, had witnessed the whole scene: her mother's pinched white face, and her father's awful triumph at his cleverness. She had slipped out of the house without even a coat and gone up to London for the first time on her own. At Piccadilly she braved the midnight queue of drug addicts waiting for their next day's prescription, and caught the last tube home. As she waited in the

41

station, two young women with long straggly hair came up to her and asked, with reddened eyes and pock marks round their sockets, if she could spare a few pence for them to catch the main line home. Scared shitless of stories she had heard of junkies plunging syringes into hapless bystanders, she gave them what she had and they went away. Not so the police in the Panda car which kerb crawled her down Balham hill. She was relieved by their presence against the dangers of the night until they stopped and asked her all sorts of questions which only her middle class accent prevented them pursuing.

That night her mother slept upstairs with her and Ingrid, saying the air there, being higher, was easier on her lungs. That was the beginning of a secret friendship with her daughter which had to be kept from her husband lest he dub it Œdipal and thus unhealthy. Minnie would often arrive home late at night to find Beryl sitting on the bottom step sobbing hopelessly. She would be paralytically drunk, and Minnie would gently prise the empty bottle from her grip and hide it in the dustbin which her father never went near. Once Minnie found her mother on the front path stark naked, rocking from side to side lasciviously, pretending to be a penguin on heat. Minnie wondered if it was this revelation of her mother's frailty which spoiled their relationship in later years, but sometimes Beryl's drinking led to amusing consequences. Like the time she had swigged half a bottle of cider as well as the valium the doctor gave her for the nerves, and they had gone off and done Sainsbury's together. They both laughed and laughed at the extraordinary things that spilled out of the bags when they got them home again: bean shoots, small brown partridges, gentlemen's relish, a chewy doggy bone.

— We don't even have a dog, Beryl chortled.

Her husband's most famous line, which Beryl never tired of repeating, was spoken one night after they had guests to supper, and Beryl, legs aching with fatigue, varicose veins throbbing, had started doing the dishes.

— Don't bother with the washing up, darling, he had said kindly, you can do it in the morning.

It was one of the girls in the office who had finally given Beryl the courage to leave home. In her impatience with the women who came to consult her bosses, she now played down Rita's part in her decision and wondered why these poor souls couldn't do as she did. But even after she had moved out she was subject to odd, inexplicable fears.

— How shall I pay the rent, Minnie? she had asked. Minnie had been puzzled at first, not understanding what her mother was asking.

— Well, she said finally, as she thought of her friends who had already left home, you keep a bit back from your wages each week and then either the man comes for it, or you send it off to him and he pays for the stamp.

Beryl's biggest worry had been telling Ingrid. The little girl might love her father, and she would have no reason not to think him perfect. If she could, Beryl was resolved not to turn her daughter against her father. She and Minnie went into the bathroom where Ingrid was sploshing and playing sheep with the soap suds.

— Ginny, darling, Beryl stuttered with great trepidation, I'm moving up to live in North London and I want you to come with me.

— Brillsville, chuckled Ingrid in delight, gathering the soap suds up to her chin, does that mean I can have a room of my own?

— It does my own precious pet, and Beryl hugged her small wet daughter to her, getting covered in soapy water in the process.

The friend at work who had provided the confidence had also provided the flat. She and her husband were going away to Oxford for a year and the landlord had agreed to take Beryl on in the meantime. The only snag was that there was not enough room for Minnie to come too. If Minnie had shown any signs of wanting to come, Beryl would have done her damnedest to find a bigger flat; if there had been any possibility of Beryl getting a bigger flat, Minnie would have asked to go too. However, Minnie was just starting A levels at the time and though her mother's life was in turmoil, she saw no reason to jeopardise her own. So Minnie went to live with Aunt Alice, the same sister that Beryl used to sneak in to see on her return from Sainsbury's.

The day she left, in a taxi piled high with cardboard boxes and black plastic dustbin bags, Beryl's pulse was racing. At the same time she felt unutterably depressed. She was a failure, she had not managed what millions of women all over

Britain managed without even dirtying their aprons, she had not kept her home together. Her children had not been ribena babies, Ariel failed to do anything but work in Minnie's understains, and her only son had died in infancy. She stared blankly at the unknown streets through which they were passing in that grey nomansland of the city on a Sunday afternoon. Kingsland Road seemed to go on forever and when the driver asked "where now?" at Stamford Hill, Beryl had to confess that she hadn't the faintest idea. She reflected that where they were going she would not even know where to buy paraffin and the launderette lady would not mind Ingrid for her while she did the shopping. For a while she was lulled by the throbbing of the engine so that when the taxi stopped she felt she was leaving the last home she had known. The driver helped her out with all the boxes and as it took so long, he accepted a cup of tea as soon as Beryl had found the gas rings. He was very cheerful and encouraging, obviously thought she was doing a moonlight. By the time he left, it almost occurred to her to ask him to marry her, so scared was she of finding herself alone.

So there she was, starting again at thirty-six in a dark cold flat where not even the faded wallpaper was familiar and there was no garden. She gathered Ingrid up in her arms and hugged her passionately. Rita had said that the window sills were wide enough for quite large window boxes, in a vain effort to encourage Beryl. Beryl cooed to her daughter to raise her own failing spirits.

— It's not so bad, she meant to say, but it came out as, it's so cold, so very cold, and no garden, not even a daffodil.

Warmed a little by the tea, she set to work to arrange the kitchen where they would sleep that night. Rita had left some bits and pieces so she was by no means destitute. She had stolen her husband's television, her one act of felony during the whole of her married life, and come to think of it, it was her who had paid off the last instalment. She now parked Ingrid in front of it, while she scrubbed the floor which bore witness to the troubling presence of mice. As she scrubbed she glared at her wedding ring and the thought came to her that she could sell it and buy Christmas presents, and that would be nice. Plops of salt water dropped down onto her hands and she viciously wiped the tears back from her eyes. She was very happy; today was the day she had done what

44

every other married woman was wishing they had the guts to do (except, it seems, her sister Alice). She had left her husband; anniversaries were made of such things. There would be the anniversary of leaving to look forward to, the anniversary of the divorce, then the anniversary of the second marriage, for she intended to remarry, someone who would appreciate her this time. It occurred to her to phone Minnie or Alice, but she determined to see this one through on her own, and all her successes would be hers as well as all her failures.

She had seen less of her elder daughter after that. Minnie was up to her ears in essays and Beryl was working overtime to pay off the furniture, but that Christmas had been magic. Minnie had come over and Beryl got a good price for her wedding ring. They had each chosen what they wanted to eat and the resulting fish fingers, chocolate digestives and dripping toasts might not have been what the average Londoner would have welcomed that day, but to them it spelt freedom, every yucky, greasy mouthful. Ingrid's little back room was too cold to sleep in because of the damp patch and the mould growing on the wall, so they all cuddled up in Beryl's double bed with the odd orange curtains for sheets and the patchwork bedspread made of all their old frocks and blouses.

When Beryl's husband asked for access to the girls, Beryl was in a mood to grant him anything, exhilarated to be able to turn the lights on and off at her own command and leave them on all night if she wished. So Ingrid spent every second weekend with her father, but Minnie refused adamantly to have anything to do with him, though she only lived round the corner.

— You know I go over and do odd bits of cleaning for him, Alice had started one day.

— Yes, Beryl said, warned by her sister's tone to brace herself for some unpleasant discovery.

— Well, the weekends Ingrid's down, I can't seem to find an extra bed made up. Of course, he's a lazy old whatsit, probably gives her his army sleeping bag to save on sheets.

Alice never spake ill of anyone, but Beryl did not mistake her message.

— Ginny, when you sleep at Daddy's, she paused, better not put ideas into the child's head, do you have enough blankets?

— Oh yes, plenty. I sleep in Daddy's bed and we get very

45

hot.

Out of the mouths of babes: Beryl yearned to give way to panic, but still she did not want to frighten her daughter. She phoned Minnie up as being more able to giggle her sister into an admission. Minnie felt her heart sink, but that Saturday she took Ingrid to the children's matinee of Chitty Chitty Bang Bang and Ingrid had to be assured that the wicked witch wouldn't really hurt the children.

— Ginny, do you like Daddy?

— Yes, said the child nervously.

— Does he like you?

— Spect so. He's my dad.

— Would you like an ice cream?

— Not half. Chocolate, please.

— Does he cuddle you?

But Ingrid's mouth was now safely full of flake and her replies more and more inaudible.

— Yes, a bit.

— And kiss you?

— Yeah, so what? He kisses you too.

— No, I mean, does he kiss you on the mouth?

— Sometimes. Ingrid was getting more and more edgy, and Minnie felt herself going bright red, why couldn't her mother do her own dirty work? But she had to go on.

— Does he put his tongue in your mouth? she blurted out.

— No, no, no, he doesn't, Ingrid screamed and raced off across the common. At last Minnie caught up with her, covered her in dead leaves and pretended it was just a game. Ingrid was asked no more questions, but by the end of the year Beryl had found and married an Australian and January saw them heading for Perth. She had been prepared to promise whatever her husband wanted; he could keep the house she had painted and cleaned and she would not ask for maintenance, but he was not getting Ingrid. Perhaps more should be said about how she met and married her second husband, of how she took afternoons off work and bought bottles of wine so she could waft seductively downstairs and ask him for a cork screw; of how she appealed to him pitifully for fuse wire and invited him up for cups of tea. But that story can be found in any one of a hundred romantic novels. Beryl forbade Minnie to go to the divorce hearing, not wanting to make things worse between the girl and her

46

father, especially as he would now be her closest relative in the country.

The month before she left was a rush to get medical certificates and interviews with migration officials at Canberra House, so the rather melancholy affair of saying good bye to her daughter and her sister was overcast by her anxiety that somewhere a document would have been lost and their visas would not be through in time. When she paused to reflect, which became quite a luxury at that time, life seemed brightened by the prospect of Australia and the obvious fact that Ingrid adored her new father. He had asked her what she wanted for Christmas, and she had been surprised as she hadn't thought men bought presents. Nevertheless, she had named two board games, either of which would have done equally well, and was thrilled to discover on Christmas Day that not only had he not forgotten, but he had bought both games and the two of them settled down to learn the rules.

Beryl had tried as far as she could, to leave all this behind her. Right up to the last moment at Heathrow Airport she had been sure her ex-husband would come striding towards them and say in his manly baritone,

— Stop! This is all a mistake; a simple misunderstanding. My wife needs help, she has left her husband, her mind is unhinged. I can prove it, I'm a psychiatrist; just as he had in court, only this time he would have ultimate proof that she was round the bend. First she had left him and their comfortable owner-occupied home to live in squalor in North London, then she had abandoned her eldest daughter and taken up with another man (to the grave detriment of the younger child who had since been refused visits to her sorrowing father) and finally she was deserting the country which had reared her to flit off half way round the world. Now, you would need strong motives for doing that if you were not already a little disturbed, I put it to you, your Honour.

Even now, years later, she would be gripped by a throbbing horror as a tall man with a grey beard came straight towards her in the street, only to hail a taxi or greet the person next to her. Other times she would wake up in the morning, before John got back from the taxi, and imagine she had awoken from the dream and must get her husband's suit back from the cleaners before he went to Paris.

In leaving it behind her, she seemed to have lost some of

her understanding of other women's problems.

— I am a feminist, she would say to her husband, but not an emotional one like Minnie; a good solid economic feminist with no time for ranting and raving and screaming "unfair". I mean, we all know it's unfair, you can scream till you're blue in the face, the thing is to do something about it.

Beryl was a staunch trade unionist who would make sure her daughters worked in union shops if it was the last thing she did for them. Right now, however, when Mrs Bolt left the office having convinced herself that if she only tried harder things would be alright again, Beryl was thinking about herself. Normally she left "introspection to the introverts", but Minnie turning up like that had revived old habits in her.

Her garden in Balga was truly amazing. While the other houses were still surrounded by failing native bush or struggling wood chips laid out on black plastic sheets, Beryl's was a landscaped wonder with hills and valleys, fish pond and rock garden. There were plants spilling out of various odd teapots and watering cans or bowls covered in shells. By the front door was a little glass bust which Beryl called the "Genius Loci". It was made from broken bottles and had sharp curly green hair like the Medusa's head and two split marbles for eyes. One day perhaps Laura's cat would disembowel itself on her, which would be sad, but in the meantime she stood protecting the house from anyone who might wish to talk to Beryl.

Beryl entertained friendly relations with her neighbours. She fed Mrs-next-door's cats when she went to Bunbury on holiday and watered Mrs-out-the-back's plants. This had to be done before work as it was useless leaving the sprinklers on during the heat of the day. When young Sandra across the road had realised that buying a house meant no money for anything else, it was to Beryl that she had instantly come for bus fares to work, with the proposition that Beryl buy her old car which she could not afford to run. It was Beryl also who had found homes for the puppies whose owners kept them locked up in a box scarcely big enough for them to waggle their silken ears. She was a comfortable, familiar sight as she waddled home from the bus stop, gazing absently into the coarse grass in case it concealed a compatible plant, and picking up odd bits of string with which to make pictures. No one would have guessed as they watched her open the letter box, stooping vaguely to pull up a weed, that she stood in mortal boredom of other people.

— People are the most important thing in the world, Ingrid had announced happily one day.

— You'll soon get over them, her mother had said.

When the children were little the most grievous crime, for which they could be sent to bed with no supper, was to be boring. To insist on anything for too long or to get serious was to be thus condemned and they had quickly learned to keep their opinions to themselves. In this way Beryl had ceased to count them as people, they were the children, part of herself. Once you had had a child, never never could you see the world in quite the same way again, but other people who talked too much or had expectations of you were something else. Beryl would be polite, she would even fulfil their expectations to a certain degree, but after that she claimed the right to be as mad as a hatter. It was easier like that. When her first husband had suggested they have his mother to live with them, Beryl said she would stick her own head in a gas oven first. She had avoided all her second husband's relations in Perth by pretexting asthma attacks and giving them bunches of plastic flowers for Christmas.

— How thoughtful, they had said, and that had been that.

Beryl liked to keep her mind free for herself. She would spend whole Sundays on the beach collecting seaweed or shells to decorate a mirror, comparing lines and angles and curves and watching them slip in and out of each other. Or she would painstakingly tear up pile after pile of newspaper and stick it all together again in the form of a bedside table or a reading lamp. She would pause over the flour paste and look out at the washing line, thinking how well the pink T shirt went with the green dress and the pale purple skirt. Sometimes she would even stop what she was doing to go and rearrange the colour scheme.

Her problem at the moment was lack of space. Normally she could clear a place for herself around a dress she was making or a patchwork quilt, but this time she felt an acute need for wide open spaces empty of any other human thing. There was a thought she had felt coming for many weeks now, but what with Minnie arriving and Christmas and all she had had to postpone it to the back of her mind. The mention of wide open spaces summoned up red desert very forcefully in her mind's eye and in a flash a naughty plan was hatched.

— Is that the government Tourist Office? Could you tell me when the next coach leaves for the Pinnacles?

— Let's see, that'll be Sunday morning 8 o'clock. Cost you 26 dollars a head. Now, how many'd you say were going?

— Oh, just the one, I think, yes, just the one.

During her lunch break Beryl slipped out to pay for the ticket before she could change her mind. As she crossed the Mall she spotted her eldest daughter deep in conversation with some women selling a feminist newspaper. She was not overly surprised, Minnie could winkle out feminists in the strangest of places, but Beryl did not wish to stop in case talking to Minnie should put her off her errand.

Chapter 4
Rottnest Island

Laura would not have been altogether surprised to meet Minnie in the Mall either. Her sense of anticipated excitement caused her to suspect Minnie of all sorts of odd acquaintances and she was shortly to have a conversation with her foster sister which would go someway to clarify where the excitement would come from. After the incident on their way home from Star Wars, Laura had begun to ask herself questions about Min. The word "lesbian" echoed through her mind, as though it were enough to throw someone's sexuality into question to contaminate the hearer. The bloke had simply said, "Are you a lesbian?" and Laura had assumed he meant Min, because she looked so butch. It was a natural mistake to make: Laura herself had been a bit taken aback at the airport but, now that she knew Minnie, she realised it was because she didn't care what she looked like. Minnie was just odd; she clambered out of cars on her hands, head first, and butted in on other people's conversations at the cinema if she didn't agree with what they were saying. Now that Laura thought about the man in the bush, she had a weird feeling that perhaps she was implicated in the insult too. It had blown the gaff on the clear everyday world of true love and common sense. Now anyone could come at you from nowhere and accuse you, and however much you proved your pent up passion for penetration, it was possible to answer "yes" to their question. You might not "really" enjoy fucking, you might be faking, you might fancy your best friend. If you cut off from females and expressed admiration only for things male, you could be a latent homosexual living in bitter denial of your own nature.

Laura stood at the edge of a precipice. Behind was the kindly but clammy world where things were as they appeared and if you worked hard at Coles you could earn enough money to go off to the Eastern States. In front was a great echoing void, the void of lesbian sexuality, where every gesture and every thought had to be reassessed. What if she was not the only woman who didn't enjoy sex? She thought of Beryl, patently delighted that all the kids were going to the Drives on Christmas Eve, so that she could be alone with her husband; of Ingrid pattering out to Boyfriend's car night after night, clutching a roll of toilet paper in her nightie. No, surely not. And it wasn't even true that she herself didn't like what passed for the most meaningful form of human communion. She didn't like sleeping in the wet patch and she didn't like the dull ache she had down there when he didn't stop after he'd come, but she loved the cuddling and the softness and the way she felt about her body afterwards. She wasn't too keen on him actually going into her, except initially just as it went in, but you had to make some compromises. Thus clarified the problem began to hinge around whether or not Minnie was gay. If not, then the taunt in the dark was simply a taunt in the dark, the big stick simply a stick and they had been right to pass by in silence. If so, then Laura didn't quite know what followed but perhaps Min could tell her.

It was the day that the four of them went to Rottnest Island that Laura determined to pop the question. Circumstances were ideal; Ingrid and Boyfriend went off for a ride in a glass bottomed boat to see the reefs and the fish and have a quiet quarrel, which left Laura and Min to go on the trampolines on their own. They got on well as a rule, Laura would talk about Y.M.C.A. camps she had been on there, when they had been woken up at dawn and forced to climb over barbed wire and have an early morning dip in the ocean because the showers weren't working. Minnie delighted in forcing Laura to admit there were some things she did enjoy.

— Don't you just love it when the water trickles over your toes early in the morning when you're not quite awake, and pulls the sand away from under the soles of your feet?

— Yis (pause) but they made us walk along the seaweed and you can't tell what's in there and boy does it ever pong.

— What about that star fish you found?

Laura did not greatly mind being petulant, especially as she knew it amused Minnie, but at the mention of the star fish, her voice mellowed.

— Oh yes, it was bright red, bright, bright red with smooth

52

sides and a leathery back. When the waves rolled away and left it uncovered, it held its breath as if it was afraid they wouldn't be back again. I picked it up and threw it onto the other side of the sand bank so it could move freely and I imagined it was grateful to me.

Laura's whimsy took Minnie by surprise, used as she was to hear her foster sister sneer at what she called Beryl and Ingrid's "treasures of the sea shore syndrome". Minnie had finally decided that she had come to Australia to tell her mother she was gay, whatever else might happen, and if that proved too awesome, she would exercise herself on her sisters, starting with Laura as the least involved with her. She was sure that once she decided, she would think of a way to carry it out. Minnie was nothing if not purposeful (once she decided who she was playing) but I suspect this was due more to an agreeable combination of circumstances which Minnie interpreted to her own liking and that in fact there was little to choose between Minnie's determination and Beryl's determinism. Minnie set herself to thinking how she would work up to it, absorbed entirely in the technical problems, not the result of her endeavour, just as she had done about coming to Perth. She would get Laura talking about sex and a silence would fall which she ought to fill with details of her own sex life. Laura would be obliged to prompt the conversation with interested questions about Min. Then it would be Laura's fault if she did not like what she heard. Minnie marvelled at her own powers of manipulation.

Laura wondered how to get into a situation where a question about Minnie's sexuality would not seem out of place. The only idea that came to her, clichéd and obvious though it was, was to talk about her own sex life first and lead on to Min from there.

— How are things between you and John? Minnie asked.

— Oh, you know, he wants to go to the beach when I want to go to the drives. In case this wasn't clear enough, she added,

— The first time it's exciting, you know, the waves pounding around you, the water licking your feet and this strong man holding you in his arms. But then you get to thinking of the sand up your bum and the salt in your hair and you know, it's never as good as in your imagination.

Minnie found Laura's constant use of the expression "you

know" somewhat alarming, implying as it did that Minnie had the same fantasies. If she said "No, actually I don't know", Laura would groan and say she was quarrelling over words. It was like the game that straight women play of chatting about their boyfriends and then asking what you think. "Yes, you too can be heterosexual"; think back to the last time you fucked a man and you can join in the conversation with the best of us. Or maybe you'd like to come up with some lesbian goodies for us to add to our sum of human knowledge?

The trampolines they had been waiting for were now free. Two sweaty little boys came skipping and hopping out of the fenced enclosure, a picture of childish innocence.

— Your turn next, girls.

They climbed onto two trampolines facing each other, and tried to bounce up and down at the same time. Not possible.

— I'm over-reacting, thought Minnie, and contented herself with the simple,

— My imagination doesn't quite run to strong men and pounding waves.

— Oh.

There was a silence. Minnie was willing Laura to say more, to incriminate herself by admitting there might be more than boy makes girl make love. Laura felt the only way to express her disapproval in a neutral way was in the negative.

— Minnie, don't you like sex?

By way of reply, Minnie took off into the sky.

— Don't you like sex? Laura repeated on a down sweep as Minnie was whooshing into the air.

So it was still up to Minnie to disturb that sunny afternoon with her abnormality. If she said it first then it was just a confession and she a perverted individual.

— Laura, isn't it obvious? Minnie sprang up in the air, threw herself forward and executed a superb somersault.

Laura began to bob up and down in quick short jumps, watching Min intently. Then, in the strange stillness of that hot summer day, with the heat haze shimmering over the sand and the weary mums giving their bodies to the waves, breaking the silence, Laura laughed. Minnie had won.

— No, no, it's not, she insisted, what do you mean? And Laura tore away from the trampoline springs in enormous bounds of nervous energy, only to be sent back imperturbably just as she seemed to be heading skyward. And Laura knew she had lost. Minnie was a lesbian. The void stood before her again. She had only Minnie to turn to.

Minnie threw herself flat onto the trampoline bed and was immediately returned to the upright,

— Laura, you know what I mean, but you want me to say it. I'm a lesbian.

— No, you're not, Laura laughed and tried to stand still for a moment, that's like kids messing around at school with rubber lips saying "Kiss me, I'm a poofta", but everyone knows they're not really or they wouldn't dare say it.

— Perhaps that's the only way they can say it, Minnie too was endeavouring to remain upright but the rippling motions in her bare feet were too tempting to ignore. Presently she shot off again into the air.

— Come on, Laura, we've only got ten minutes, don't waste them.

Both women hurled themselves upwards, trusting only to gravity to bring them back down again and at one point both managed to hit the same height at the same time. Finally, however, they let themselves fall back and be rocked gently by the still reverberating trampolines.

— Of course it does, thought Minnie, but she trusted Laura to think it through.

— You can see right out to the sailing boats from the trampoline, Laura glowed. Minnie smiled, and at that moment in the most natural way in the world, Ingrid and Boyfriend hove back into sight, still squabbling, having peered at the fish and the blue ocean bed from every possible angle. The sky was still cloudless, it was 42 degrees centigrade, and the sand was too hot to walk on without thongs. Laura looked around desperately for facts to hold on to but it was no good: if Minnie was a lesbian, then the sky was only cloudless because at other times it was black with rain, and the temperature was 42 because it wasn't quite hot enough to be 43 or cool enough to be 41. Laura had to accept the awful truth, there was no 42, it simply didn't exist. Heterosexuality wasn't normal, there wasn't a normal for it to be.

Before she appealed to Minnie for help she would try one more acid test. Laura's horror of change dated from when she was very little. Perhaps she had always suspected that things were only what they seemed, and if she had allowed this thought more leeway Minnie's abnormality would not have affected her so much. She had been in a good position to realise that though Janet & John, Mummy & Daddy & Rover were not every child's experience of domestic bliss, there was nothing else to replace it with except lack of Mummy or Daddy or Rover. Her reaction had been to hanker after the ideal state, pictured on every Weeties packet, and when she did not find it in the world around her, she had hidden it in the depths of her own past for which there was no proof but her own word. She could remember to this day, she must have been seven or eight, saying proudly to her friend Kathy at school,

— I've got a new uncle.

— You can't have a new uncle, Kathy had protested, same as you can't have a new Mummy.

But Laura had a new uncle. Her mother had come home one night, rather pissed, laughing a lot and saying gaily,

— Come and meet my little weeds.

A man's voice had protested that it was too late to wake the children, but Irene had been adamant.

— If you're going to live here, you must meet the inhabitants.

Laura turned over and shook Moira, who blinked crossly.

— Come on, Moira, wake up, Mummy's brought us an uncle home.

Irene came into the bedroom with a strange man who stood in the doorway saying,

— I'd far rather see you in bed than these little shrimps.

Laura felt an acute sense of failure, perhaps she should have smiled and offered the uncle some peanuts, like you did at grown up parties. For the next few years, however, she had had an answer to those awkward questions they ask you at school.

— What's your father's name?

— What does your dad do?

— Is your Daddy coming to parents' evening?

In a fit of gratitude, Laura had taken the new uncle's name because the children at school had their father's names and, if she was to pretend that her uncle was her father, she had to have his name.

This seemed to make him happy, for her mother always said she was his little favourite.

She hardly ever saw the new uncle; he worked very hard and would come home late at night and go away with her mother at weekends, but nevertheless this period was the closest she ever got to perfect happiness. When she was lying awake crying, in the stream of Homes to which she was later sent, she would summon up the picture of all others most reminiscent of those times. It was the photograph of four little girls, a man and a woman, standing in front of a wooden gate. The part of it which was fixed indelibly in her mind was not their grinning faces or the ice cream melting in their hands, but the newly painted sign, beside the mail box, proclaiming proudly, John Johnson and Family.

As Ingrid and John, Minnie and Laura made their way back to the ferry, Laura inwardly resolved to go back to Kalgoorlie and see John Johnson again as the last bastion of her faith in the world. They walked past the log cabins made by convicts when the island had been a penal colony, before it was given over to holiday makers. No more building was allowed now and the place was overrun with bicycles. There was a rickety bus which would take you round the lighthouse where generations of keepers' daughters had collected butterflies to stop them going mad, two cannons which were going to save Australia from aerial attack by the Japanese, and such vans as were strictly necessary to transport pie, chips and Swan Lager from the Temeraire Two to the Quokka Arms. You could buy sun-hats with the motto "GottogotoRotto" on them and apart from that there were the trampolines, boats and quokkas (as well as the sand and the sea and the sun, not to mention the surf, which you will find on any one of Australia's beautiful beaches. Your local travel agent will be delighted to give you a brochure but believe you me, the other attractions pale in comparison with the uniqueness of the afore-mentioned sun, sea, sand and surf). You cannot go to Rotto without seeing a quokka, a small furry creature rather like a rat, which explains the name of the island (or I suppose it does if you happen to speak Dutch or German or whatever damn language it is in which "rott' means "rat"). It is in fact a marsupial, smaller than a wallaby, much much smaller than a kangaroo and not nearly so good in the water as a duck-billed platypus. The other interesting thing about it is that it is ideally adapted to drought; it can, at times of great stress, recycle its own piss and, once gestation has started, prolong pregnancy for years at a time until conditions are right to give birth.

The male of the species is similar to the prototype with obvious exceptions.

It was this small rat thing which stopped our gang of four in their respective tracks. As they passed the log cabins with the romantic history it hopped out in front of them, demanding its tithe of Chiko roll or pastie. Ingrid bent down to pat it and confirm how sweet it was, more from a sense of this being what one does to small furry animals than a genuine love of failed koala bears.

A close observer would have noticed Laura not bending forward like Ingrid to stroke the mangy animal and a trained psychologist would have wondered that a girl who was so fond of cats and star fish should prove insensible to this fairy tale creature, however unacceptable its name. No such observer was present, however, only me, and I wasn't looking. At a rough guess I should say that Laura's ontology (so what? I had to look it up too) had been so profoundly disturbed that had you asked her,

— Do you like cheese?

She would have replied,

— I don't remember.

Of the quokka she exclaimed in disgust,

— Leave the dirty thing alone, it's got fleas.

All animals have fleas, it's what makes them human, so why hadn't she noticed this characteristic of the charming beasts before? Her tendency to think in terms of Before and After was to remind herself that Something Momentous had happened, in case she caught herself slipping back into her old habit of believing that if anything untoward should occur, at least it was intentional on someone's part. She had never felt quite the same about the weather after she realised that in fact her mother had no more control over it than she did and, far from doing it to spite her, was just as pissed off when it rained.

However, despite the inner turmoil of at least two of the party, our faithful four made it to the Rottnest Islander in time to get standing room on deck. Ingrid and Laura opted to spend half the trip back in the toilet in front of the mirror. The room was so small that if anyone came in to go to the bog, a not infrequent occurrence, one or other of them would have to go and wait outside and continue applying the moisturiser out there. Ingrid was an advocate of Bronze Sun because it allowed you to brown as you baked; Laura, however, being of fairer complexion and blonde hair, preferred Block Out which prevented the harmful UV rays from ever touching your skin. Either way, as they peeled back cotton shirts and bathers, the mirror threw out an image of two young women in the first throes of sunburn. Bikini marks and watch straps shone out brilliant white on a scarlet background; fetching if painful.

Ingrid wondered why Dolly had those long articles about emphasising the sensual colouring of the lips, when boys only turned round and said,

— You shouldn't wear lipstick, doll, I can't stand the taste.

Laura was finding great relief in covering her entire body in lanolin, a ceremony she had performed on myriad previous trips to beach, river and lake. She was conventional in appearance, "just normal" she would have said, but living at Balga had made her branch out a little and Beryl had bought her a black T shirt.

— Jeeze, black, mum? I've never had one this colour before. The aunties used to say only French prostitutes wore black.

But Laura had worn the T shirt and had even been known to go skinny dipping at Swanbourne, though the sight of all those men purving at them from the sand dunes, fully dressed down to their shoes and socks, made her wonder if naturism was liberation, or just more of the same. She could never quite banish from her mind the feeling that women who wore low cut dresses somehow deserved what they got. A hangover, perhaps, from the time when she didn't mind what happened as long as someone was responsible. Then she could watch from the sidelines and not get hurt.

Laura felt affronted; there was nothing in the rules about finding your foster sister was a dyke. Lesbians were either strong and bossy like Nora in Prisoner or ugly masochistic women who couldn't get a man, like that Violette woman in the scruffy paperback that had been passed around in the Home. Above all, lesbians were never anyone you actually knew, let alone someone bouncy and fun.

— Minnie should put something on her shoulders, they're

the texture of Dunlop Radials. She'll burn.

— Aw, we spent most of the time in the water.

— What were yous talking about when me and Boyfriend came back?

— Sex.

— Mmph, that's funny. So were we.

— How far had you two got?

— I was saying it was too hot to sleep in the panel van and he was saying you didn't buy a pair of wheels so's you could sleep in the house and where would Min sleep if he slept with me.

— With me.

— Oh, you'd got that far.

Laura had offered her bedroom to prove that she did not hold Minnie's sexuality against her. Ingrid was less complicated, certainly about other people. If Laura offered to have Minnie sleep with her, it was because she wanted her to. This in no way affected her confidence in the world as a place that loved her, what other people did in bed was their own business. She had been surprised that Johnny was camp because she had previously assumed that gay people were alright. She was quite undisturbed by Minnie's gayness, the latter had made no great point of telling her and she had not been expected to react in any particular way, so placidity could keep her plodding on till it was no longer an issue. Always best not to act surprised, let alone shocked, then it could never be later established that you had in fact heard.

— Boyfriend said if it was really hot, we could leave the back door up.

Laura did not have the same problem with her John. He made his weekly visit to her every Saturday and as his mother thought it immoral for them to sleep together at her house, they fucked at Beryl's. Beryl positively encouraged the activity as a cure for adolescent spots, but John slipped out of the house at two in the morning, shoes in hand, not liking to spend the whole night away from home. He only got tiring when he'd been to see a film and had erotic notions about the beach at night.

Ingrid was standing on one leg on tip toe, twisting her whole body round so that her flab was compressed and her muscles strained, trying to peer at the small of her back to see if her bikini mark had gone. You don't burn your bum

60

raw skinny dipping for nothing. Suddenly she stumbled and was propelled across the room against the back wall. The lights flickered. For a moment she wasn't sure if it was her head or if Laura felt it too; where was Laura?

There came a groan from one of the cubicles, then two hands and her foster sister's face appeared round the edge of the door.

— Strike! What happened? You right, Ing?

A buzzing noise took over the air around them, a crackle and,

— During the present turbulence, we request all passengers to remain indoors.

— Turbulence? muttered Minnie, Where does he think he is, on a fucking Jumbo Jet?

If the truth be known, however, she was feeling a little guilty, well though she knew that this was an i.u.* emotion. At the exact moment when the sudden storm had blown up, she had been praying for an act of goddess which would wipe her sister's boyfriend from the face of the Earth.

From the upper deck had cascaded a veritable torrent of rusty bicycles and the pent up wrath of hoary Speedwells and back pedallers had vented its spleen upon the hapless Boyfriend seated below. The fury held within their girded spokes had finally been liberated when the wind's howls hit the exact frequency of their all-steel frames. The freak storm was evidently the result of unusual air currents set up by cyclone Felix in its passage over Geraldton, 380 kms up the coast. To poor Minnie, however, who had just witnessed the main enemy bounced to death by the worn tread of a hundred seamed frames with buckled rims, it seemed like an answer to her prayers. It does not rain bicycles, even a kid's solid rubber chopper, every day, but to be hit on the head by a 50 lb Raleigh Roadster with brazed frames and cutaway lugs, you have to be really unlucky. It was the revenge of the cheapo cheapos, the Richard's rejects and the rugged but weighty.

— Bummer, said Boyfriend as he toppled over.

To explain the cause of Minnie's anger towards the pulped pathetic mess which now lay spreadeagled on the deck, left cheek bearing the imprint of a hundred sandy tyres, we would have to look back thousands of years when man (sick) first discovered both his sex's part in the reproduction

61

*Ideologically unsound (Ed.)

problem and the insecurity of being individually irrelevant. Failing that, I will take you back a mere half hour of our human life span, the time it took Laura to lanolise her legs and Ingrid to map out her sunburn in the tiny ferry toilet where we have just left them.

Minnie and Boyfriend had both remained on deck when the other two went below.

— Aren't you going to powder your nose with the other chicks?

— No, I'm getting a stubby, do you want a beer? Minnie returned with two tubes of Emu Bitter and a cup of tea.

— Strewth, you've gotta be a Pom! Afraid the bubbles'll get you all excited and you'll need the tea to calm you down?

— Listen, mate, if it's got bubbles in, it's gnat's piss. You wait till you've tasted Fuller's ESB.

Boyfriend tried another tack.

— Wanna ride in the sinbin when we get back?

— Yer what?

— Shaggin' Wagon. We could go for a hack, do a few burn outs, lay a little rubber.

Minnie refused to rise to this show of lexical prowess. It is, what's more, extremely difficult to take anyone seriously when they persistently stare at your breasts. In London you could wear quite open, low-cut shirts, but shorts, even of the most boring sporting white, were right off. In Perth suburban housewives wore bathers to the local shops; you could have legs "right up to your bum" but breasts were asking for it.

— That all yours?

— What big round eyes you have.

— You bounce beaut when you run.

— Ever been to Speedway? Boyfriend continued. The front yard at his mother's was littered with old Hillmans on wooden platforms and he spent his Sundays chroming the engines.

— I'd rather go to Hell.

— That was my next suggestion.

Minnie was furious. What a fool, she'd walked right into that one.

Boyfriend was worse when he was being earnest.

— Look, I was only kidding you around. I know you're women's lib and all. Ing told me. Well, I'm right with you;

62

chicks should get the same money as guys, but in Australia, well in the West at any rate, I wouldn't know what happens out East, it's all equal anyway. Girls can get apprenticeships, look at your sister's hairdressing.

Minnie felt tired, took a deep breath and said patiently,
— It's not only about equal pay. In England the Yorkshire Ripper has just killed his thirteenth victim, not to mention the hundreds of other women whose murders don't hit the headlines because they didn't manage to get killed by the same man.

— Oh, I quite agree, rapists should be hung. In the Eighteenth Century and in those Arab countries, if you stole something they cut off your hand. It's an eye for an eye and a tooth for a tooth.

Minnie thought about how sweet Boyfriend was to Ingrid and did not believe he was being deliberately annoying, but that was the problem.

— You know yourself that rape isn't all it's cracked up to be. I mean, when I'm out cruising with the other guys, we often stop to pick up a bit of skirt, not nice chicks like you or your sister, but the sort that'll get into a panel van.

— Ingrid sleeps in your panel van every night. Minnie spoke slowly. She was beginning to get angry.

— You know what I mean. You pick up some Sheila, pash on in the back and the next moment she's yelling "gang bang". You don't know if it's a complaint or a suggestion. He sniggered at his little joke.

— And in places like Kalgoorlie, he continued, warming to his theme, you only have to get off the train to be offered some black fella's sister. They're Gins of course. Have you heard of the Gin Run? No, I s'pose not, you being a girl and all. You wouldn't like it. You drive round town and pick up a Gin, you can usually get one for the price of a flagon, and if you haven't had one by your second night, you're not one of the lads. Well, I mean, who's to know if she's willing or not?

It's alright to listen to this kind of shit when you know the speaker is about to be knocked unconscious by a herd of wild bicycles, but you feel awfully powerless otherwise. Minnie was sick to the pit of her stomach. Was there nowhere she could escape to? Here she was on this beautiful day, gently sprayed by the water as the ferry bobbed up and down, sharing a beer with her sister's boyfriend who seemed to want to show his good will. And here was this monster, coolly telling her that she knew very well that rape wasn't rape when the woman was black, sold by her brother, without her own transport, or simply "not a nice chick". She did not deign to reply, but stared at him with grim hatred.

There was a prolonged silence, then, realising he was not being approved of by his Girlfriend's Eldest Sister, Boyfriend looked for a way of changing the subject without retracting. He started to whistle, gazing unconcernedly out to sea, as if they had agreed to differ.

— Did you know you can't whistle directly into the wind? It whips all your breath away and the sound gets lost, he remarked in that affable way men have of viewing Life as an apolitical curiosity.

Then he glanced back at her from the prow where he had been conducting his aerodynamic experiments. His look of boyish discovery turned slowly through resentment and paranoia to aggression at her unblinking, icy loathing. He moved towards her, and she recognised in him one of the young men from the Mall, when suddenly the boat gave a lurch. He put down his glass and his face turned green. He crumpled up before her eyes and Minnie felt as guilty as if she had poisoned him.

— Here we go again, she thought.

— Groog. You shouldn't have given me that beer, I'm going to throw up.

Just as he was bending his head with the time-honoured words, dear to all who have travelled long distances with small children,

— Quick, a paper bag!

a great cry of wrath was heard, which rent the heavens asunder. A neat brown hand appeared from out of the sky bearing a trim toasting fork and directed a blast in the direction of the retching figure. Minnie gaped in horrified anticipation but with the total absence of anything untoward befalling the wretched young man, she sighed,

— Bloody Women's Movement, never do anything on time, assuming the thunder bolt, or whatever it was, had simply missed its mark as Boyfriend keeled over.

— Nothing so old hat, said an ungodly voice which Minnie recognised as that of the goddess. We feminists use only the most modern methods. You should join, sister.

— I'm a life member, Minnie growled. Honestly! After all her footwork on abortion demonstrations, the one time she asked for something it was bungled. Surely Hyde Park to Trafalgar Square year in and year out, as Private Member after Private Member tried to hit the Big Time over women's bodies (a fertile area, as the joke went), deserved more than a faint sizzle and a drop in the ocean?

It was at this moment that the heavy metal avalanche began and Minnie saw that the heavenly figure had melted the chain which held the bicycles together.

— Must have been that flash of lightning, the Captain was heard to say later, with the knowing look of an old sea dog. Tough luck, sport, see you later, he added to the prostrate Boyfriend. In a free enterprise society there is no monopoly on rational explanations.

The passengers flocked indoors, ignoring the loud speaker which they could not hear anyway due to the wall of sound, but persuaded by the heavy rain. The bicycles were rounded up, their little wheels still spinning in the air, and reprimanded severely to behave themselves in future. The stewardess' heart was not really in it, however. She had lost a Dawes Galaxy Deluxe, Reynolds 531 frame with cotterless chainset, the only bicycle casualty and the like of which she feared she would never own again. Furthermore, she had seen the arm descend from the sky and had rejoiced, as would we all, at this latter day Sign. If she'd been consulted, she might have agreed that the death of a potential rapist was worth the loss of a Dawes Galaxy. But she hadn't been asked.

Once the lights came on again Ingrid and Laura, now convinced it was the world which had blundered, not them, picked themselves up and helped each other climb the stairs. The first sight to greet their eyes, when they entered the bar, was the stretcher, carried on board for just such emergencies, bearing Boyfriend's body.

— Bloody oath, he looks crook, cooed Laura, always quicker off the mark than her foster sister.

— Should do love, he's dead . . . , said the stretcher-bearer. At a look from the Captain she pulled the white sheet up over Boyfriend's treadmarked face, all that now remained of the green bike she would so sorely miss. At the thought of its little lugs, picked out in gold, her eyes misted over; she would never save enough for another. The Captain, already feeling embarrassed that such an incident should happen on any vessel in his charge, noted the mistiness and harumphed that women were allowed on board at all. They always brought bad luck.

Laura, Ingrid and Minnie were pale and shaky by the time the Rottnest Islander finally reached Fremantle. They had all been sick on the ferry and were wondering how to get home now their driver was laid up. Ingrid felt a bit pissed off that she'd lost Boyfriend, but it solved the problem of where to sleep. Beryl was waiting for them when they got back, worried that they were so late, but all sympathy when they explained.

— Oh, poor lad. His mother will be very upset, she had said comfortably as she washed the dishes, I do hope he wasn't her favourite.

And that had been the last word on the matter.

Chapter 5
Historic Guildford

New Year's Eve was a Saturday, and Saturday morning found Beryl busy cleaning the house. Normally she did this on a Sunday when the kids were not underfoot: Laura went to see Moira and Ingrid would be out with Boyfriend. Beryl did not wish to explain why she had altered her usually fixed routine, planning to be out of the house early enough the next day to avoid awkward questions. Her husband would be tired from the taxi, and nothing could wake her daughters.

Difficult though it was to deflea the carpet at the best of times, it was still worse if you had to pretend you were really doing something else. Bending over airily to look at her nephew's wedding photo, she pulled the powder from her pocket and dusted the ground beneath her. Sitting calmly on the sofa, *Middlemarch* on her lap, hand playing with the upholstery awaiting its prey until 'snap', one of the little brats was caught between finger and thumb and squeezed till it clicked: to perform this with an air of total unconcern as though tensing her muscles at an exciting passage in the book? No, it wasn't on and besides it wasn't terribly effective. What a pity she couldn't just send the girls off to Mass or a nice meeting.

Laura flounced in from her bedroom, demanding to be done up.

— What are you doing with the flea powder?

She was always asking questions in a friendly sort of way, but never listened to the answers.

— Painting the ceiling.

— I'm bored.

— Why don't you go and see Moira?

— We're not speaking since Christmas Day.

Desperate measures.

— I thought perhaps we should take up Sandra's offer.

— What? Buy the Kingswood?

The deal was soon clinched. Sandra's husband had gone off to Cairns to start a new life in pawpaws but had decided against Sandra's aura and had not invited her along. Sandra would just about pay off the house on her wages as long as she didn't get extravagant and start eating. It was cheaper to go into town by bus as the big six seater just ate gas. Left out the front the car would rust away, even if it did look flash in the driveway.

— Can I go for a spin?

Beryl was hoping Laura would ask, but found it wiser to feign maternal concern.

— Darling, I've only just bought it. You'll go up a curb or get yourself lost.

— I won't, mum, I'll be ever so careful, honest I will.

— Well, I suppose it's alright, only don't go too far.

Ingrid and Minnie came in from the pool as Laura ceremoniously backed the Kingswood from Sandra's front yard to theirs. It hadn't seemed worth turning as the drives were opposite each other. It was much cheaper to buy a house and a plot of land all in one, but it meant that every detail of your unique family home was repeated at regular 10 metre intervals along the line of little red houses set exactly 5 metres from the road.

— It seemed like a good idea, Beryl apologised, fearful lest her daughters wonder at her sudden extravagance, Sandra needs the money, and it is a family car. Besides, now we've lost Boyfriend and my John's always out in the taxi . . . She trailed off, not wanting to tread on any toes.

— You win some, you lose some, Ingrid said wistfully, wondering what control she'd have over Laura; the arrangement with John had at least been clear.

Laura, sensing this, rolled down the window and asked brightly,

— Wanna go for a hack?

Beryl was delighted.

— Why don't you go too, Minnie? You know how you love a drive.

— Yes, and you, Mum; we'll all go! We can go to Historic Guildford.

Everyone liked this drive. Beryl would gaze at the enormous giraffe-necked church, built in the days when the settlers thought they were still in England and before they were glad they were not. Laura sniggered at the really foolish railway crossing where it was actually possible to be stuck at the lights and on the railway track at the same time. Minnie's heart missed a beat when she heard the word "Guildford", that was where the party was being held and to go there during the day meant a tying up of the two worlds she was finding increasingly schizophrenic. Ingrid had no particular love of the town itself, the sight of miserable aboriginals sitting in the church garden with its litter of beer rings did more to rock her faith in a good world than anything else (the fights had become so numerous that bottles were no longer sold and tinnies rusted in the couch grass), no, what she liked was the ride along Alexander Drive through Dianella where the road was lined with startling white Italian houses who vied with each other for the number of arches and pillars they could display. It was better at night when the sweep of ghostly staircases was set off by grim colonnades which snapped like gappy teeth.

Beryl was tempted. Everyone was in a good mood; they would drive down singing through the open windows at the tops of their voices, and very probably she and Minnie would burst into quotation: "In Xanadu did Kubla Khan" as they passed through Dianella, then they would have a cup of tea in a cafe (which she would pay for) and wander round the shops, sneering at the clothes. But, being slow to deviate from her normal routine, she was loathe to attempt any contingency plan at so late a stage.

— No, darlings, you go. I'd rather have a potter while you're out.

"Potter" felt sufficiently vague as to be unchallengeable. They could not come home and in righteous indignation exclaim,

— Mum, mum, you haven't finished the pottering! You said you'd potter my jumper and you haven't even started.

The verbal equivalent of "potter" was "mutter", or "natter" if it involved more than one person. Her daughters accepted the excuse, having need of the same line of defence themselves on occasion.

— Are you and Moira really not speaking? Ingrid piped up as Laura drove off.

— How do you know about that?

69

— I was hanging my towel on the line and I heard through the fly screen.

Now that Laura was in Guildford and the Great Eastern Highway lay before her, it seemed like the ideal opportunity to zoom off to Kalgoorlie. Like it or not, she was going to have to tell her sisters so they could provide Beryl with a pretext for her staying out all night. Minnie she felt reasonably sure of, but Ingrid had become something of a mystery to her since they had started living together. There was the rivalry over Beryl, and she even wondered if Ingrid objected to her calling her foster mother "Mum"; then there was her own jealousy over Ingrid's apprenticeship, bad though she felt about it. However, she needed Ingrid, and could only hope that at some later stage, Ingrid would realise she needed her.

— Yeah, Moira was angry that I let her make a fool of herself on Christmas Day.

— What, you mean the bubble?

— No, she knew we didn't really mind about that.

— Oh, saying The Fox was disgusting?

— Yis, well Minnie was bound to get upset but Moira said I hadn't explained things properly and I'd let her get drunk and silly.

Minnie pricked up her ears in the back seat but went on looking out of the window, not yet ready to join in.

— I thought she was just pissed off that you'd come to live with us after your own mother . . .

— It's more than that, you see (Laura took a deep breath), I told her I was going back to see John Johnson and she said I was a crawling arse licker.

Minnie sat up and looked at Laura, wondering what it all meant.

— When are you going? she asked.

— Well, said Laura vaguely, you know we didn't have a car before and here we are on the Great Eastern Highway . . .

— OK, we'll tell mum you're watching the fireworks in King's Park and staying the night at Simone's, said Minnie decisively.

Ingrid resented Laura going off to have a nice time with Simone and had got as far as imagining what Simone would say about the Ocker Pig when she remembered it was all just a story.

— Won't mum want the car this evening, seeing as she only just bought it? she said, not wanting to foul things up, but sensing trouble.

— Bound to; you'll have to act the thoughtless daughter who kept the car out all night. Mum knows nothing about speedos, so she won't know how far you've gone, Minnie solved the problem to Laura's satisfaction at least. But now she was actually going, she began to feel apprehensive.

— Good luck tonight, Minnie, she ventured, I hope you have the nerve to turn up.

— Now that I've been here it'll seem a lot less terrifying.

It occurred to Minnie that Ingrid needed some kind of explanation.

— I'm coming to a women's party here tonight where I won't know anyone.

— How brave, was all Ingrid could say.

— I'm not really into tracing lost father figures myself, Min continued, but as you're going to anyway, I just hope it all turns out alright.

Laura felt irritated at the way Minnie had taken over and made a friendly chat into a public meeting with speeches for and against. After all, she hadn't said a thing about all-women parties. Must be all those conferences Minnie went to.

— What 'bout you, Ing? What are you doing tonight?

Ingrid looked from one to the other, thinking what exciting lives they led and said firmly,

— I thought I'd eat.

— Eat? the others chorused blankly. For Minnie this hardly even counted as an activity; it was grabbing a hasty sandwich and gobbling it down before a lecture. For Laura it was something to be avoided if possible; you invented all sorts of allergies to the commonest foods like tomato and curry so that well meaning women would stop piling your plate.

Ingrid's face was set, in great contrast with the soft curves of her chins. Given the prevailing air of tolerant sisterhood, neither of the others felt they could pursue their sense of natural indignation; each wondered if her own project sounded as outrageous as this simple desire to spend the evening feeding one's face. Minnie would have liked to protest that it wasn't the same; compulsive bingeing was a very real problem whereas women coming together in a social setting was essential to the movement. Laura could think of nothing so homespun as a girl setting out to find her long lost uncle, even if No 96* had rather soaped the market. Ingrid was perfectly aware of both their disapproval and their tacit acceptance.

Finally Minnie grinned.

— I'll bring you back some prawn crackers, there's bound to be some tonight.

Laura promised one of John's rock melons. He was the only person she'd ever known who managed to grow them outside captivity. The sudden sharp memory of that enormous overgrown garden where all the water had to be piped in from Mundaring Weir but still they had fresh vegies, reminded her that she must set off soon or she wouldn't get there before dusk. Ingrid and Minnie got out and waved goodbye. As she drove off, Laura was ruminating on the Everychild's folk Australia story of C.Y.O'Connor who had had the brilliant idea of piping water out to the goldfields and who had hung himself only a few hours before the first few drops trickled into Kalgoorlie, believing the venture a failure. She too would soon be following that great white pipe, set half a foot in the air; and when it stopped, so should she.

By unspoken consent Minnie did not stride off to find the place where the party would be and Ingrid did not waft away to the market buying here a mango, there a lamington, (those disgusting little mounds of cake covered in grey coconut which ressemble nothing so much as cold hedgehogs). And if Minnie shot an eye out to examine the houses they passed for women's symbols, sun streamers and other tell-tale insignia, she did not let on, any more than Ingrid, whose roving gaze told her that kiwi fruit were very cheap for the time of year, but bananas probably over-ripe. As they walked towards the station, they talked instead of Beryl and Laura and London.

— Did you go to John's wedding? Aunty Alice sent Mum the photos.

— Yeah! It was quite funny really. They know what I think about weddings so it wasn't worth not going to make a point. If you see what I mean.

— Cut the politics, Minnie, this is your sister you're talking to. You went along for the wedding cake and a sight of old

*All Australian disaster series (Ed.)

Veronica in white.

— Partly. Minnie didn't like being deflated when she was feeling righteous and she always told her funny stories from the beginning, interruption always messed up the story.

— Anyway, I went dressed in black with a dyke earring and gave Veronica a 26 blade Army knife and John an electric element so he can make his own tea when she leaves him.

— I bet you did, said Ingrid, teach them to invite you to anything. Was granny there?

— Yeah, but John's mate John warned me she was sitting right up near the altar on one of the front pews, wouldn't miss a good ceremony. I told him I didn't really want to talk to her because she always says sadly: "Of course Minnie has no one to keep her warm." So he said, "Tell her you're a pinko commie queer" and I said "but I am, John, I am". So he turns to John in the middle of the bloody church and yells, "Have you heard the one about the bridegroom whose cousin's a pinko commie queer?" and John goes up to the organist in the middle of "Jesu Joy of Man's Desiring" and says if the other John hums it he'll get the organist to play it for Hymn.

— You are awful, Minnie, you set it all up just so's people will talk about you. Ingrid was unimpressed and made her sister tell her about dear Aunty Alice.

— Sometimes I think that because of mum and dad splitting up I'll never see Aunty A. again.

Ingrid never spoke of her father and Minnie was too aware of the solemnity of the moment to ask any questions. When they reached Wellington Street, Ingrid elected to go North to Wanneroo to do her shopping, and Minnie took the Surfers' Express, courtesy of 61X radio, to the beach. So the sisters split up, Ingrid musing on the Perth bus system which Beryl always referred to as "Socialism in Action" because there was a flat fare anywhere in the met area during a two hour period. To Ingrid this was simply convenient, she could not see why politics had to be dragged in. Minnie meanwhile, was puzzling as to how her sister could have had the childhood she had and still shy away at the word "politics".

They parted the best of friends and neither returned home till evening, by which time Beryl had scrubbed the floors, shampooed the carpets, shoved the chair covers in the washing machine and taken down every single ornament from the lounge room shelves, washed them gently in soapy water, and put them all back again more or less where they came from. It occurred to her that perhaps she ought to worry where the girls were all day as she sat down to lettuce, radish and an artichoke, all produce from her own garden. On reflection, however, it seemed a little late now to start acting like a proper mother. Minnie had been most aggrieved, when at the tender age of 14, she had started going out with boys and not been given an evening deadline. Best friend Gillian at school said it meant her mother didn't care about her; she herself had to be in by 10.30. Beryl had known that Minnie would not go out without best friend Gillian and it was inevitable that Gillian's mother would have come up with some formula for the regulation of young adolescent sex life. Beryl was from an age which believed in promiscuity, though she herself had not slept with anyone before she got married.

— Damn well made up for it afterwards, tho', she thought with an involuntary grin which faded softly when she remembered no one was there.

As soon as she got home, Minnie ran herself a bath, unusual in Australia where, though baths do exist, they soon fill up with pot plants. She wanted time and luxury to plan out what to wear. The problem of transport had miraculously vanished without her having to lift a finger: Boyfriend would have copped 50 demerit points had he attempted to drive in his present condition, and Laura had upped and offed in Beryl's new treasure. When the water was steaming, the mirror dripping with white mist and the bath foaming at the mouth, Minnie unzipped her jeans and slid meltingly in.

Whatever she wore, the colour scheme would be pink and black. At the usual age of sixteen, she had decided that black was the only colour. This had soon worn off, but left an elegant aftertaste. When, a few years later, an artist friend had declared,

— Pink is a much maligned colour, confined to the coventry of little girls' hair ribbons and strawberry ice cream, she had added pink to her colour scheme. When the hot pink triangles on a black background had come out, her choice had been confirmed. When feminist colours had mutated from the lurid green and lavender of the suffragettes to the pink and black of later Spare Rib diaries, she found her clothes provided her best feminist credentials. In a flash it came to her: Pink boots from Camden Lock, hand made by Sue and Barbara to accommodate bunions and corns; Brutus jeans; black Harrington; the whole set off by triangular perspex earrings. She gushed out of the bath, threw on said items and made for the bus stop. As the sweat dripped down her neck she knew half her outfit would have to come off.

It took ages to get to Guildford, which was plenty of time to agonise and when she did arrive her nails were too blunt to scratch her dandruff. By following the route very carefully on both bus and road map, she managed to get off two stops before hers. This gave the hour hand sufficient time to reach nine o'clock and she bought a bottle of Yalumba while she waited. But perhaps Australian feminists didn't drink wine.

— All the more for us, Milly snapped at Minnie crossly.

As before when Minnie couldn't cope, she switched into emergency overdrive, i.e. Milly. When a friend's mother asked Minnie what she planned to do with herself, Milly would speak gravely about her university course and PhD. At Christmas when Steppo had shown her photo after photo of little steppos, whom she had never met and to whom she was not related, she had called on Milly to examine each one attentively and ask intelligent questions as to their whereabouts and proximity of kinship, while she slipped out to the pool with the others. Their worst excess, which had very nearly landed both of them in serious financial trouble (the only kind that Minnie took seriously), had been due to the London housing shortage.

At the end of the university term, Minnie was chucked out of her hall of residence and forced to seek an alternative. There being nothing in the immediate vicinity of Camden Town, she had looked further afield. When her old friend from People Against Sexism days had offered her a room in her house in Crouch End, she had accepted without waiting to see the room, not entirely convinced that such a place existed. Anyway, the price had been right, and homelessness was looming large. The woman, Barbara, had driven her up then and there, suitcases piled on the back seat. The room was full, absolutely full, of the most staggeringly awful furniture, the wallpaper was bright yellow, and the landlord lived underneath. It might still have been alright, if only

Barbara hadn't talked so much. What can be dealt with in a friendly way in a CR group, becomes a deadly bore in your own home. Barbara went on and on: Man United; the launderette; the neighbours; her mother; home-made beer; her diet. It was awful. Minnie froze up completely and lay on the sofa in a paralyzed heap while Milly, darting furious looks in her direction, brightly fed the conversation with: George Best; use the extractor first; you can always phone the police; my mum's just the same; fizzy though, and have you tried cottage cheese, only 33 calories an ounce. At this Minnie had intoned "fat is not about lack of self control", the opening bars of Fat is a Feminist Issue. It was not a tune Milly knew, and after a few more hours, Barbara went to bed. Minnie and Milly had shared the single bed in Minnie's room, as so often in the past.

— It's impossible, it's just completely impossible.

— Seems alright to me. Very clean.

— Oh scrupulously! Look, it's no good, I can't stay here. Milly held out for propriety as long as she could.

— One simply does not sneak out of one's future home after midnight without so much as a forwarding address.

— I haven't got an address at all, let alone a forwarding one.

— Minnie, vagrancy just isn't on, but if your mind is made up, what can I do but follow? At least leave a note.

— A note? Minnie repeated in terror.

— Look, pretend you're quite quite mad. Then Barbara will forgive you, won't want to come near you, and won't take it personally.

— I can't bear people to be sorry for me.

— You can't have it both ways.

Dear Barbara,

What a lovely house! so warm and attractive! (but I hate exclamation marks, they're so obvious. Shut up and sprinkle them, make it look like a profound religious experience). *But really! all that yellow! We just couldn't. And the beer bottles! There is one in every drawer, we looked. We peeped under the washing machine and thought it only right to warn you, but there's something going on down there. Perhaps it's fond of you, as you're an old inhabitant, got used to you in a way, but we could just feel as we stared at it, that it wanted us out. Saw us as intruders. It's probably best to sneak up on*

76

*it in the dark so it doesn't know you're coming. We suspect
it feeds on home-made beer. And yellow.*

Yours in sisterhood,

Minnie (hey what's with this "we" character? You wrote
it, you take responsibility for it. But you've been dictating
what I have to write. Look, Barbara doesn't even know me.
She's been talking to you all evening. Oh, alright, but she'll
think you're completely off the wall).

& Milly.

Well, how would you feel if you found that on your
cooker one morning? Never trust the washing machine
again, eh?

They waited till the last sound died away through the old
house: dripping taps, creaking boards, coughing; counted
another hour after that, put their clothes on and crept downstairs, shoes in pockets, a suitcase in each hand. Minnie wondered how ever she would have managed them without
Milly. At the bottom they slipped their shoes on, whispered
open the door, then pelted along the street, giggling, as fast
as the cases would let them. As they paused to get their
aching breath back and ease their overexcited lungs, they
spotted a taxi and went back to Aunt Alice's, the only place
on which they could descend at four in the morning.

Barbara, who was alright really, only a little garrulous
when nervous and trying to put someone at their ease, read
the note next morning and felt the breath kicked out of her.
It hurt. Then she felt angry, which was easier to deal with,
and demanded that Minnie pay for her rank irresponsibility
in the form of one month's rent, room or no room. In the
end it was Milly who went round, Minnie shaking her head
pathetically and declaring she could never go near the place
again and were she ever to meet Crouch of Crouch End, she
would tell them what she thought of them, and explained
to Barbara that her twin had been very overwrought over the
exams and moving house, and would love Barbara to come
and see her. Milly was tactful enough not to mention the
washing machine. Barbara reckoned she was under enough
strain as it was not to take on anyone else's and regretfully
declined the offer. But she dropped the rent demand, having
found a less sensitive housemate.

Minnie hoped it would not prove necessary to call on
Milly's services now; Milly had a tendency to lecture when

nervous, which was rather hard to conciliate with Minnie's bouncy ebullience. Besides, surely one of the reasons for coming all this way was to dispense with Milly's services altogether.

33, 35, 37 ... Minnie had to peer at the mail boxes to make out their numbers in the dark.

39 ... This was it. She pushed open the rickety gate, trod softly up the path and opened the door of the house. The wind chimes rattled melodiously as she went in, putting paid to any hope she had of inserting herself gently into the flow. Eight pairs of eyes looked up at her. She advanced awkwardly. Why were there so few people?

— G'day, nice to see you, what's your name?

— Er, Millicent, but they call me ...

— Milly? OK, Milly, get yourself a drink.

— No, thought Minnie rebelliously, not her, but she trotted obediently into the kitchen, cut the palm of her hand on a cork-screw and poured herself some wine.

— Here, she said to Milly, handing her a glass. Only don't drink too much, I might need you later.

Minnie went back to where the wimmin were sitting in a closely-knit circle, discussing the festival they were about to plan. Minnie could think of nothing to say, so, in abject gloom, she allowed Milly to ask interested questions concerning the place, date, and numbers expected. Milly was beginning to sound like a reporter.

— Do you think there will be anyone from Darwin? she enquired politely.

Silently, Minnie cringed, how on earth could someone who was leaving the country in a week, be interested in whether anyone from the Northern Territory was going to a festival in Western Australia? She herself would be 12 thousand miles away by then. To her horror, Milly got up and crossed over to another wombon and started gruelling her on West Australian Refuges, their politics and policies.

— Where do you get your funding from?

— What's the average turnover of wimmin in a given period of, say, two months, or would that depend on the time of year?

— Do you have male counsellors/counsel men or do you feel the word "counsel" is inapplicable?

Taking her twin aside, she hissed,

— This is a party, no one wants to listen to you talking shop.

— I'm NOT talking shop, I've never worked for Women's Aid in my life.

— No, said Minnie grimly, but I have. She was sure nothing would stop Milly except outside intervention. It wasn't until Milly had conducted an informative conversation with someone called Lilith about the circulation and availability plus distribution figures of Rouge, that Minnie heard a familiar voice which, coupled with three glasses of Yalumba, allowed her to grab Milly by the shoulders, shake her non-violently, and propel her out of the room. (But not before Milly had blown her cover as an ordinary human being and appeared unmasked as a "talking head". Minnie had a lot of sympathy for the womon who asked laughingly, trying to suppress her rising suspicion, whether Milly was with the CIA or MI5).

Minnie emerged into the open air of the back veranda where the sound which had broken Milly's spell welcomed her with full-throated ease. It was the dark brown voice of Gina Birch:

— I met her in a bar down in old Soho . . .

Minnie jumped up, kicking over the wine, and leapt onto the bare boards of the veranda. There were three womben dancing in what looked suspiciously like a couple, but I doubt if she even noticed them: she was on her feet, pink boots pumping up and down, bopping to the music as free of care as if Kate were with her. Linda, the wumin who had invited her, went past and declared,

— I don't like this kind of music, as though this were the official Perth bulletin.

— Philistine, Minnie yelled, it's the Raincoats; she had begun to enjoy herself. At last she paused to draw breath and went inside for some more booze. A leg was blocking her way.

— Got a light? it said.

— I don't smoke.

The end of a budding friendship. But somebody else produced a match box and Minnie asked for one to chew as her nails had given up the ghost.

— What amazing earrings.

They were luminous green with a feather attached. Earrings, like compulsive nibbling, provide an instant introduction.

— Fishing tackle.

Gosh. This was Minnie's most enthusiastic exclamation; it was what went through her head when she orgasmed, to the deflation of her lovers at the beginning of their relationship.

After they had covered number of holes, how to reopen same after a period of abstinence and would you ever put one through your nose (plus accompanying hygienic observations), the conversation showed signs of flagging. Minnie set off again to get that drink. As she raised the bottle to her glass, a womun threw her arms around her theatrically and husked,

— How would you like to be raped by me?

Minnie freaked out completely at the word, wondering how anyone could imagine that was funny, but not confident enough to say so. Milly stepped ponderously into the breach.

— I don't think it would be rape.

She meant of course that rape necessarily implies a patriarchal power struggle which can therefore not exist between two wymyn, though other intrasexual power struggles are indeed possible and to be condemned wherever found.

— No, hissed Minnie aghast, she thinks you mean I fancy her.

— Oh, I give up. You got yourself into this, now you can get yourself out. It's your scene not mine, and with that Milly returned from whence she came, having unearthed a very nice specimen of Barossa Riesling with the most tempting bouquet.

Minnie grabbed the now empty bottle.

— Why wouldn't it?

— Because I'd smash you over the head with this.

— Isn't she cute? the woman drawled, aware that it wasn't a joke but too slow to unsay it.

Minnie related the incident to her newly found friend.

— Bloody Hell! said the friend incisively if boozily.

And Minnie felt understood.

— What's your name?

— Erica. Yours?

— Minnie.

— Oh. I expect you get very tired of people calling you "mouse".

— Not really, it's a constant source of amusement, said

Minnie drily. I'm not called Minnie because I'm small, that happened afterwards when I stopped growing. It's short for Millicent and I can't stand Milly.

— Thanks, said a tipsy voice by Minnie's ear.

Minnie worried that she was talking too much, as usual. She took a calculating glance at the faint oil stains on the inside of Erica's overalls. Maybe, maybe not.

— Did you come by car? she asked disingenuously, willing the answer "no".

— Yes, spat Erica with disgust, I would have ridden, only my bike was swept into the sea.

— Wow! Another bike dyke.

And that was that for another few hours as

— Yeah, but tubs and sprints are no good for city cycling, spend your life sewing up tyres, succeeded

— My last bike was a Dawes Galaxy, but I lost it overboard in a freak storm, while other wumin clambered over them unregarded.

Soon, however, they'd have to come back to the sexed world of wimyn. Minnie wondered how they'd make the transition.

Erica grinned,

— Come on, she said, let's dance.

They spent the rest of the evening watching some weird and wonderful wiming from Melbourne who were in a theatre group and looked it. At about 3 am when it was useless to pretend to phone a taxi Erica suggested they go home. There were two other wyming going to Updike Street and the four of them drove off together.

— This is Sky, Erica introduced, she's staying at my place tonight.

It was the wimon with the bizarre attitude to rape, but she now looked too smashed to be freaky. She crept into a corner of the car, rolled up into a little ball, and groaned. Minnie laid her head on Erica's shoulder, closed her eyes and immediately felt sick. It seemed safer to open them again. At Updike Street, they half carried Sky through the house into the back yard where she asked only for a drain to be sick into. Minnie knew the feeling.

— Look, yous can both go to bed, I'll come in when I feel better.

It sounded inviting, Minnie felt dead tired, but Sky had

begun to crawl all over the garden and Erica said,
  — I think she's really crook.

Chapter 6
East Perth Infirmary

— No, no, don't take me to the hospital, I can't afford the hospital. Just give me some milk.

Sky was holding her stomach together and writhing in the back seat of the car. Minnie didn't know what to do. She looked at her arms lying clumsily in her lap and put them gauchely round the other woman, her stomach tying itself into sympathetic knots.

— You don't pay anything at Outpatients. They'll just give you something to coat your ulcer a bit better than milk.

— Ulcer? puzzled Minnie, looking at Sky with respect, I thought only business men got ulcers.

Sky's face had lost all its urbane self-assurance and she looked scarcely older than Minnie herself.

— They used to give me this stuff to take, but I'd get high on it and drink the whole bottle.

Erica put her foot down and they shot off along the road, narrowly missing an ambulance, siren screaming, coming from the opposite direction. Both cars turned into the "Emergency Vehicles Only" entrance.

— Well, we're a bloody emergency, Erica gritted through her teeth. If we don't get her seen to before she starts spitting blood, she'll die.

The ambulance screeched to a halt just in front of them.

— Probably only some man choking up a little paraquat from his long suffering wife.

They stumbled into the building, supporting Sky between them; Erica marched up to Reception. A stretcher appeared for Sky who vanished behind a green screen.

— I'd like to stay with her, please, Erica ennunciated clearly.

— I'm afraid the Doctor can't allow that.

— I am a nurse, said Erica, her trump card. And in my hospital we do allow patients their basic human rights. She resisted the urge to ask the woman how she felt about compassion as a non-participant.

— Oh yes, and where's that? the other nurse asked politely.

— Adelaide.

— The Eastern States, said the sister, as if modern medical knowledge had not yet reached those parts.

Erica was ushered out protesting and joined Minnie in a dejected lump on the bench. It suddenly felt very late and rather grey. The elation of the party had quite died away and even the pleasant inebriation was inexorably turning into a hangover. Sky was not a close friend of either of them, and, now the danger was over, they could almost wonder what they were doing there. Erica offered Minnie a cigarette, despite the "NO Smoking" sign, and Minnie accepted a match, her nails were now down to the cuticle.

The waiting room of a large city hospital is not the most pleasant experience at the best of times, with its seedy coffee machines, dirty plastic cups and spilled ash trays plus the ever present fear that someone is going to wheel a stiff past you at any moment. It must have the highest mortality rate of any public building in the city. On New Year's Day, 198- it was positively garish, with a dirty cotton wool snowman and a christmas tree whose faery lights blinked on and off in desperate good humour.

— Bloody 42 degrees today, and they still have a shagging snowman.

Minnie curled up on the bench and twisted round to see the other revellers. There was a very smart couple sitting bolt upright in their seats despite the late hour and regulation low backs to the chairs. Opposite them was an old Aboriginal woman with horrible sores and bruises on her legs and arms. Her toes stuck out at an odd angle from her laceless shoes as if she only wore shoes on special occasions. Next to her was a fat woman fidgeting nervously, eyes trained on the clock. Then came an elderly gentleman and finally, taking up all the remaining benches, the cream of Australian youth. They lolled in various poses of swaggering indifference. Decadent elegance, perhaps, their hair was certainly long and their feet sensuously bare, yet their toe nails were too black and their beer guts too pronounced for one seriously to suspect them of more than passing existential angst,

nineteenth century spleen, or plain old mal de siècle. However, fashions change. Who is to say that the youth of yester-
year were in any way more gifted than our own lads?

Minnie's attention was rivetted on the smartly dressed
man. All his actions were precise and deliberate. He could
have saved the world from the invading reds with his slow
determination. He raised his left arm from the shoulder of the person sitting next to him, and with his left
hand pulled his lapel exactly two inches away from his
breast. He raised his right hand and inserted it into the folds
of his jacket. On the third jerk, it travelled smoothly back
down from breast to knee. Here it was joined by the left
hand which lifted the top of the leather case. The right
hand now tilted the case at an angle of 45 degrees. A coin
slid from one side of the case to the other. The man opened
his mouth.

— Would you like some coffee?

— Yes, please, black no sugar.

The man stood up and walked towards the machine. He
stopped, looked at the black writing above the first button.
He looked down at his hand, then back at the sign. He turned
outwards to the room, looked round it, then moved towards
Minnie and Erica.

— Can you give me two 20 cent coins for this 50 cent
piece?

His request cut short Erica's wandering as she fished around
for some change.

— Would you like some coffee?

Minnie nodded and Erica got up.

The young men had not been watching the smartly dressed
man and were tired of teasing the Aboriginal woman. She sat
on her bench satisfyingly terrified but seemed too ill to react
with real drollery to their taunts.

— I would ask you to suck me off, but I'm saving my piss
for the alco-test, one particularly happy specimen whispered
in her ear so that only she and his mates could hear.

— Go away and leave me alone, said the woman, paralysed
lest one of them touch her. Then she would scream and be
thrown out of the hospital for drunkenness and the doctor
wouldn't see her.

The lads creased up at her pathetic attempt at dignity, but
really she was only a Gin and they could play with one of

85

those anytime. Unless she did something screamingly funny, wet her knickers or something, she wasn't worth bothering about. They looked around. The fat woman looked possible, but as they leered she grinned nervously and they promised themselves fun with her later. They glanced over the straight-backed couple and the elderly gent. Nothing there, though they sniggered at the young man's suit and called the old man "grandad". Then they felt bored.

And it was then that they discovered Erica. Cropped hair, faded overalls and as she turned with the two coffees in her hand, her jacket fell open on the words "Lesbian Liberation will never come under Fraser" written in lavender letters on a round metallic disc.

They curled their lips at her with delight. She could have been made for them.

— Hey, tranny, can I turn you on?

Minnie would have tried to ignore them, but Erica replied,

— At least get the name right if you're going to insult us.

To Minnie this approach seemed rather too intellectual, but perhaps she was wishing Erica hadn't worn that badge.

— We're not insulting you, you're an insult to the whole human race.

They smirked at each other. One strutted towards her, pelvis thrust forward, prick leading the way.

— I'm a doctor. I can cure you with my big injection. Now, just lie still like a good girl while I stick it into you.

It sounded like something from a text book for poofta bashers. Minnie was tempted to tell them to change their script writer.

— I've got enough of the sticky white medicine to cure a thousand lesos.

The young men moved forward, though one was slower, being slightly drunker than the others. As he lurched along, Minnie thought she recognised Boyfriend, come to get his revenge. They were now, all four, uncomfortably close and their crotches were almost on a level with Minnie and Erica's faces. The women were surrounded by anxious young bucks, maddened because their one attribute was scorned.

— Didn't know chicks had muscles.

— Why don't you buy a Lady-Shave?

Peels of happy laughter.

— Never seen a real leso before.

86

— Looks like Nora from "Prisoner".

— Shouldn't put lesos in a woman's prison, that's not punishment, it's paradise.

Erica had run out of cigarettes and Minnie didn't smoke, blast her. She tugged a thin packet from the leg pocket of her overalls: Drum rolling tobacco, kept there for emergencies only. Normally no emergency emerged before she forgot about it completely and was surprised by odd brown shreds in the washing machine and a dank soggy wad in her pocket. This was not the first time the mere sight of her had caused a flutter in the hearts of men.

— Are you a boy or a girl? had followed her down the street since her appearance had started seriously challenging the norm. The anguished enquirer usually calmed his age-old terror at this walking question mark with the philo-sophical,

— Don't matter anyway, you're so fucking ugly.

However, to say that Erica was used to it was not to say she could handle it. Every time, her heart would beat violent-ly while her feet maintained their even tread to prove she wasn't scared. And every time she would take a deep breath when she reached the corner and swear to let her hair grow and buy a dress. Naturally she never did, but she could not quite banish the thought from her mind that if she did, she would be safe, and if her life style caused her unpleasant-ness, she must change her life style. Whatever happened, she always ended up feeling guilty. She rolled herself a cigarette to stop her hands shaking, and put it to her mouth.

Golden flakes of tobacco lay all over her lap.

— Who said girls don't smoke Drum? sniggered one of the lads, quoting a well known bill board.

— She don't look like a girl, added another turning to Erica.

He tweaked her overall straps playfully, like a father caressing his daughter's golden curls. Boys must have their fun. Minnie seemed forgotten for the moment and she was undecided whether to join the game now or save her energy for later.

— You're a transvestite, aren't you?

The unexpected nature of the term made the two women laugh.

— Obviously been watching the Rocky Horror Show.

Milly giggled. Bad move.

— See, they're loving every minute of it, bloody perverts, one of our fun loving band said to the poker, who stretched both sides of his mouth, showing no other signs of life. Another swaggered up to Erica with a women's magazine, pointed to a photo in it and said,

— That's what a real woman looks like. I've never hit a chick before, but you're not a chick, you're a, you're a . . .

— Lesbian, supplied another, reading out Erica's badge.

— Step outside, Sheila, said a third, grabbing hold of Erica's jacket and forcing her to her feet. We're gonna help you give blood, people could die without it.

Minnie looked across at the man they had given change to; he was sitting bolt upright on the edge of his seat, his right hand lying palm-upwards on his knee, fingers bent to reveal the nails, which he was examining intently. He didn't move a muscle.

— Fuckwit, muttered Minnie.

The fat woman smiled nervously and the elderly gentleman had fallen asleep. Minnie stood up, preparing to throw herself bodily on these dick-heads who dared to touch her friend, when, out of the corner of her eye, she saw the old Aboriginal woman get up slowly and hobble on bleeding legs to Reception.

— I wonder if I could have a glass of water?

Her voice, soft and deferent though it was, awakened the night nurse, who had been on duty since noon the previous day. The nurse who was supposed to relieve her had phoned to say he was at a party and could she hang on in there for him. He would return the favour at a later date. She had stayed at her post, not knowing what else to do.

— Why she can't get it herself . . . the night nurse grumbled, cross at having been woken, and crosser still at having fallen asleep. Nonetheless, she walked over to the tap and gave the woman what she wanted.

— Thanks very much, the woman smiled gratefully and put the water down beside her.

— I suppose she couldn't afford coffee, mused Minnie vaguely, thankful for the break.

At the appearance of the night nurse, the men had slouched back to their seats.

— Would Miss Anita Tucker's next of kin please come to

88

reception.

— That's us, said Erica. She had her work cut out convincing the nurse she was Sky's sister.

— Full name.

— Anita um Tucker.

— M?

— M for er Minnie.

Minnie spluttered.

— Date of birth?

— 25.

— What, 1925?

— No, she was born in (quick calculation) 1955.

— Day? Month?

— She's a Scorp.

— You don't seem to know your sister very well.

And the doctor was adamant, Sky could not leave.

— Except in the care of a responsible person. Now, where's the girl's father?

Erica snorted, thinking: He's the reason she's got an ulcer at age 25.

— My family live in Adelaide, my sister and I are here on holiday visiting friends. I rang home as soon as we realised dear Annie was ill, but of course it would take them ages to get here by car. Her voice was fluid and convincing.

The doctor still seemed reluctant, but she had other cases to deal with. A young girl had been brought in from a road accident and the drunken louts from the other car were making a nuisance of themselves in the waiting room.

— One last thing, said the doctor, indicating that Sky could go, were you in a position to see what state those young men were in when they first came into the hospital?

— Drunk and disorderly, said Minnie firmly.

— So was their chauffeur, said Erica, he nearly ran into me.

— But they came in an ambulance.

— Exactly, responsible position, should have known better.

— There's a gent in there in a city suit, he was watching them all the time. Could be very informative.

As they walked through the waiting room with an aggressively somnolent Sky between them Erica hissed,

— If the police take his name and address those yobs will lynch him.

— Shame, said Minnie.

Neither of them dared look round, for fear of attracting more attention. This was a pity: had they done so, they would have seen that the old Aboriginal woman had not touched a drop of her water. The full glass remained beside her. The young men were all called together and the old woman heaved a sigh of relief. Now she was sure of getting her treatment.

The doctor was in consultation with the nurse. The young girl from the road accident had no identification on her save a family snapshot of four little girls and their parents in front of a post bearing the legend "John Johnson & Family". Their names were scrawled on the back, and 'Laura' was ringed in red. Road accidents were always awkward; you treated them same as anyone else and in the end they refused to pay. Perhaps one of the lads knew who she was; it was worth a try.

— Would Miss Laura Johnson's next-of-kin please come to reception, said the night nurse over the speaker, or anyone who knows her.

— Sounds like a radio request, said Erica. I'd like to say a big hello to Mum and Dad and my boyfriend John, all the inhabitants of Warrawarra and everyone who knows me. She looked at Minnie to see if she shared her contempt. Never had the description "green and weepy" fitted Minnie so well, the shock made her leave go of Sky's arm and the latter slumped slowly to the ground intoning,

— Asked me if I was allergic, said I was only allergic to one thing, male doctors they said, yeah, I said, make me vomit . .

— Bloody oath, mate, said Erica, What's wrong?

— That's my sister, Minnie burst out, she's sposed to be in Kalgoorlie.

— They'll never swallow that, we can't spend our lives in hospitals rescuing dykes in distress just because they're our sisters.

— But it's true, Minnie wailed.

— Your name's not Johnson.

— No, it's Jay.

- - Let's have a little practice; you'll have to get your story straight. Now, is your father's name Johnson or Jay?

— Débar, but only my sister Ingrid kept it.

— So your mother's Débar?

— No, she took her second husband's name.

— So all the women in your family have different names?

— So you're Millicent Johnson, are you? asked the doctor when Minnie finally got to see her. She wondered which of the little girls in the photo this was. Minnie reckoned hospitals didn't really mind who was called what as long as someone was responsible. She was scarcely listening to what the doctor said, her tone reminded her of the nurse at King's who had told her her father was dead.

— She's dead, isn't she? she asked bravely, bursting into tears. The doctor's financial worries were very communicative.

— Don't be melodramatic, your sister just had a nasty shock. We were anxious to get her name and address. Oh, and has she had any contagious diseases in the last few months?

Minnie stared. Nothing made sense. She had gone to a party yesterday, or was it the day before? She had danced a lot and someone had asked to rape her. She thought it was a woman. Later the same woman had got very sick and some men had threatened to kill Erica. Who was Erica? Now the woman had turned into Laura. And those sores on the Aboriginal woman's legs, red with black crusts around them and yellow liquid seeping out. How she hated yellow. Was she in King's? Had she had another migraine?

— Looks like you're in a worse state than your sister. Why don't you both go home to bed? said the doctor with the look that goes with the bedside manner. Funny old world, one sister gets hit by a car and the other one gets shock symptoms; Government raises nurses' wages and closes their quarters. There was no accounting.

— Do you have a private insurance or are you under Medibank Public?

— I thought you didn't pay for outpatients, insisted Minnie, brought back with a jerk to the here and now by this mention of her pet phobia, spending money.

— Yes, but there's the little matter of the ambulance fees . . .

— Bloody ambulance fees, Minnie repeated, what a country.

- - Our doctor bulk bills, said a pale but upright Laura from the doorway, and anyway, I came in the police car.

Minnie and Laura went back to the waiting room. Sky had just vomited on the man in the smart suit. The corners of his mouth were turned down and his eyes were opened wide, his neck was bent forward at a 45 degree angle to his chest, his right hand held an impeccably white pocket handkerchief which hovered above the sick patch in his lap as if it had not been programmed to face this contingency.

— Wanted to check my blood pressure, said I was bloody pressured enough as it was, Sky was confiding to him. The puke left a nasty taste in her mouth so she picked up the Aboriginal woman's water and with a hasty "scuse I", knocked back the contents. The night nurse, ashamed of her previous brusquery, glared at Sky and insisted that the old woman be seen next to get her away from these yobbos.

— Taxi's wha' she needs, Sky slurred, she's sick. How's she gonna get home on those legs?

Once championed, the night nurse could not now drop her protégée, but there were no taxis free on New Year's Eve and no ambulances could be spared. There was only a police car going the same way to check out a crash. For the first time in her life, the old Aboriginal woman got a lift home to Guildford in a squad car.

The four young women left the building, two in hospital blankets, but all walking.

— Your place or mine? said Erica.

— Thought you'd never ask, said Minnie. Lets go to mine. It's miles away, but at least we all get beds to sleep in.

Chapter 7
Meanwhile, Back Home In Balga

Ingrid watched as Minnie swept out to her party, telling Beryl not to wait up. Her sister's capacity to make friends amazed her; she had lost contact with most of hers when Beryl had moved out to Balga, except for Laura whom she seemed to be losing by a reverse process. She could not understand why Laura wanted to go all the way to Kalgoorlie which was hot and dusty and full of men whose wives had given them metal detectors for Christmas to get rid of them on the weekends. But Laura's Kalgoorlie was a strange faraway land where the streets were wide and John played frisbee with you in front of the hotel. For the late Boyfriend it was a brothel, and for Minnie, a ghost-mining town. Similarly, "women's party" spelt jeans and an old jumper to Ingrid, a suit of armour to Laura, a shot gun to the dear departed and pink perspex earrings to Minnie. And Beryl? "Statistically abnormal", probably. "Barren" was the adjective which immediately sprang to mind — a woman without a man was like a town without water, it would have to get what it needed by artificial means. But no-one ever dared ask Beryl, so she went on writing her letter to her sister.

— Going out tonight, pet? Beryl asked, seeing Ingrid hovering dangerously near Alice's letter.

— Yes, said Ingrid, guessing that this was the answer most likely to give her the evening to herself. If necessary she would get dressed up, go out and then climb in through her bedroom window. She was a practiced eater and had faith that if you spent half your wages on food, you would find a way to eat it.

Beryl had been thinking of going out but did not like to leave her youngest alone, especially on New Year's Eve. Ingrid was sure to find it symbolic. John had promised to take the evening off, there were never enough taxis on New Year anyway. Beryl had not pointed out the absurdity of this argument because she rather liked it, and she was tolerably pleased with a taxi driver husband. His encyclopaedia sales had given her a bad moment but then the lawns made him faint in the heat. The only problem with the taxis was that she never saw him. Anyway, tonight he was going to take her somewhere nice. Wherever that was; it was so long since she had been there.

— That's good, dear, where are you off to?

Her daughter was quite capable of fantasising a whole evening full of witty remarks, flattery and exotic food from the privacy of her own bed. In order to be left alone, Ingrid had grown adept at producing descriptions of the sort of night out her mother would have wished for her, down to the finely observed small detail which authenticated the whole. Before his demise, Boyfriend had taken her out to fantasy feeding scenarios, demanding for his part only to keep his hand on her thigh and turn the car radio up loud. While he sangalong, she was free to muse over the crepuscular kangaroos as they drove back down from the Darlings, or gaze in adoration at the strong silent metal containers, 50 metres high which lined the coast road to Freo. She had by now an eight month back-log of imaginary locations which she had thrown into her memory, all higgledy- piggledy, forever promising herself time later to sort them out. Only it is rather difficult to wander peacefully off into your own world when you are obliged to sleep in the back of a car, your face a mere foot from the roof. Had anyone pointed out the contradiction between her chirpy faith in herself as the centre of creation and her inability to make any effectual intervention on her surroundings, she would have laughed and explained,

— Boyfriend did everything to please me, I just didn't tell him what I wanted.

Having anticipated her mother's question, she replied,

— I'm going to meet Laura and Simone in King's Park.

It didn't do to give too much too soon.

— But the fireworks aren't until midnight.

— No, but they're having a barbie before, and Simone's dad bought her mum a gas fondue set for Christmas.

The fondue set was a hall mark. How could Beryl, knowing Grazyna's purple and orange lounge suite covers, not believe in it? The family was not rich enough to eat at the King's

Park restaurant, but a fondue set would just set theirs above other New Year's Barbecues. Furthermore, John, Grazyna's husband, a lorry driver, might easily have brought the set back from a trip out East.

— How tedious, Beryl said, the fondue set had evidently caught her imagination, Grazyna will spend all afternoon dicing beef only to have the oil catch fire or the skewers fall into the pan. Do you want us to give you a lift? John and I are going out too.

— Thanks Mum, but the Czajkowskis are picking me up.

Beryl looked at the clock. She would just have time to finish her letter before she went.

Dearest Alice,

John's wedding photos are blissful. His skin seems almost translucent in that funny fuzzy light. Veronica's a darling, isn't she?

Veronica's parents had been friends of hers since Beryl had first married. After her divorce she had hardly seen them, perhaps they sided with her husband, aghast at her own fall in the world. They had invited her to a party shortly after her decree nisi and, having something to celebrate, she had gone. It was not a success. Not knowing what to do with Ingrid she had brought her along. They arrived early and were roped into the sandwich making. Ingrid obligingly trotted to the fridge and laid out marge, cucumber and salmon on the table. She had spread her way through two whole loaves of stone ground bread before Mrs Upper-Crust discovered her error.

— Marge! my dear, she squealed in a shrill, shocked tone, malignant with disapproval. Her Veronica had passed the Stork test at the age of 18 months.

Ingrid had offered to scrape the offending slime off again as she had seen them do in cafes, but Mrs Upper-C. insisted that the bread was quite ruined. Beryl was tempted to get Ingrid to slip the spurned sandwiches in her bag for future consumption, but the sight of Ingrid's tear stained, satiny face determined her to cling to her Mother's Pride as the last bastion against snobbery.

So here was Veronica marrying Alice's John. While his father-in-law footed the bill.

... What a weight off your mind to have your John married, the letter continued. *I'm sure I would not have*

95

given up as much for my two, but then they're girls and it's different. Men seem so helpless, don't they? My first John couldn't even boil a kettle; if he remembered to put the water in he'd forget to switch it on, and if he'd got past that stage he'd have left the plug out of the socket. Ho hum, those were the days. With a girl you know she'll muddle through somehow.

"Muddling through" was like "puddling along", it described more a state of mind than an action. If you didn't want to go into details of meals of bread and dripping, or eating the baby food mum-in-law had sent for the youngest, you said you were "muddling along" and your sister didn't press the point. Beryl, like Mrs Bolt or Sandra or Alice, had spent most of her life "muddling through" and the height of luxury had been enough money for both a cup of tea in Brixton market and the bus fare home. "Puddling along" came later, when the children were old enough to be left on their own for a while. You put on an old coat and gum boots and went for a walk on the common. The earth would be wet and the benches too damp to sit on but it got you out of the house for an hour and no one could accuse you of not going where you said you would.

— Women are all so vague, her first husband would say, no wonder they can't drive.

. . . It's wonderful having Minnie with us again, I'm crossing my fingers she'll meet someone she likes and stay. She's out at a party at the moment with some people she just found in the street. I hope it's alright; perhaps one of them will be "the one". Laura and Ingrid are out together for the first time in months, and John and I are going somewhere too. I do worry about John, I see so little of him and I wonder sometimes if . . .

Beryl hastily scribbled out this last half remark, sure that in any case Alice would read between the lines. She began to muse instead, wondering just how much longer she'd be able to keep it all going. Dear Alice. Leaving her first husband had meant losing her sister. Beryl was afraid to concretise her fears on paper where a kitchen table chat would have seemed all right.

After Ingrid, Beryl had had a hysterectomy. At the time she had been very glad, though it was John who had suggested it. He seemed to see her as an uncontrollable breeding machine. The new baby had terrified her with its short tongue, unable to suck and the great red V on its forehead where the forceps went and she was easily persuaded there was something wrong with her. Now, however, since her remarriage, she bitterly regretted it. She would not be able to have John T's child.

— Silly me, she thought out loud, pen still posed over Alice's letter, I was forgetting.

The first time she had woken up in drenched sheets she had reached philosophically for "Our Bodies Ourselves" and leafed through to the chapter on menopause. Minnie had sent it to her for her birthday. She read that having her ovaries removed caused her to get the change much earlier, sighed and flicked through the rest of the book. She glanced at the pictures and finally threw it down in disgust. All those pages on birth control, babies and menstruation, and only 19 pages for older women. Evidently feminists agreed with the rest of the world that women were only women for as long as there was some hope of them having children. When would they realise that after you reached sixty the whole world was a matriarchy? She had started taking low dose oestrogen as soon as the change had begun, and cheered herself with the thought that she was less likely to die of cancer than her daughters who were on the pill. The worst aspect of menopause, which no one warns you about beforehand, was not being able to go to your doctor with any ailment whatever without having it blamed on your age.

She looked forward to being called "an old woman" when she could at last be sure no one was looking at her and it wasn't worth calling her eccentric. She thought of Laura's flat little tummy, of Ingrid's bounteous breasts and of her own sagging stomach which had lost its elasticity to three children. Her legs were criss-crossed with the scars of varicose veins; she no longer knew the colour of her hair, the first grey had appeared when she was 25 and she had been dyeing it ever since. One night the bus driver, having no other passengers had driven right up to her door instead of continuing on down the Wanneroo Road, saying it was too late for her to be out on her own. Did she still want men to fancy her? She couldn't decide. She wanted them to leave her be, but she wanted them to admire her as well.

Gone were the days when she wandered round the Tate Gallery, staring at her own reflection in the glass over the great masters, but she still watched Laura's tight little buttocks with regret and put on her make-up with greater care than ever. Would it be easier for Minnie, she wondered, who had never been pretty and so couldn't miss it? Perhaps she could persuade John to have an early night.

Ingrid took a shower for good form, though really she preferred her own smells to new Camay. She had grown so used to pleasing other people that she had turned to food as the only thing over which she could exercise control. When she was very little, her sister had come back from the bus stop, nose dripping with blood, having been set upon by a gang of skins. It was Ingrid who opened the door.

— Back so soon, she said calmly, as Beryl bathed Minnie's face and called the police.

— Saturday night in Balham, they said at the station, what do you expect?

While Minnie and Beryl were busy being furious and frightened, Ingrid had reached for a Mars Bar.

— She's too young to understand, Beryl said, but she was wrong.

After her shower, Ingrid was tempted to stay as she was, wrapped in a damp towel, the air felt oppressively hot.

— Hello, darling, I am glad you're home, said Beryl as John arrived back. While he was changing, Beryl hastened to finish her letter. She was so happy, happy that both the girls had jobs, happy that John had settled for taxis, happy that Minnie was there.

... I feel so depressed, Alice dear, I wonder if it's the change of life that's doing it. Do you get that way too? The doctor gave me more valium for the nerves, but nothing seems much fun any more. We're so stuck with the house and the mortgage, every penny goes into the bank and we're practically living off the girls. Laura wants to buy a car, but we can't afford a new one. She'd get a fearfully expensive one that went like a bomb and drive it into the sea and I'd be so worried about her. So with the money Mummy sent for Christmas I bought a second hand one which I hope will put her off for a while. If it was me I wouldn't have one

98

*at all. You know my two gears: very slow and stop. I'd like
to be saving up to see Australia. It's ridiculous, we've been
here five years and I've hardly been out of Perth. I do miss
you and the girls in the office; there doesn't seem to be
anything to look forward to . . .*

Beryl paused as John came out of the bedroom, freshly
shaven and showered.

— What am I saying? she thought. Poor Alice will think
I'm miserable.

*. . . Must dash, there's John now in his new silk shirt; I
wonder where we're going. Things are looking up.*

Feeling once again desirable and desired, Beryl picked up
her black shawl and whisked out of the room, knowing
they would probably end up in the Balga Tavern, but not
particularly caring. The Czajkowskis would arrive soon for
Ingrid and everyone would have a night out.

After they'd gone, Ingrid jettisoned the towel, not
bothering to put it away, and wandered from room to room
naked, picking things up and putting them down again not
always in the same place, respecting neither privacy nor
difficulty of approach. She went into her mother's room
and looked through the family photo album concealed under the bed. It contained all the details of her unknown
little brother's death, but she soon lost interest. She took
Laura's diary from the drawer and replaced it without opening it, likewise Minnie's bank book. She climbed to the
top shelf of the kitchen cupboard and examined the good
dinner service that was never used. She went into the laundry
room and peered behind the washing machine. All her
actions were permeated with a sense of desultory enquiry.
She felt as light as a butterfly, despite her belly's evidence
to the contrary. She gorged herself on the freedom of the
house, doing just as she pleased, with Edith Piaf on full pelt
and no Laura to say,

— Not that French crap again, don't understand a word of
it. Be a sweetie and put Abba on.

No Minnie to yell from the depths of "Sexual Politics",
— Be a darling and get us a cup of tea.

No Beryl to say in that exhausted voice which was so hard
to resist,

— Petal, as long as you're ironing your uniform, would
you ever do John's shirts?

99

Ingrid picked up the bottle of Brandivino they had got giggly over on Christmas Day. "No" she thought to herself and let her hand wander on to the Brandy.

— But you don't like brandy, Angel, said her mother's voice somewhere in the back of her head.

— How do I know? she protested, I've never tried it.

Down came the good dinner service complete with fish knives and grape fruit spoons. She laid it all out on the carpet in the lounge room, the one they rarely went into: a candle-light dinner for one. Mum would kill her if she saw, the wax would ruin the carpet, and why was she eating on the floor, might one enquire? A person had some standards. The carpet was thick white pile which cushioned Ingrid's feet and tickled her heel.

She could do whatever she liked: break the crockery, smash the windows, sit in the basin, piss in the sink. She could even open all the windows and let the flies in. She got high on all the awful, naughty things she could do should she choose to, just as she used to whisper "shit, shit, willy, bum" under her breath as a child. The sound of smashing glass would echo satisfyingly throughout the house for a minute or so but then her mind filled with the piteous vision of her mother scraping away at the old putty, arms aching as they reached up to do the top of the frame. The only thing she really wanted to do was tear her newly starched uniform up into tiny shreds and throw purple dye all over it.

Failing that, she pulled her box full of goodies out from under the bed. For a moment she surveyed it all, not yet attempting classification. As she contemplated, she gloated and rubbed her hands together in motionless glee. She would start off with french bread and paté de foie as an hors d'oeuvre, waiting on herself first to make sure she had every-thing she wanted, then slowly munching through the deli-cate morsels, washing each mouthful down with brandy. No. She would do it all just right. She would start off with sherry, that was what Mum served to Dad's associates, then red wine during the meal, followed up with port. The entrée would be a choice between avocado pear and stuffed eggs; she would pick both. She wondered whether to skip the fish dish, uncertain whether it came before or after the entrée, and anyway she didn't like it much. But this was her treat and everything was going to be just so, besides there was those ducky little silver fish knives. There was a tin of tuna in the cupboard, she could have that with olives and fresh lettuce from the garden.

— Grown on the premises, Modome, she said as she served herself. Her pièce de résistance was irresistible, as they say: a delicious looking paella full of capsicums and tomatoes and liberally sprinkled with cashew nuts. As a side dish she would have creamed spinach with one, no three eggs beaten up in it. Next came dessert, in the plural: fruit salad made of the mango and pawpaw she had bought that morning, covered in cream, sesame seeds and coconut. She might add a drop of sherry for the tang. Then she would heat up the christmas pudding with the brandy butter and some whiskey to make a blue flame. Perhaps she should blow it out and make a wish. Pity she wasn't having chicken, because she would easily win the wish-bone. Finally coffee would be served with camembert cheese and optional after eight mints. She would eat the whole box; after all, she bought them.

Normally when she pigged herself it was on the sort of cold congealed left-overs that no-one could possibly want to eat: stale water biscuits or the remains of the rice at the bottom of the pan. She had known herself to snatch greedily at the ryvita packet and cram whole, tasteless rusks eagerly into her mouth. But this time she prepared only what she wanted to eat and made sure there was so much that she could not be afraid it would run out before she finished.

The bread and pate was amazing: the bread crisp, the butter salty and the pate not at all fatty. Unfortunately she was already beginning to feel full after she'd eaten them. The eggs and avocado tasted vaguely weird as she had them in quick succession and the egg yolk mixed curiously with the vinaigrette. She gave up on the brandy at the third sip, it was true: she didn't like it. The tuna fish was good, but she had to stop half way through the paella, which posed the problem of what to do with the left overs. It would be a sin and a shame to throw them away, but if she left them in the fridge the others would find them. She decided to eat them later on when she'd had a breather. She slurped her way through the fruit salad and pudding, washing it down liberally with sherry to keep her stomach sweet. After that she found she was beginning to feel rather full. The coffee and mints would have to wait a while. Her stomach was demanding a tea break.

She lay flat on her back. The most comfortable position for a distended tummy, but one often frowned on at more formal dinner parties. She usually took the precaution of wearing a dress when she knew she was going to eat, so that whatever abdominal swelling might occur could take its own course unhampered by zip or waistband. She stuck her tongue out and gave a lick around her mouth, experimenting with the different combinations of tastes which had encrusted themselves on her person. There was lemon juice on her chin from the fruit salad, and bits of tuna between her teeth. She felt thoroughly satisfied, her tummy was full, her mouth felt milky and there was loads more if she started to feel anxious. The carpet caressed her back, Edith Piaf regretted nothing, and neither did she.

— I must look very odd, she thought, I wonder what Boyfriend would think if he could see me now? And she got up to fetch a mirror.

Staggering bloated to her feet made her feel rather ill, she swayed as she found her balance and plodded off to the bathroom. The mirror, from its perilous position at the top of the book case, threw her back at herself, not the sybaritic fantasy of Roman gorging orgies, but an enormous peeling monster with wagging double chins, and a belly big enough to hide a child.

— You pregnant cow, she accused herself, you're obese. Obese, obese, obese, echoed round the room while the kindly "plump", "round", "chubby", "dimpled" fled off to the outer recesses of her approving self.

Around her sprawled the guilty remnants of gluttony: avocado skin, cherry stones, bread crumbs.

— A whole avocado and two boiled eggs, her mirror image screamed, you are disgusting.

It was true, she was not delightfully uninhibited, fat and friendly; she was grossly overweight: an insurance risk. The sight of her whale blubber body would put people off their dinner. She began to examine every inch of her revolting frame; she pinched her sides till they hurt, bent over, squeezed her spare tyres together and counted the rolls, shook the padding on her upper arms, pummelled her thighs and even puckered the loose skin on her feet. The fat she had once regarded as comforting, smooth and soothing, a wall

102

against the world, was in reality just excess which should be sliced off with a razor.

She could see herself doing it. The sharp tongue slicing into her soft flesh, tearing off the extra layers, ripping open her bulges, leaving the unprotected, streamlined self that she alone knew was hiding underneath. Grimly she went to the bath room and sought out a bottle of ex-lax; she was too chicken to cut the flab off nobly so she would let it seep out ignominiously from the inside. Then she picked up a box of salt, poured it into a glass of hot water, and drank it down.

— No half measures, my girl, she warned herself. You ought to have thought of the consequences before you shovelled down all that paella.

— Don't bother making me feel guilty, she groaned, don't I feel bad enough as it is?

She held the basin with both hands, her forehead pounding, gulped for air, and was sick while the cabinet mirror above her reminded her she could never be sick enough to expiate her dissipation. When the retching was over, she allowed herself one glass of water to take the taste away, as long as she spat it out afterwards.

— No sneak swallowing, she warned herself, You've got to kick the habit completely, that's what they say to druggies.

Poor Ingrid, yet how could she protest, she had been caught as red-handed as if her mother herself had walked in. While she was waiting for the familiar churning in her stomach and bowels which would tell her that the vicious circle was nearing completion, she taunted herself with the delectable remains. Presently her insides turned to water, and she made a quick dash for the toilet. There she stayed, bowels caught in the squelching spasms for upwards of ten minutes. Sometimes it rocked her with pain, as her anus muscles ached to stay still. She put both hands on her stomach, and a nasty, unpitying voice said,

— Don't clutch your stomach, girlie, it's big enough to lead a life of its own now.

When the spasms stopped, she groped to her feet and the blood rushed to her head. Then she pushed off to her room, shoulder to wall for support, and collapsed into bed.

Beryl and John had gone to the Balga Tavern, which was jolly and full of people. The local band played a slow version of "Rock Around The Clock" which made Beryl feel

103

inexplicably sentimental. She and John played kneesy and held hands under the table. They drank double whiskeys and remembered other occasions in pubs in London when there was grey slush in the gutters outside and an icy draught blew in whenever anyone opened the door.

— It's so warm here, Beryl smiled gratefully as they walked back to the car, little fingers interlinked.

— I wonder where the Kingswood is, she murmured as they walked up the path.

— It's not yet twelve o'clock, give the girls a chance, said John as he nuzzled the nape of her neck.

Beryl and John were just cuddling warmly up in bed, arms and legs lovingly entwined, when Ingrid let off what she thought was a fart, and turned out to be diarrhoeia.

— Mum, she whimpered, but before she could turn it into a wail, another voice interrupted her.

— You made your bed, now you can lie in it.

Ingrid squirmed damply.

— Have the pride to stew in your own juice.

Not for nothing had Beryl spent the last twenty years as a mother. Through the thick muffling of John's body she heard her youngest daughter's bleat.

— Speak Lord, she shouted, half sitting up in bed, but the cry was not repeated.

— Must have been a nightmare, she said to reassure John.

— How selfish, just as we were getting to know each other, he snuggled up to her.

Chapter 8
Kalgoorlie

Twenty-four hours had passed between Laura leaving the house in a Kingswood and coming back in an Escort. She had set out happy, almost smug: got her licence only three months ago and here she was driving the all-Australian dream. The said Australian-dream went like a bomb; in minutes she was the other side of Midland and heading East to Northam. She planned to take a break at Southern Cross and reach Kalgoorlie around five.

She had learned to drive on the Ute that John had bought for his lawn round via a loan from his mother.

The Ute was a great big bugger with only three gears, but this one was a beauty, wide and fast at the same time.

— Power, she yelled gleefully out of the window.

In the end she felt quite glad to be going alone. Her scene with Moira had not been quite as she described it. She had sat down on her sister's bed in the tiny room Moira shared with Pam. When Laura arrived, Pam was out.

— She's started going to the Pavlova and meeting men in the lifts, Moira explained. Probably meet mum too, she added bitterly. I don't give a shit either way, but she keeps borrowing my blouses and coming back with them ripped.

— Moira, listen, said Laura to change the subject. Six years in Homes had inured her to tales of personal tragedy.

Moira turned on her.

— You give me the shits, Laurie, you really do. You're all set up with your sugar mummy and you don't give one fuck about the rest of us. As long as Madame has her private swimming pool and use of family car everything's just bloody great.

— Moira.

— Don't bother, because I'm not listening. I'm through with you, sister dear, any attempts to reform me will be treated with the contempt they deserve. Pam may be an old pro, but what was good enough for my mother . . .

Silent with rage, Laura reached behind her into the little wash basin and gripped a bar of soap between her fingers. As Moira's brace flashed with fury, Laura shoved the soap into her sister's mouth.

— You wash your mouth out, you filthy slut. You don't know what you're talking about. If you didn't have braces, you'd be on the game yourself. I saw you making up to Ingrid's boyfriend.

Moira spluttered into the sink.

— I'm going to Kalgoorlie, Laura continued calmly. If you want a ride, then speak up.

— Yes, Moira yelled, though the soap was still sticking to her teeth, I can hitch East from there. Laura was, after all, her big sister and a lift was a lift. She could get even with her later.

— You're not hitching bloody anywhere; you'll end up raped and murdered by the side of the road. I'm going to see John Johnson, and if you come that's where you're going.

— Bloody oath, that old bastard. Laura, you're not serious.

— Deadly.

— Oh Laura, take me to Sydney. You and me together. We'll have a wild time. Is the car outside?

— No, stupid, I'm not going to Sydney. I'm just asking you cos I'm your friendly neighbourhood sister, remember?

— Funny way of showing it.

It was then that Moira had called Laura a crawling arse licker and this morning Beryl had bought Sandra's car. Laura sped on past a circle of giant black boys which looked like they were having a prayer meeting, all their bushy green heads bent towards the middle and their grassy fronds swayed their agreement in the wind. They could have been four metres high.

— That whimsy's catching, Laura mused to herself, suddenly reminded of Ingrid. A year ago she would have seen only trees. No wonder Moira scorned her. Gradually she felt she was being sucked into the family, the cosy middle class world of simultaneous quotation and food at every meal. She could imagine Minnie gazing out of the window and lecturing earnestly,

— Did you know the Xanthorrhoea was a member of the

106

lily family? It's one of the few remaining prehistoric plants, and trust it to grow in Australia.

Something bounded across the road ahead of her. Her driving instructor told her never to swerve for anything smaller than a human being. Her love of furry animals told her she could give up stroking her cat if she wilfully ran over anything on the roads. So she stopped dead. The creature stared at her with enormous eyes then zipped off into the bush. The way Laura saw it, there were two ways of tackling her car journeys; either you assumed the passenger role and recorded the scenes from a side window or you looked straight ahead like the driver, and concentrated on the road. Beryl, for example, was quite capable of sitting at the steering wheel, concentrating intently on her mind's eye. Laura, on the other hand, was a born driver, and knew the number of gear changes John averaged from Balga into town. She watched every pedal pressure and memorised every dial reading. And this was before she got her licence. It was said that she knew how to double-de-clutch before she learned to drive. She rather despised other chicks who learned to talk car only to communicate with John.

— Perhaps it's the big ends, they would contribute cheerfully when the car's suspension had been wracked by an unsealed road, and John would be delighted that his girlfriend was so stupid. If she hadn't said anything at all, he might have thought she simply wasn't interested. Laura would open up the bonnet, throw a swift glance around the engine and mutter,

— Sparking plugs need cleaning, and she would extract an emery board from her manicure set and do the job herself. She kept a little tin of quickies in her hand bag to clean up afterwards.

Exhaustion and starvation set in k.m.s. before Southern Cross. Her first long trip and no co-driver. At first she put a lot of effort into driving, and it amused her to play with the gears, but on a straight road with very little traffic, there wasn't much work to be had. There was the occasional pleasure of overtaking, but after a while she had been forced to sit back and let the tyres grip the roads as they did in the ads. The car kept itself politely in the middle of the lane, and even the steering wheel could get by without her. She was beginning to feel unwanted, hard shouldered, as it were.

Flies bombarded the windscreen from all directions with the deadly accuracy of a meteorite storm committing hara-kiri. They lay there, entrails like blobs of pus on the glass, as if waiting for the great director in the sky to shout "cut". Then they would clamber to their feet and go back to being whatever it was they were before they became bit parts, extras in an unseen film. Meanwhile, little by little, the windscreen was filling up with dive bombers. Laura squirted it with water and turned on the wipers. These latter performed one or two laconic turns, smearing the now diluted viscera in long auburn streaks against the silver screen. In the end Laura had to stop and clean the glass by hand, and even then there were tiny yellow spots which refused to go away. It reminded her of the bathroom mirror. The car was simply covered with dust; it was going to be quite obvious that she hadn't stayed in the metropolitan area. Even the wheel hubs had their own coating of fine red powder.

Laura took advantage of the stop to go for a piss. Everything was still. The heat rose in horizontal waves over the tarmac. She hitched down her knickers, and was about to crouch down behind a burnt out tree trunk, as she would if there had been anyone to see her, when she realised she could piss just as well standing up. She took her knickers right off, stood with legs firmly apart, and aimed at an empty beer can.

— Rust, you bastard, she said.

It was comparatively easy, you needed only to tense your muscles a little and the shoot took roughly the direction you planned.

The waterfall burrowed into the sand like a laser, drowning columns of ants in its wake.

— Power, thought Laura, once again. From now on I shall stand on the toilet seat.

She sat down on the tree trunk for a while and observed that though it was black and charred from a recent bush fire, it was still obstinately sending forth green shoots which were bursting into leaf higher up.

— Time for some home spun philosophy, she said and giggled.

The giggle echoed around her in the silence and was sucked into the shimmering heat. There was sweat behind her knees and her cotton dress was drenched at the back and clung to her with salty insistence.

— Bet my armpits stink, she revelled, and bent her nose down to sniff. Sour and humid. A litmus paper would have a field day.

When she got back into the car the plastic seat burnt the tops of her thighs. There was something awfully naughty about driving a car with no knickers on.

— The defendant was discovered barebummed in control of a vehicle.

She was sorely tempted to leave the offending garment flying from the cheeky green stalk. There was just enough wind to have fluttered it. She was thankful further on that she had not given in to this impulse when she discovered that the sunshade could not cope with the light on its own and she was going to have to stop for some glasses. She pulled in at Merredin and crossed to the nearby roadhouse. There was no air-conditioning and the fans clicked and whirred as they turned.

— Chocmilk, she ordered.

She placed her elbows on the counter and turned to look at the yellow posters on the wall.

— Five pound passage for Respectable Females.

You were promised a job when you reached Australia and in some cases the fiver would be waived against your future earnings.

— They must have been desperate, she remarked, pushing the straw to the side of her mouth, and thinking of all those women leaving their homes and everything they knew to get on a boat bound for god knows where.

— They needed women like the goldfields needed water, the man said noting Laura's youth and cotton dress.

The paper straw had gone mushy in Laura's mouth, it was time for her to move off.

— See you later, she grinned. Something about the barman reminded her of John Johnson. Maybe it was the way he looked at her.

The road to Southern Cross was uneventful. She had discovered the curse of the long distance lorry driver: long distances. Somehow she had not remembered the journey as being so long. She had slept most of the way in a nest of downy sisters last time she had come this way, waking only to open her beak for orange juice every 200 kilometers.

John Johnson. So far she had avoided thinking about him at all. Her only sign of nervousness was a terrible pain in her stomach. Once she had taken her tummy aches on face value and plied herself assiduously with bicarb, complaining of acute indigestion. Now that she knew it was nerves, she refused to complain at all. What did he look like? She didn't know. What do men look like? Sort of big and bushy with enormous arms that bent down and carried you off. When she was little she could only distinguish them by their smell. John smelt of cigars.

— G'day, Laura, he would say. And then what?

What was she expecting more than a pleasant seven hour rush through the bush? She was determined not to start getting her hopes up; she would go and see him as if she was just shooting through. He was not going to welcome her with open arms after all these years, she knew that. He might be an alcoholic or married; in Kalgoorlie all things were possible. Best just wait and see. The creeping suspicions which Minnie's declaration had stirred in her, as well as certain other small incidents, would be allayed. She would have a father, however once removed and avuncular, and the world, as in former times her school, would keep its misgivings to itself and accept her for what she professed.

She drove on. Next stop Coolgardie, then home. In the days of the gold standard Coolgardie was a thriving community; half eaten wooden buildings bore witness to a civilisation not unlike our own. Whole streets had crumbled away when the gold ran out and, though a recent revival had sent the flocks back again, this had been no more than a flutter. Most people prefer Kalgoorlie with its split level, fully air-conditioned museum displaying objects that most English tourists are used to seeing in their own grandmother's kitchen: moustache cups looking like someone's taken a bite out of them, cast irons that you heat up on the Aga and white lace petticoats hand sewn by the Irish needle women. The English cannot go round a foreign museum without exclaiming,

— But, my Aunty Vi's got one of those, it can't be very old.

They are contemptuous of Australian centuries because they are small in number, never dreaming that Aunty Vi's treasures were either exported by force, or filched from a less imperial nation.

There are also camels at Kalgoorlie, brought to Australia in the Early Days (before centuries were discovered) by Afghan guides, in whom, it appears, the English had more faith than in the native Aborigines.

Today, as every day, there was a trickle of tourists photographing Johnny climbing on and off camels, just as he had the lions in Trafalgar Square, the Sphinx in Egypt and the running dogs in Peking. Laura, however, hardly noticed the men in their white knee socks, their tans a shade too puce, or the pink women in their new batik dresses which had already come and gone in Australia. It recalled vague memories of childhood: feet on the bottom slat of the wooden fence with a row of sisters in a diagonal line up to the highest slat in descending order of thong size, or holding the reins while a larger child clambered onto a camel refractory. She could not yet dwell on it as her mind was engaged on the execution of a Uee in the main road without seeming to do anything illegal.

She shot off up a side street and pulled up in front of Dun Raven no. 33 Domestic Terrace. No need to count the houses, or peer at the front doors this was no. 33 because it came after a dip in the road, acknowledged by the left wheels only, and there was the oleander growing right outside. So many times her imagination had brought her home in a flash car, the grown up daughter with a driving licence, and she had taken John for a drive. The tree could have died off in the drought of 79; John could have moved elsewhere; the RTA could even have filled in the dip in the road. But no, everything was as she had left it. She pulled the old photo from her pocket and compared it with the real thing. Exactly the same. Not a blade of grass out of place. There were John and Irene, arm in arm, still smiling at one another; there were Moira, Donna and Tracey, the white fence and the sign, still bright with new paint, declaring proudly to the world,

— John Johnson and Family.

— OK, you can all relax, picture taken. I'll have them delivered to you in about a week, Mrs J. We have to send out East to develop black and white. Little ones would have looked just beaut in colour with their blue eyes and those yellow dresses. Still, you're the boss.

— Sweet old-fashioned girl, my wife. If you could have

111

done them in sepia with furry edges, she would have been rapt.

Moira, who was a head taller than Donna, bent over and licked the luscious pink cornet, which was melting in her sister's hand.

— Mum, shrieked Donna, taking this gesture as an invasion of her person, Moira's eating my ice cream.

— Dondon can have my i ceem, Tracey piped up, feeling dizzy from standing still so long in the sun.

— Pack it in both of you, get in that house and wipe your faces before I wallop you.

Laura remained serenely immobile, leaning against the fence, licking her cone with a neat pink tongue which permitted no drop to fall on her dress. She didn't really like ice creams, they were too sweet, but she liked getting a treat and was anxious to show her appreciation by keeping clean. Perhaps then John and Irene would take her with them this time.

— Just one more in the back garden, Irene pleaded, the light's much better there.

So the family trooped round the house and Donna and Moira re-emerged, faces scrubbed.

— Stand still, Irene ordered, and they all cuddled together, a picture of domestic happiness. But the unfortunate Moira could not resist tweaking her sister's hair, and Donna, predictably, squealed.

— It didn't hurt her, it didn't hurt her, not really, mum. She's bluffing. Moira blurted out in dread anticipation.

— What's she blubbing for then?

Donna pinched Moira on the arm in retaliation. Then Moira thumped Donna and they both fell into the melon patch, yellow dresses ruined. Irene picked them up by the hair and dragged them indoors. Laura turned to Tracey and straightened her ribbon.

— Moira and Donna are naughty, aren't they, Daddy?

From the house came the sounds of her two sisters being beaten with the clothes brush.

— Hurry up, doll, we'll be late, John shouted, still posing for the camera, hands on Laura and Tracey's shoulders.

— Nearly ready, Irene sang out brightly and appeared in the doorway carrying a tartan overnight bag. At the sight of this, Laura's heart sank, however good she was, they always

112

left her behind.

— Couldn't we bring the big one with us? John whispered, she's real pretty, and very grown up for her age.

— No, said Irene coldly, she has to look after the little ones.

Laura overheard them, but then, she'd always known John was her friend.

Irene wished John hadn't been so mean about the photographs. He said she alternated betwen pride and jealousy over her daughters' good looks. The four yellow dresses with matching hair ribbons had been bought specially — (would the cost of a colour film really have made such a difference? John's financial priorities were bizarre) and at the moment pride had the upper hand. The audition John had landed her at the "Sexy Sheila" would restore her confidence that she was as attractive as ever, babies or no babies. Motherhood merely enhanced her assets: a woman with four blonde daughters must be a natural blonde herself. The publicity photos would show her and the girls at cutesy angles, a humorous contrast with her stage act: kids were a great selling line among the male clientele. Irene wondered sometimes whether John got sucked in by his own slogans.

— Bye bye now, girls, and be good. Don't eat us out of house and home.

— Where Mummy going? Tracey asked.

— Perth sweetie, to buy presents for you all.

— What presents? A dolly, a train, a ship, a house, a koala bear? Tracy chirped, she knew her mother would forget, but it was fun imagining.

Tracey and Laura held hands and waved good bye as John drove off.

— I do hope they'll be alright, Irene murmured.

— Should have thought of that before, John said crossly, family obligations did not suit him, despite the sign on the gate. Besides if you really loved them, you wouldn't leave them.

Irene was irritated. She would much prefer to stay home, thank you very much, but one of them had to work.

Laura led Tracey back into the house where Donna and Moira lay sobbing on their beds.

— I hate Donna, I hate Mummy, I hate photos and I hate my yellow dress. Moira's voice reached fever pitch at the end.

— I hate Moira, I hate Mummy, I hate photos and I hate my yellow dress. Donna's voice echoed from the room she shared with Tracey.

Slowly the echo become a song and the song became a chant. Laura and Tracey joined in, and the four sisters stamped around in a circle banging saucepans, speeding up on "I hate", and rushing into the middle on "dress". One by one they divested themselves of the offending garment and threw it into the middle of the circle. Moira looked at the yellow pile with a malicious glint in her eye and went to fetch the matches and kerosene. Solemnly the plastic container was passed from sister to sister and each poured a large dose onto the pile.

— We havin' a barbie? Tracey asked, recognising the plastic bottle.

— Yes, said Moira firmly. She picked up the reeking clothes, carried them outside and placed them on a stone slab out the back. When the others were duly gathered around her, she and Donna held hands, feeling themselves to be the most injured parties, and lit the pile like a birthday cake. The flames whooshed almost instantaneously into the air and each of the girls made a wish.

— I hope they never, never come back, said Donna sanctimoniously.

— Ssh, said Moira, you mustn't say or it won't come true.

As the flames died away, Tracey got tired and sat down.

— I'm hungry, she said, looking at Laura.

Laura went to have a look in the fridge.

— Pumpkin again? asked Moira.

Laura nodded,

— But they've left us some bread money and there's loads of vegies in the garden.

The others were exhausted from crying and running and let her pull up the carrots, clean the potatoes and chop the pumpkin. As she shook the carrots against the back step, she longed to have her licence and drive to Perth in a flash car and find John and Irene. She called to Moira to take over from her, told Donna to watch the potatoes and walked round to the front of the house. As she passed the charred remnants of their new dresses, a cold shiver shuddered up her backbone. Laura senior marvelled at the quirk of fate which had saved them from being burnt alive, and Laura

114

junior wondered how on earth they were going to explain it to their mother. She was tempted to go back to the house for some bicarb, but instead she untied the hair ribbon, which looked very silly on her now short hair, and tied it to the freshly painted sign. Then she climbed into the driver's seat, turned the keys in the ignition and never looked back. She had been in the house five years or five minutes and everything was just as it had always been, down to the pink ice cream stain on Donna's dress. If ever she felt the urge, 33 Domestic Terrace would be waiting for her; the potatoes boiling dry because Donna had got bored of waiting for them and gone off to eat jam sandwiches instead.

Hunger followed Laura from the house, and she headed for the hotel, looking for signs of modernisation, of changing with the times, but found only the past. The hotel bar held some relief for her, she had never been in it as a child. She ordered a salad roll and went to eat it in the car park. Feeling the strain of her seven hour drive, she wound up the windows, mindful of stories of drunken youths, and fell asleep in the back. As she drifted off to sleep she thought,

— I mustn't tell Moira that it's all still here. She hated it worse than me.

She awoke again around ten o'clock, drenched with sweat. It was true what Ingrid said about sleeping in the backs of cars, especially with the windows shut. She stretched her legs, but her back felt like a curvature of the spine and her arms like rigor mortis. She opened the car door and slid out. Where the day had been boiling, the night was pleasant, and the stars very clean and bright. As she moved her legs, her blood remembered to circulate and presently she drove off. The return journey was going to be one hell of a long haul. It seemed as though the engine hadn't stopped since the previous morning and its purring joined forces with the cats' eyes in the middle of the road to mesmerise her. It was the same road she had come in on only a few hours before, but it seemed like a different world. What had changed? Nothing. Nothing whatever had changed here; while elsewhere prices rose overnight, erstwhile best friends got married and even milk went sour if left too long. Here the hunger and the smell of pumpkin and the desperate striving for mum's approval were still patiently waiting for her. You couldn't jump into the same river twice (or was it once?) for the waters were ever flowing on, but Kalgoorlie was a stagnant pool whose muddy, murky depths you could keep on churning away at while it gave you its solemn promise that it would remain just as it was for ever and ever. Laura felt like a criminal with a penchant for the scene of the crime.

-- Laura, Laura, Donna was calling, the potato water's all gone and Moira's hurt herself.

Moira raised her scalded arm and whimpered in pain.

— Poor darling, here, Laura make it better, and the elder sister carefully ran the younger's arm under the cold tap and tied a clean tea towel lightly round it.

— There you are, mouse, now you're a wounded soldier, she soothed, just as Irene said to her.

Moira went off to play hospital with Donna, and Laura finished making tea by herself, adding loads of marge to the potatoes to compensate for them being burnt.

— Tea's ready, kids, she yelled, and they gobbled down what there was and washed up what there wasn't. When all visible traces were gone, each picked up her plate and licked it clean. This was fun if you had a see-through plate, as your tongue, flattened against the glass, looked like a pink slug and made the person opposite you giggle.

— Wash up quick, and then bed, Laura ordered.

— Tell us a story.

— Can we all sleep in your room like last time? I'll sleep with Moira and Tracey can sleep with you.

— You'll kick Moira to death and she'll take all the blankets.

— I know, let's all sleep in mummy's bed, shrieked Moira, surprising even herself by the boldness of her suggestion.

Laura drove on through the night. A road train thundered past her about every half hour, but that was all. In between there was only her, Moira, Donna and Tracey and their games were all the reality there was.

All four little girls crept in awed voices into their mother's room,

— We'll have to top and tail, Donna whispered, or the one on the end will fall out. Moira stomped off to fetch more pillows and Laura put Tracey, who was already asleep, snugly between the sheets.

The mere thought of Tracey's soft hair and sleepy burrowing face made Laura yawn.

— I should have brought a thermos, she thought, then I could have got one of these road houses to fill it. But soon she arrived in Southern Cross. She had driven for three hours without noticing. It was a relief to be somewhere less familiar and the electric lights cast an artificial glare which contrasted oddly with both the bright sunshine before Kalgoorlie and the total blackness afterwards. Laura was discovering half tones. Dimly she ordered pastie and coke, not in the least peckish, but wanting to keep her body functioning normally. Even while she sat at the greasy table, someone else's egg yolk in front of her, Irene's voice came back to her,

— Why don't you ever clean the lipstick off the mugs, Laura?

Irene was the only one in the family to wear lipstick, and Laura liked to see this mark of her lips, as if she had been kissing the mug.

Luara turned over and kissed Tracey good night across Donna's legs. Donna tickled her under the chin with her big toe, crawling half way under the covers to reach her. Moira shuffled forward to tickle her too. Laura snorted with laughter, caught both their legs, and softly stroked the balls of their feet. Instantly both bodies leapt into the air, the toes recoiled and Donna and Moira dissolved in mirth.

— Not so loud, you'll wake Tracey.

— You awake, love? the owner shook her roughly by the shoulder. Come on, you can't sleep it off here. I don't know what you're doing out on your own at this time of night, and I hope that's your car you're driving, because if the cops come round asking questions, I'll be sure to recognise you. I don't want any trouble.

— It's my mother's car, said Laura, and I don't drink.

— Maybe not, said Mr Niceguy, but you can't sleep here.

Laura drove off again, thinking all the time that she should pull off the road and wait till morning, but wanting more than anything to get back to the safety of Balga and away from those horribly familiar, clinging little voices.

— G'night, Laurie, whispered Moira.

— G'night, Molly, g'night, Dondon.

There was a silence. No breeze, no other traffic, just the rhythm of the engine and Tracey's regular breathing.

— It's too hot with the blankets on, Donna complained,

so they threw them off, and slept, four naked bodies under a big white shroud.

Laura's mind was blank, the car knew the road as well as she did, and needed no outside assistance.

— Oh for an automatic pilot, she thought. I wish I was in bed with all my clothes off.

Another semi-trailer, another roadhouse, the speedo seemed frozen at 90. There weren't even any bends to navigate. And then, just as Laura was thinking she was too tired to go on and would have to pull into the bush and spend the night with her sisters, she passed a signpost saying: Midland, 10 kilometers. Another hour or so and she'd be in Balga. She opened her eyes wide, took a deep breath of air and set her sights for home, soon the lights of the great metropolis would keep her awake.

— Krreek, krreek.

Something was wrong. At first she thought it was herself snoring, then she realised it was the small ball of wool lying next to her. Tracey was rattling as she breathed and her small body seemed wracked with chains.

— What's the matter, poppet, can't you breathe?

— What's the matter, darling, is it the big ends? Irene asked John, anxious to get moving if they were to be in Perth by morning. They had made a late start with a couple of drinks at the hotel.

— No. I don't know what it is, the car won't start.

— Battery flat?

— Possibly. Anyway, it won't get us to Perth. You'll have to phone the Sexy and tell them you'll be coming by train.

The audition wasn't till Saturday night, but Irene had wanted to arrive early to have time to sleep before the show. Now they would have to go home and wait till morning.

Laura got the remaining pillows from the other beds and propped them under Tracey so her chest was easier. Then she found T's asthma pills and gave her two with a gulp of water. Tracey looked frightened.

— It's so heavy, she said.

Laura threw off the sheet, even if it made no difference, at least Tracey thought it did.

— Krreek, krreek.

There it was again. Laura listened to her nose as she breathed out. That wasn't it. Then she listened to the engine.

There was definitely something wrong. She slowed down; hoping at least to pass Guildford before she had to stop. It might even be the petrol, a big car like the Kingswood must use up an awful lot. She looked at the fuel gauge, the arrow was determinedly middle of the road, and she was pleased not to have made such an elementary mistake. She must find a garage, but as she sped on no roster sign appeared to her. Guildford flew past, along with the crazy level crossing and the high roofed church. She slowed down some more and it occurred to her that if it was the battery, she would never get started again on the hill. But the engine had finally konked out. All she could do was a Uee and park on the down slope, facing the oncoming traffic. She opened the bonnet and stared into the engine.

John slammed the bonnet down again in a temper, he couldn't see anything wrong with the damn thing. Irene climbed into the driver's seat and steered while John pushed. The engine choked, coughed and then started, kicking and spluttering all the while.

Tracey coughed and spluttered, and Donna kicked from the depths of her sleep. Laura pulled Tracey close to her, and tried to coax her back to sleep too, stroking her back all the time to smoothe out her lungs.

She could see nothing wrong with the engine, though she had checked oil, water and petrol. She peered over the radiator into the blackness.

Suddenly she became aware that John was peering over the bed at them in the darkness. A switch clicked and light flooded in. She screamed. Irene, slower out of the car, because of her high heels, clicked into the room at her daughter's voice and caught the look John cast over the girls.

— You perverts, she screamed. What do you think you are doing in my bed, all four of you, stark naked and without even the bed clothes on?

Laura was aware only of loud raucous male voices, singing at the tops of their lungs and at break neck speed, then two piercing lights careering at her out of the darkness as if the SS were about to commence the inquisition. Then came a loud crash and Laura was thrown backwards to the side of the road. Their car must have turned over several times because two subsequent crashes came to her out of the air.

As she lay in bed, stunned by her mother's explosion,

Laura pinched herself to see if she was really there. She held her breath lest even that cause offence and tried not to move a muscle. She could do nothing but await the maternal decree.

Laura lay by the side of the road, dazed by the lights and the collision. Slowly she tensed each muscle in her body, her fingers moving lightly over her skin to check everything was still attached. Face, eyes, nose, two arms, breasts, one legs. What was that she said? She froze with horror. She could not feel the other leg. Her fingers groped an inert lump of flesh which lay on the ground, buckled under her at a peculiar angle. At least it was still there. Perhaps she could leave it to science. She shuffled her body so as to examine this former part of herself at closer quarters. It had all the softness and curves of a human limb, but hung there limply, reproachful as a cast off boot. It began to prickle. How long had she been lying there? The prickling started to hurt neurotically, sending spasms of pleasure and unpleasure up her thigh. When the hysteria got too much for her, she moved her leg slightly and clenched her toes. This both eased and accelerated the throbbing. Her leg was now alive with acupuncture.

— Pins and needles, she thought.

— What you need, said her mother, is a damn good hiding.

Irene never really knew if she was protecting herself from her daughters, or her daughters from their uncle. She needed the job in Perth, but they would have to leave Kalgoorlie, and with her out working every night, the girls would have to go into a Home. For herself she hoped it would be temporary but maybe they needed stability more than they needed her.

The drive into East Perth Infirmary remained a dark mystery to Laura, with odd flashes of gum trees. She found out later that she had gone in a police car and been asked her name and address. She had stuttered clearly,

— 33 Domestic Terrace, Balga.

— She's raving, one of the police murmured, I used to be a taxi driver, and there's no Domestic Terrace in Balga.

They tried her on her name, and she answered without hesitation,

— Laura.

— Laura what?

— Laura Johnson, she thought, but it sounded ridiculous.

120

She was a girl, how could she be anyone's son? and John's son? How could John have sons, let alone daughters?

— Laura, Irene's daughter, she trembled.

— Sorry, love, don't know any Irenes. What's your Dad's name?

But Laura's answers remained vague and inefficient, presently they left her alone. At the hospital, the sergeant had a private word with the doctor,

— Must have had a bang on the head, Miss, she's not the full quid. Don't even know her name.

— Brain damage, surmised the doctor, if only we had more staff.

— You'll have to go into a Home, said her mother firmly. You can't be right in the head.

Laura, from the fuzzy depths of her terror, listened to the verdict in silence. There was no appeal. She had no voice. She was an outcast in society: her brain was sick and her mind was in need of attention.

Chapter 9
Sunday Morning, Eight O'clock

Beryl had asked her elder daughter, six months after she met John, how often Minnie and her John made love. An odd question, but Beryl had no standard to go on. John Débar had given up the habit shortly after Minnie's birth. Beryl had not liked to ask why, however closely the question touched her personally, and Ingrid had been a complete surprise. In consequence, Beryl found it difficult to broach the subject with other women. It seemed odd to discuss something she had scarcely ever known and did not particularly miss. From certain half-laughed remarks of Alice about her John getting affectionate after Doctor Who,
— I think it's the sight of all those Daleks,
Beryl surmised that her sister's marital relations were what might have been termed normal. If nice Rita had not had to go off to Oxford with her husband, increasing intimacy might have prodded Beryl to ask, over a brandy at someone's farewell down the pub,
— Are you on the pill or what, Rita? I was wondering for my Minnie, you see, as I don't use anything myself, not after the operation.
When John T had appeared on the scene, and with a gentleness and sensitivity that Beryl thought miraculous, introduced her to orgasm, she felt anxious to compare this achievement with that of other women. Finding it difficult to believe that her own experience could vary so much from the average, Cosmopolitan, multi-orgasmic Superwoman featured in her daughter's magazines, she decided to apply to Minnie directly.
— About three times a week, came the factual reply. Minnie had no idea how to talk to her mother about sex. This had not been covered by her PT teacher's little chat.
— Mmm, yes, so do we, but I only come about once. That's enough though, I wouldn't want it any oftener. I

mean, I don't feel the need to masturbate or anything.

Minnie said nothing and Beryl worried that she had embarrassed her daughter. Parents and children should not know too much about each other. When she had had a low key affair with a married man at work, she had strenuously kept all trace of it from her daughters. She did not want them growing up cynical about their parents' love match or it would spoil their own chances of marital happiness. Up to the date she left she spoke no evil of her husband in front of her children. She might have talked to them now about sex, but the younger ones would giggle so much as to stifle any clear transmission of thought, and she feared to approach Minnie lest she receive a stream of anti-male abuse. That female conversation which takes its unerring route from things of general interest through one's own John's latest demands to birth control and sex, reflected the circuitous route one followed to reach it and was always jokey and anecdotal. You could never apply it to yourself, except as a spring board for another anecdote.

John and Beryl were less often joined in marital harmony now with John's job, than during the old romantic days in London when they would both rush through Ridley Road market on a Saturday so as to be home a good hour or so before Ingrid came back from the Mare Street children's matinée. Then early nights were a permanent feature of life. When Ingrid stayed up late in the kitchen watching the telly, Beryl feared for her morality through the thin plasterboard. If she missed anything about London, it was those damp days of sexual exploration, when it always rained on the weekend and the market was aswamp with squashed tomatoes and one-off cabbage leaves.

Last night had been wonderful. While Minnie was at her party, and Ingrid and Laura enjoying themselves in King's Park, Beryl had been revelling in John's newfangled kindness. Though she no longer compared with Debar's "Roll over, darling, I want to use you" technique, she still felt obliged to her John for not being like other men. It had been a joyful surprise to discover other positions than "staring at the ceiling". She had wanted to spread the good news, but 36 years and three children might cast suspicion on her adolescent enthusiasm.

John lay asleep beside her. It was 7 am. She would have

to get dressed and go if she wasn't to miss the coach. Luckily she had the car now, so she wouldn't have to fuss around with buses. She took a shower, put on some old jeans and sunglasses and packed a thermos. They never gave you enough tea on these excursions. She also packed a change of underwear, a water bottle and a cotton sleeping bag.

— Ready for any contingency.

You never knew when a vehicle would break down and you would be forced to spend the night. On this reflection, she packed her toothbrush and paste as well. She lingered over breakfast, noting that the tin of tuna was gone, which meant Ingrid was back, and therefore Laura with the car.

Beryl's getting up noises wakened Ingrid, whose sleep had been fitful and whose dreams had been filled with mud. She awoke out of a quagmire into a bog. The wet shifting swamp had localised itself into a brown squelch beneath her. Contact with the cold ooze troubled her. She was going to have to get up. She tumbled the bedclothes onto the floor, crumpled the sheets together, and shuffled into the bathroom. Hot water and a nail brush purged the guilty remnants and another scorching, cloudless day would dry out the evidence. As she stood barefoot in the early sunlight she remembered it was Sunday and Mrs Bovis' family friend would be calling for her at eight o'clock sharp. Where was the inspiration? The neat little almost truth which would convince and pity at the same time? What if she did want to go after all? If Mrs Bovis recognised in her latent piety which she herself did not know existed? She could not set up an excuse and dismantle it in time to change her mind. Realism took time.

— You're up early, darling, Beryl called through the fly screen.

Before Beryl's embarrassment at being apprehended in hot pursuit of a life of her own, and Ingrid's at the evidence of a self-indulgent evening could cause either of them to voice an attack on the other or a defence of themselves, a loud thud was heard as of a soft object hitting the front door.

— The papers, Ingrid yelled, I'll go.

In letters to Kate Minnie had cited this phenomenon to show how much space there was in Australia.

— *It's so big. The towns are just one long suburb and they have grass verges not pavements because there's too many streets to line. If you go for a walk, the dogs come and bark at you, like in the English countryside, because they're not used to pedestrians. They deliver papers by bike here, and just fling them into the front yard as no-one would have time to walk up every garden path and push them through a letter box.*

What to Minnie was Australiana, was to Beryl a relief, and to Ingrid a godsend.

It was surprising that, given this enormous superfluity of space, as witnessed by barking dogs and loud thuds, such a thing as a traffic jam should exist at all. One rather imagines young Ossies gazing at a tailback of traffic round the New South Aldwych with the same wonderment with which they might behold snow.

It was even more surprising, therefore, that a traffic jam should choose, of all the square metres of that vast island continent, Beryl's front yard as its first venue. The loud thud was only the trumpet call which heralded an army of horns and hooters, as a green Escort tried to park beside a white taxi carelessly left in the middle of the drive the night before. Following it was a stately family sedan whose driver was looking at her braceleted wrist and ascertaining that it was 8 o'clock and if the police car which had pulled up behind her did not reverse immediately she would be late for church. The police car's retreat, however, was inadvertently blocked by the paper man who wanted to be paid.

— Oh good, thought Beryl, that'll be Laura with the car, and she ran her eggy plate under the tap, left it to drain on the side, dried her hands on her apron, and went to the front door.

— What is going on at number 64? said Mrs-Diagonally-Opposite.

— I expect they're having a house-warming, said nice-Sandra-across-the-road.

— At eight o'clock in the morning? said Mrs-Next-Door-But-One, who had never forgiven Beryl for setting the Cruelty People on the caged dogs. She was sure she could have found homes for them,

— I think I'll call the police.

At least that's what their twitching curtains seemed to suggest, though it would take an experienced neighbour to interpret all the ins and outs.

The man in the blue van opened the door and strode purposefully out. Minnie, Erica and the two bundles slid out the right hand side of the Escort, the left being jammed by the taxi. Meanwhile the police person (sex: male) and the church-goer were having an exciting shouting match as to who had right of way on a private drive.

One taxi, one Escort, one Sedan, one police car, one little blue van: the only car Beryl couldn't see was a Kingswood. Ingrid, with eyes only for the personally relevant, immediately picked out the family Sedan as just the car for a Presbyterian, and, having no more convincing plan, hid behind her mother, who was surveying the scene arms akimbo.

— You owe me thirty dollars, Mrs T, said the delivery man, not beating about the bush, and if you don't pay up, I shall be forced to foreclose on the Nation Review.

— Does one Laura Johnson live here? said the police person of the opposing sex, slamming his car door on the church-goer, if not on her fingers.

— Which one of you is Ingrid? said the church-goer, from the depths of her hat.

But Minnie and Laura, Sky and Erica, stood as a rampart to these latter day invaders of Church, State and Capital. Their demands on the maternal figure were enough to block out any less personal petition.

— Mum, I've stacked the Kingswood, said Laura, aware that she had just passed her initiation ceremony into the Australian youth sub-culture.

— Mum, I'm a lesbian, said Minnie; Sapphistory is made of such moments.

— Mum, I'm going to church, said Ingrid; the Festival of Light glimmered briefly.

But Beryl, spurred like Ingrid by personal relevance, committed an act of gross individualism. Her first.

— Ask my husband for your money, she said to the delivery man, it's him that reads your papers, and, ignoring the other supplicants, walked across the road to Sandra's and phoned Pioneer Coaches from there.

Her lightning assessment of the situation told her that none of the vehicles there assembled would get her to Perth in time for the coach. Her maternal instinct, constructed by patriarchy, doubtless, but useful nonetheless, had informed her in one swift glance that none of her offspring were dying. A mental picture of the route to the desert, such as women are not meant to possess, showed her that she had time to walk to the end of the road before the coach passed that way and a quick phone call would let them know of her intended presence. She picked up her bag and set off down the road. She was tired of being a mother.

The delivery man grunted and knocked on the door, exchanged a few masculine words with the sleepy John and drove off thirty dollars richer. This released the pressure on the police car's boot which now backed out to leave the church-goer room to manoeuvre. Ingrid trembled at the loss of both her own shield and her tormentor's attacker. As soon as the sedan was free, its driver would renew her questions and an answer would have to be given, even in the shape of silence.

Beryl's departure left a breach in the family's defences and John went back to bed. As elder sister, Minnie felt she must shoulder the burden, but Erica got there first. For a moment Minnie drew back from the battle and thought how wonderful it would be if she and Erica really were in it together.

Erica was talking to the police offender of the next sex down.

-- Laura is ill, she stated, she is in a state of mild shock and the immediate application of warm blankets and sucrose in the form of a cup of tea is indicated. Help me take her indoors.

This effectively silenced the young offender, convinced by Erica's medical tone that his legal knowledge might not be relevant in this case. Docilely he became the young man to whom gallantry is a second nature, and carried Laura to bed. As Sky looked a little off-colour too, he resumed his shining armour and bore her into the house.

While Erica was dealing with the police, Ingrid approached Minnie.

— She's come for me, she said prophetically.

The church-goer was still disengaging her car.

— Whatever have you done?

— I partook of the forbidden toffees, and they're going to take me to church.

— Oh dear, said Minnie, thoughtfully, tell her you're ill.

— But I can't be ill every week, and I know they won't let up.

— Then just tell her you don't want to, how ever did you let it get this far?

— Don't be so disingenuous, said a voice in Minnie's ear. Ingrid shrugged, Minnie would never understand.

— Have you forgotten Barbara? Milly continued. You got as far as telling her that you'd move in with her, and then look what happened.

It was true; Minnie knew perfectly well how you could get into that position. You tried so hard to be the person the other wanted you to be, and they began to believe you really existed. She was going to have to introduce Ingrid to Milly; it was the least she could do for her sister.

The church-goer had by now parked her car neatly on the grass verge next to the drive, mistaking Beryl's flowering teapot for a discarded hub cap now that her back wheel had squashed it flat. While she went to check her car's paintwork (it didn't do to put off the examination, especially if the other party was a police car), Minnie whispered urgently to her sister,

— Do you really not want to go?

— Yes, wailed Ingrid, or rather no, I don't want to go to church, but I do want to go on being Mrs Bovis' friend because she's a nice lady and she makes me laugh and if we met here mum would be horrible to her.

— Right then, said Minnie purposefully, get someone else to go for you, and she told her sister about Milly. But you'll have to call her something else.

— ?

— What about Fran? Wouldn't that do?

— How do you know about Fran? scowled Ingrid, no, she can't go, she's a sucking up toady who does everything Johnny Francois says.

At which point, the church-goer, who had completed her sketch of the bumper with tally marks to count the scratches, stepped up to the two sisters.

— Well, my dear, are we ready to go?

— Yes, smiled Fran considerately. Let me take your bag, you must be quite fatigued. Really, some police officers have no respect.

— No, Ingrid barked, but at that moment the officer-knight,

128

finding his arms temporarily free of young maidens, seized upon Ingrid, the pale and wan, and carried her off.

Erica came out with cups of tea, but unfortunately she had forgotten the strainer and Plodperson, detecting leaves at the bottom of the cup, was reminded of luke warm tea at the station and became a police man once more. He pulled an accident report from his breast pocket, the one with the button on, and began asking pertinent questions.

— How old is Laura?

— How long has she been driving?

— Why did she park on the wrong side of the road?

Erica and Minnie answered his questions as far as they could whilst plying him for information as to the nature of Laura's crime.

— Well, the young men were certainly drunk, he admitted. We have a very full statement from a witness who saw them at the hospital. I ran out of paper getting it down. But now some bloke's come forward from the Southern Cross to say your sister was so smashed she fell asleep at one of his tables.

— So what? Erica interrupted impatiently.

— It seems these yobbos crashed into Laura's parked car. This is borne out by the position of the cars afterwards relative to each other, which we have since ascertained.

— Oh, insurance! said Minnie nonchalantly, let the companies fight it out.

— No can do, said the officer of the lore, staring gloomily at his dangling roo bar, you see, a man was wiped out in the collision, went by the name of John Boyfriend.

— Thought we hadn't heard the last of him, Minnie tutted. How masochistic can you get, only geezer I know to notch up two tragic deaths.

But out loud she said,

— He can't have been, officer, I'll vouch for him, he was dead already.

The lawmonger continued,

— We haven't found his body yet, and the other yobs were so pissed they can't remember if he was with them or not.

— What makes you think he was killed, then?

— Just a routine investigation. The super gave us strict instructions during the RTA blitz on drunken drivers to treat every traffic offence as if it was a murder hunt.

— If the blokes were drunk and ran into Laura's stationary vehicle, then it doesn't matter what state she was in, they're the guilty party, Erica insisted. Minnie marvelled at her staying power and wondered what she was like at crosswords.

— They're saying they were dazzled by Laura's headlights into thinking they were on the wrong side of the road. They pulled across sharp to remain on the right side of her, thinking they must have gone off the road in the darkness.

— So they crashed into her to teach her to stay on her own side, sounds pretty territorial to me.

— Well they'll fight it anyway, and they're in with a chance because one of them's a professional driver and stands to lose his licence if the judge finds against him. I mean, no one wants another fellow to lose his job.

— So Laura pays damages because she's only had her licence six months?

— Goodness, thought Minnie, Erica's been listening.

Plod sucked his pencil and completed his report. He would be back later for a statement from Laura. Meanwhile, she was not to leave the country. There was something about the case he didn't like. He puzzled over it awhile, wrinkling his eyes to help and giving the ozzie salute to frighten away the flies. Then he realised what it was.

— Did you say your sister only had her licence six months?

— That's right.

— Then she couldn't have driven from Southern Cross in five hours, she'd have been wacked.

Minnie and Erica shrugged,

— No, they said firmly, of course she couldn't.

Plod drove off in his squad car, the roo bar going rattle rattle. He hadn't even taken the church-goer's number. His mates at the station would laugh at him.

Minnie practised picking up gravel with her toes. She was quite happy for Erica to deal with authority, if that was what she was good at, but it made her feel frivolous and she was afraid Erica would take her at face value.

Erica was rolling a cigarette, knees spread, back curled, face calm as a mask, but when she reached for the matches the tobacco fell out in a blob. Minnie put her arms round her.

— I'm sorry I left it all to you.

--- It's not that. I was really worried for Laura. I didn't realise it wasn't serious.

For a while they held each other, then went inside with the empty mugs. Ingrid was sitting on the floor in her dressing gown eating a bowl of ice cream, her crimes of the night before expiated.

— You can't eat ice cream for breakfast, pudding, Minnie picked up the words her mother had left out for her.

— Yes I can cos I am and don't call me pudding, Ingrid shovelled the last hasty spoonfuls into her mouth.

— Call yourselves sisters, scoffed Erica, looking around with interest at the place which called itself Minnie's home. Lots of arty things on the walls, probably perpetrated on the premises. She could imagine them with a nice antique shop in Subi.

— How was the party?

— Great, what did you get up to?

Ingrid saw that Minnie had forgotten the prawn crackers, she obviously did not take eating seriously.

— Oh, I went to the Rocky Horror Show, she was sure this was on, because John had told her about it before he snuffed it.

Minnie and Erica exchanged looks.

Sensing disbelief, Ingrid continued,

— It's a real cult movie. You all bring rice with you and someone in the audience makes paper hats. Then, just when Janet gets married you throw rice at the screen, and when it rains you put on the hats, everyone sings along with all the songs and there's this triffic character who's a transvestite from Transylvania.

— How amusing, said Erica drily.

— Who's your friend? asked Ingrid, surer of her own position with the ice cream safe inside her.

This was the moment Erica hated, and after a night of momentous happenings, Minnie quailed at explanation.

— This is Erica, she said flatly, she's a stewardess on the Rottnest Islander.

— Who's your sister? asked Erica.

First name, profession or description? Minnie wondered.

— Ingrid's a hairdresser, she said, her ambition is to travel.

— We went to Rottnest, said Ingrid cheerily, to make up for past surliness.

— Yes, said Milly resolutely, every visitor to the West should take the opportunity to visit this historic island and have a close look at the quokkas which breed there so plentifully.

Minnie chewed miserably on a match stick. She could face a completely strange party, a night in a hospital waiting room, attack by adolescent youths, her sister's car accident and even chit-chat with a police officer, but Ingrid still reduced her to helpless lecturing.

Ingrid felt her friendly advance had been spurned.

— Yes, she said to Minnie, we all read the tea packets.

Erica felt the heat was off her.

— Let's call it a day, she said.

Could Ingrid keep up bingeing and vomiting indefinitely or would she run out of sheets? Would Minnie and Erica sleep together? They were all too tired to find out and these pressing questions were temporarily refused predication.

Chapter 10
The Pinnacles

Lex was proud to be a professional driver. Her father had owned a garage in Marble Bar and she had helped him mend the assorted land rovers, motor bikes and semi-trailers whose cursing drivers were forced to sleep in her mother's freshly washed sheets until their vehicles were road worthy. As most of the roads in the area bore the inscription "passable dry season only", trade was brisk and profitable. Lex had attended the School of the Air and done all her lessons by correspondence. She had grown up an only child in a world of men and had learnt to be as much like them as possible. Her mother offered only the dreary image of someone living in a permanent nightmare, unlikely to capture a young girl's enthusiasm. Her grey, crow-lined face seemed to ask how she had come to this awful place, only to wake up in it, year after year. The house was an air-conditioned sanctuary that she didn't dare leave, and she punctuated her miserable existence by trips to the hospital with pneumonia. An English doctor, used to the thousands of pensioners carried off every winter by bronchitis due to cold might have been puzzled that heat should produce the same results. Yet it was true that the wives of miners at Tom Price, lured by the offer of company houses and fat salaries, showed the same distress symptoms as old women living in tower blocks at a distance of some 70 degrees centigrade. Those north western towns are weird places, with their floating population of a few hundred thousand men who leave the failing industrial towns of Wollongong and Newcastle to make a fast bucket in the north and return home loaded. Perhaps they are like the giant oil rigs. The companies try hard to establish a stable community but few women want to live in the burning dust. This absence of female domestic labour obliges the companies to pay men to cook and clean for other men, using the most advanced machinery, but at

133

great cost to their self respect.

In the end, Lex and her father had had to give in to her mother's dumb misery, and the family had moved to Perth. Her father led land rover expeditions to Alice Springs for people who wanted to get there the hard way. Lex applied for a job with Pioneer coaches, but somehow a woman driver destroyed what little romance there was in a day trip to the desert and she had been turned down. The male drivers, however, used only to the odd gentle trip to Bunbury, were forever bringing the coach back with bald tyres and one had even been turned over. In despair the company had tried Lex, who had learnt by her previous rejection to behave as little like a woman as possible and saw this second chance as a sign of acceptance into the streamlined masculine world.

Lex's eyes were now peeled for the lady passenger she had to pick up. Women were never on time for anything, she could hear her father say so,

— Except you, Lex my boy, and you know I don't count you among the women folk. I sometimes think they have a totally different idea of time from the rest of us. Give your mother a nice gold watch for her birthday and she treats it as an ornament.

Not that her mother had a gold watch, but Lex knew what was meant. She was pleased not to be included in this contempt for the fair sex and had inherited it from him. She could not identify with those pretty creatures trailing around on high heels in summer dresses.

Beryl reached the end of the road with ten minutes to spare. She sat down on a low sandy bank, and waited for the coach to appear. She hated to be late for things, just as she hated to be dirty, and allowed an extra half hour every morning to assure herself of a shower, but something always happened. Ingrid was in a decline and hadn't ironed her uniform, or Laura's cat had been sick in the living room.

She chose a middle seat on the coach, squeezing past another woman to get to the window. She was pleased to note that there were a lot of women her age or older which meant no one would pay her any attention. Coaches reminded her of harems, with their cargo of female passengers under the control of one male driver. The woman at the wheel made driving appear easy. Bad though she was at driving herself, since Laura had passed her test with such

ease Beryl was no longer sure it was a miraculous skill. She
tended to be contemptuous of anything she could do herself.
Cooking, sewing and painting she classified as activities which
would not have been beyond the average hen. Sorry, chook.
She experienced a little difficulty in assuming the language
of her land of adoption. She had just about mastered rising
intonation, but used it indiscriminately as if permanently in
doubt. Men found this rather attractive, but women suspected her of trying too hard. She was not sure who to respond
to, flattered by the men but only really trusting the women.
She always had trouble with accents. When meeting Ingrid
from school, her daughter begged her not to open her mouth
lest the other children say she talked posh. The next day, at
Balham Public Library, she had stuttered so much that
Minnie had taken over.

— Don't mind my mother, she stammers, Minnie had smiled nicely, and continued, she wants a book on famous
poisoners.

— Are you from Perth? enquired a polite voice beside her.

Beryl wished neither to appear rude nor to be engaged in
conversation. She was finding her own thoughts rather interesting and direct antagonism would result in silence, yes, but
an arched speaking back and bristling muscles would en-
croach upon her far more than a pleasant exchange of the
merits of Perth's climate versus Adelaide's celebrated clean-
liness. She smiled and nodded vaguely.

— Some aren't, said her neighbour, to no one in particular,
and, polite relations having been established, settled down
cosily to her knitting. From the care she put into it, the
quick changes from purl to plain, and the way she was keeping on myriad different colour wools, Beryl surmised that the
garment was not for herself. From her deftness, even on the
far side from the window, and her air of knowing what her
fingers were doing without looking, Beryl guessed it was a
pattern and size she knew well and imagined from the
woman's age it must be a jumper for a beloved grandson, now
grown up. Beryl smiled as she watched the waving fields of
lucerne lumber past the coach; the grandson would never
wear it, he had a drawer full of such sweaters already. The
woman knew this too, Beryl decided, but knitting was such
a peaceful activity, a vehicle to anywhere your fancy took
you, as the needles clicked and your fingers whirred. You

could evidently not be called upon to darn this same grandson's sock — No darling, can't you see granny's knitting? — as you could if you were simply reading a book. If interruption threatened to persist you could always start counting stitches and everyone knew it was not you being difficult, but the wool itself which was refusing to turn into so many knots.

The grandson would remark casually as he opened his birthday present,

— Oh, dear granny, she puts so much effort into these things, she mustn't know I don't wear them.

But the product was not the point. Perhaps this is why so few men have learnt to knit; their pride is to possess someone who loves them enough to tire their fingers making the beautiful object they are now wearing. They can think only of the time and energy that goes into the manufacture and not of the reflections which come out which are quite unmarketable and scarcely properly phrased. At the same time they have the naivety to wonder how it is that women understand things before they do . . . The woman now placidly knitting had been to Bali with her daughter. They had gone for a walk in the market, bought a flat orange drink each to quench their thirst and been followed thence forward by a little girl of about ten. The son-in-law, who prided himself on his Indonesian, had questioned the little girl, assuming she was admiring the beautiful dress of the white lady. His wife was very pretty and looked stunning in green. The little girl jabbered something so quickly that though he hated to admit it, he didn't understand: the difficulty was knowing where one word ended and another began. His wife was sniffing some purple orchids, but his mother-in-law, who had noticed the little girl at the drink stall, quietly handed her the three empty bottles. She trotted back obediently to her father.

— She says you're very pretty, said the son-in-law as his wife turned round.

— Oh, what's Indonesian for pretty? his wife smiled.

— Of course one wouldn't like to translate the actual words, she's speaking in dialect, you know, but one picks up enough of the general gist.

The old woman was still watching the little girl who was solemnly washing out the bottles.

— Don't they know there's a deposit, growled her father in Indonesian.

The little girl shrugged.

Knitters learn to put themselves second in conversation, needing half their attention for the pattern. Thus they can let their attention wander, noticing who is absent, what is left unsaid and when the silences come.

— We are now travelling through the Swan Valley, announced Lex over the loud speaker, where most of our West Australian wine comes from. I expect you gentlemen beer swillers have already noted the Swan brewery on Mount's Bay road.

There was polite laughter. There were few men on the coach, but the women laughed good naturedly.

— I'm going to make a little detour now so you people can take a look at the church that marks the location of Captain Stirling's first camp. It was 1827 and he was the first white man to venture this far up the river.

One of the earnest young men took hasty note of the date.

— Now, in the old days, the vicar lived on the other side of the river, so on a Sunday, he had to roll up his trousers, with his sermon under his hat, and swim across, watching out for abos while he did it.

— How brave, said an earnest young man.

— Why didn't they ordain a priest on the right side of the river? thought the old woman through her knitting.

Beryl wished they would turn the loud speaker off, but the others seemed to be interested. She did not want her new found land put in boxes of consumable commodities ready for translation in a Michelin guide. How could she have her own thoughts on the origin of the Pinnacles when they were already packaged as "unique limestone formations projecting from sand dunes caused by the strong ocean winds which swept the area"? Thousands of years ago, the sea retreated, laying bare vast beds of sea shells which were deposited inland on slightly higher ground and then blasted with sand, which accounted for their moth-eaten appearance.

Beryl pricked up her ears, had the guide really said "moth-eaten"? But no, the words came ringing back to her, the term was "eroded"; about as interesting as the South Downs. Beryl would be pleased to learn later from the Nambung

137

Park Ranger that actually no geological survey had been done of the area. She could imagine that strange eerie desert with its shifting sands and harsh crumbling rocks carefully dissected by pompous men in shorts and sun shields, mapping the fault lines and placing everything in squares. They shared a common ancestry with the man who covered Bondi Beach in plastic or Alan Jones and his constricted female nudes.

— Some people say the formations are actually the remains of fossilised trees and quote the existing forest surrounding the area as proof.

Beryl perked up again. The peaceful co-existence of two equally cogent arguments was so much in her way of thinking that she was pleased such a sensible attitude was being shown to the Pinnacles.

— But, continued Lex, putting paid to Beryl's pleasant plurality, conclusive tests have been performed on the limestone which prove they are not fossils of any kind, though shells are of course encrusted.

— Not fossils of any kind, it sounded like the policebod warning Laura not to leave the country.

— Facts, thought Beryl, figures, nouns. One explanation is correct, it wins the Miss World Contest, but there is room for runners up in the form of second place or ingenious argument.

Once the geologists came, there would be an end to speculation, the answer would be published in a delightful coffee table volume with full page colour illustrations of the intriguing shapes silhouetted at sunset. It would hit the Do You Know cards issued free with the tea packets and John Brillo-Pad would win points for Cambridge by solving the controversy, your starter for one, no conferring. It was not that she disliked technology; roads, for example, proved very useful in getting from Appleton to Balga. She just saw no purpose in drawing lines round things, and then pretending you were merely tracing lines already there. Roads had a tacit agreement amongst themselves that they were where they were but could very well have been elsewhere, had Balga or Appleton been a little further left or right.

A conversation with the ranger, who drove up in his land rover while the less hardy passengers were wilting on camp stools in the shade of the coach, confirmed Beryl's preconception, that even men could see the weakness of evidence.

— I'd be fascinated to hear what the university blokes say, but I'll tell you one thing, Mrs T, I'm in holy terror of their report. You see, they might think they were examining limestone, but if Charlie Court took it into his head to get interested in this here desert, he could read their findings to say there was bauxite or alumina or god knows what down there. I mean, there might be, for all we know. Overnight this "world famous tourist resort" would become "an essential source of the nation's aluminium".

— Both would be true, Beryl nodded gloomily.

— Not to a politician. It's got to be either or. If a man's not bloody innocent, he's bloody guilty. The Ranger scratched his ear admiringly at the wisdom of his words. He was tempted to repeat them.

— I swear, if they thought there was uranium under Ayers Rock, they'd blow "the biggest monolith in the world" sky high, sacred sight or not.

Beryl had joined neither the anti-uranium, nor the Aboriginal land rights lobby. She felt a certain sympathy for the young man, obviously out to change the world, and agreed that lots of people needed changing, but she did not imagine he was going to listen to her, too much needed changing for that. So she smiled vaguely and murmured,

— That would be a great pity, the rock is such a pretty colour.

The Ranger, finding her ignorant of the social issues involved remembered he had an important message to relay about an abandoned car in the Park, and returned to the Rover to do so. The other passengers did not seem as entranced by the desert as Beryl, though they had taken lots of photographs. The earnest young men asked Lex how many Pinnacles there were exactly and she, feeling a sense of personal failure, had not been able to tell them, though she was sure her father would have invented a number on the spot. She was not entirely sure that the young men didn't already know and weren't just testing her. She set them all down about 20 minutes walk from where she intended to park the coach, to give herself time to set out the smorgasboard luncheon. Some of the older women declared themselves unfit (including our lady of the knitting) to walk so far in the heat. Lex was annoyed, why women had to come on so fragile. She was sure they would peek out of the back of the coach while she unloaded the food and she would have to wash out the cups in water instead of flicking the dust with a tea towel. And then she would have to stop at Cervantes to fill up the bottles again; her brief was to stop at Cataby in the afternoons to divide custom between the two roadhouses. Besides, that fuckwit, John, was on in the afternoons and he would make stupid jokes about lady drivers and offer to check her tyres for her. For their part, the older women had no desire to trail their orthopaedic heels in the dust, and although their supportive stockings eased their varicose veins, they did not promote free perspiration.

Beryl adored the walk over the sand dunes and her legs were eager for more though the coach was in sight and the table set. It would have seemed the most normal thing in the world to have simply gone on walking smoothly over the fine dust, up and down, like waves over a beach, the light breeze wiping out her foot prints as she made them, until her thought had run its course. Her eyes, too, were tired of the continual end-stopping of city buildings where they had always to focus on some neat object which stood in their way, unable to run their natural course. Beryl was long sighted, the sort who has one pair for reading, another for seeing, and bi-focal sunglasses permanently perched on her head, and it seemed that her natural focus point must be much further away than most people's. Glancing down, she discovered a thin layer of tiny formations scarcely sticking up above the ground. She stooped and picked one up. It felt like the red paths of ants' nests in Africa, made of saliva and mud, as though the sand itself were turning to little feathery sticks jutting up above the dunes. She put it in her pocket. The jolly television cartoon of naughty Norm picking wild flowers, only to be stung by a red back spider for his pains, had never had much effect on her, her civic conscience being not the most finely tuned.

Lunch was the usual lettuce with mounds of cold meat and sponge cake. It was difficult to see what one was eating as black clouds of flies descended upon it as soon as it was uncovered, and munching was accompanied by buzzing and shooing. Beryl, having left the young ranger, sat on a rock at a little distance, sipping a surreptitious cup of tea. Her third, but they never gave you enough anyway, and she didn't like coke, which was the only alternative, now melting

140

in the Esky. Observing her fellow travellers from this vantage point, she could see there were colonial squabbles going on over who could claim a seat in the shade. The older women, who had stayed on the coach, had naturally reached the chairs first. Their implacable obstinacy was a ready match for the noisy twittering of the young men, who returned from setting up tripod and lens to find all the prime seats taken in their absence. They stood aloof, surrendering chairs they had never possessed to women whose claim had never been challenged. Lex, spurning a seat down among the women, joined the young men, on a pretext of showing them a particularly interesting formation called "the Indian". She felt they suspected her of clandestine femininity, and it was up to her to prove the contrary.

— What a big nose he has, said one of them, pointing to the limestone Indian.

— Yes, it's interesting, said Lex.

— Interesting, I could think of another word.

One of them hummed Melanie's "A thing's a phallic symbol if it's longer than it's wide".

— You're obsessed, said Lex, with a note of approbation. She knew she'd be one of the lads the day she too could make this kind of joke without other men thinking her an easy lay.

Beryl was amused by it all. No one engaged her in conversation, and she was free to observe. She liked men, personally, but that was because she had learnt how to handle them. It was convenient to have a man around to mend fuses, put up shelves, or take a look at the record player. They did not, on the whole, wash up or clean, but this was because they were incapable of doing anything without an obvious goal. Cleaning was repetitive and boring. Men, too, had noticed this, but, lacking inner resources, they needed a lot of stimulation. You could give them one-off tasks to do, and they seemed to enjoy that, but could not think ahead to when the paint brushes or tools would need putting away. Why this obviously competent young woman should wish to be ridiculed by these boys was beyond her.

The meal was over now. Lex managed not to let the old dears catch her eye. If she ignored them for long enough, years of training would make them heave a sigh, shake their head in nodding agreement at her slatternliness, and clean up the plates themselves. Then one of them would shuffle over to her pointedly and ask her where to put the litter. She would turn round, note that all the clearing up had been done, feign embarrassment, and point vaguely to a cardboard rubbish box. She could cope with waste disposal, having often helped her father with the dustbins, but washing up had been strictly her mother's job. The young men would insist on taking photos of her beside the coach and ask her about its electrics and transmission system. This lot were having a heated discussion about which of them had the best Nikon, but Lex was able to recommend some particularly photogenic rock formations and advised them to take the sunset tour.

— How much longer are you staying here? one of them asked.

— Oh, just long enough to clear up and get all the old biddies back on the coach.

— Well, we'll go on ahead and you can pick us up as you pass us. This is a very important project, you know, I believe it's the first time any university team has been out here.

Beryl took an enormous dislike to these clever dicks who disguised themselves as ordinary tourists only to come back later, no doubt, and carve up the desert to stake their claim in the book titles.

Lex felt let down to have her audience so brusquely ended and there had as yet been no light tap on her elbow, or reproving "Excuse me . . .". Perhaps these women had managed to find all the necessaries themselves, they looked the institutionalised type.

Beryl was sitting blissfully on her mound, surrounded by Pinnacles of whatever stone they proved to be. She had taken off her shoes because her bunions hurt and was wondering if the hessian she had picked up in the road would do for an embroidery picture of the desert or whether she'd better dye it pink.

Lex stared across at this middle aged woman in jeans, hair hennaed red, feet bare, gazing intently at the sand. Obviously not a cleaner upper. She turned towards the coach and saw, to her astonishment, an elderly lady knitting.

— Well, strike a light, drive five hours into the bloody desert, and this one sets up as if she had never left her rocking chair.

The woman did look remarkably at home, perched on a small canvas camp stool, needles clicking, spectacles poised on the end of her nose, with the prescription shades in the air as she looked down at her stitches. As Lex walked round the coach to the picnic party, she was amazed to see, not a row of neatly packed tupperware boxes, piled obligingly on the folding table, too heavy for the dears to lift, but a rough circle of knitters of which the woman round the corner was merely an outpost.

Lex was furious. Unspoken mutiny to her unspoken command. Around them, nestling at their feet lay cans, bottles, wrappers, all the debris of the picnic down to the ribbon of ham fat in hot dispute among the flies.

It had been touch and go at one point. Mrs R-W, whose knitting capacity we have seen already, found it very difficult to resist the urge to shoo the flies away and put the meat under cover. After all, she could knit anytime.

— It's such a waste, her eyes said to the other women.

But they knew that if one of them lifted a finger, they would all feel obliged to help.

Mrs O., who had just had her hair set at Johnny François' in town, wanted to wash her hands of chicken grease so that she could pat her head and check her perm. She itched to pull a few hairs over her wart, she was sure the wind must have ruffled them out of place. Fortunately she was deaf, and more sensitive than the others to the tacit. She wished Betsey Bovis had come, more resentful than usual of her lover's religious activity. Blanche, however, sensing her unease, passed her a tea towel to wipe her hands. Cleaning them would have been a preliminary to washing up, and once that scenario is allowed to start, there is no stopping till every plate in the area is clean, rinsed and dry.

— Is that pure wool you're using, or a mixture of acrylic?

— Oh, it's natural, that's why it's this harsh yellow colour. It hasn't even been dyed.

— I couldn't wear that next to my skin, make me go all over prickles.

— Oh, I'm right with you, but this is for my grand niece, she bought the wool for it.

The conversation flowed on as Lex glared at the softly intransigeant circle. The women hardly moved, and scarcely

143

looked up except to smile a

— Do you knit, my dear?

— No I do not, Lex snapped, I'm not an old woman
She kept this addition to herself, but the knitters heard it
just the same.

— You turn a very good heel, Mrs O, remarked one of
the women, careful to face her fully as she spoke.

The men were away down the track by now. It was too
late to call them back, even if Lex hadn't been loathe to
suggest they belittle themselves. She gathered the remnants
together and prepared to knuckle down herself.

— Can I help you, pet? asked an English voice, and Lex
handed Beryl a dish cloth.

— You dry and I'll wipe.

In all politeness, Lex was bound now to talk to this rather
odd individual. Beryl felt that you did not share the washing
up with someone without exchanging a few words.

— You're English, Lex tried.

Beryl nodded.

— What about you?

— I'm from W.A., Lex's answer was short. Was this woman
suggesting she might be a migrant? Just because her skin was
more tanned than most. And if she said anything about her
driving, she would splash dirty water over her. Bad enough
stick from men, let alone sympathy from women.

— Oh really, Perth born and bred?

— Actually, I spent the first twenty years of my life in
Marble Bar.

Why did she bother, no pom had ever heard of the place.

At the words Marble Bar, Beryl's ears lit up.

— Oh my, she gushed.

— She's going to tell me it's hot up there, thought Lex,
still, at least the name rings a bell.

— How wonderful.

English enthusiasm grated on this dour Australian.

— Name takes your fancy, does it? she asked sarcastically.

— Not just that, but the heat and the stars and the silence.

Lex was still not quite convinced she was not being made
fun of. Had the other woman guessed at her sensitive core?

— My dad used to have a garage, and my ma ran a motel.
Lex clung to the factual.

— What fun, said Beryl. That was what she would do, as

soon as the girls left home. John could keep the garage, he liked tinkering with engines, and beating the met. office to the weather forecast. The motel would be a bore, but she could go bush walking, and no one would invite her to coffee mornings.

— I've always wanted to live up there.

Lex was struck by Beryl's candour.

— Yes, she said simply.

But the clearing up was now done and there was no excuse for mutual exchanges. The knitting was put away, and the coach filled up again. If Beryl was going to carry out her plan, then she must do it now. In her bag was enough water to stay in the desert over night; she had protective clothing of a bright enough colour to attract an aircraft if necessary. She knew the signaling code for emergencies, (but not "I'm perfectly alright where I am, will you please leave me alone"). She had chocolate and raisins for energy, and a small packet of flour to make damper. Unlike most Australians, she believed in those early pioneers who carried salt and water on their horses and made flour of the grasses they found around them. The fire would be quite illegal, but then you weren't allowed to stay overnight either, unless you were a passing Aborigine on your way to a sacred site. The ranger would be back at 6 pm for a last look around if she panicked, and then there was the sunset tour. She had even remembered a raincoat, so that if she was not found for several days, she could dig a little hole in the ground, cover it with a plastic sleeve and suck the night's condensation. She had only to drift off behind a rock and no one would notice her absence. The driver was caught up with starting the coach, which appeared to be stuck in the sand, and if she remembered Beryl at all, she would never remember which trip she had been on. Instead of going over to the coach, Beryl must make as if for a pee. She looked around for a suitable spot.

Lex had let go the hand brake and opened the choke a little, worried that the coach was so unresponsive. The women seemed to have settled down for a nap. The engine revved. After ten years driving on the toughest roads, to get herself bogged in a pitiful little desert on a route she did every day.

— Everybody out, she yelled, worried that the women

would not move.

Slowly they creaked to their feet, and trod carefully off the bus.

— What's the matter, dear, engine trouble? asked one kindly, but the others prodded her on, nudging her not to make matters worse.

Lex took the question as unanimous spite against her. She expected them to wash up when she herself couldn't even drive a car. The deaf woman was dying to tell her never mind, anyone could get bogged and it wasn't really a reflection, but she didn't trust her monotonous pitch to convey the necessary kindness. The little group of grannies stood in a geriatric cluster, watching Lex's antics.

First she set her jaw, and tried again with the accelerator. Then she got out and gave the back of the coach a determined look, but knew she could not move it single handed. Then she ran nervously back to the front to try and catch sight of the men. She was about to ask Beryl to go after them, when the grannies came towards her bearing odd sticks and pieces of wood.

— This is no time for a bloody peace offering, she shouted, exasperated beyond self-control, you look like a bunch of retired red Indian squaws.

The women ignored her, except to smile placatingly, and proceeded to place each bit of wood just in front of each tyre. Beryl watched fascinated. There seemed to have been some kind of self-selection whereby the less good on their legs stayed by the coach and arranged the wood for maximum efficiency. Beryl wavered. Torn between staying in the desert and helping the coach back on the road. Finally she joined in the wood gathering and helped shove it under the wheels as her back was suppler than most. Lex sulked, but finally took charge of operations and told the women where to look for wood.

— She's deaf, one of them explained when no one listened to Lex.

— But you can't all be deaf, she exploded.

— Old women generally are, said the same woman who had been knitting on the journey out, with an ambiguous wink at Beryl.

After the wood was laid, there remained the problem of how to move the coach onto it. Lex was all for calling the men to help her.

— But there are only six of them, and twenty four of us, came the mild protest. Perhaps we could toy with moving the bus until they come back and help us out. We promise not to strain our muscles, put our backs out or sue your company.

One of the older women took the steering wheel, which left Lex free to push. It was not much effort between 25 of them, more a problem for 50 hands to find a griphold on the coach. Some of the women were panting by the end, but then it was a very hot day.

Just as the coach was setting off, the men appeared over the slope.

— Been for such a long walk, they cried, you took your time, didn't you?

They were eager for a cup of tea, but the older women were anxious to get back.

— I suppose you have heart pills to take at prescribed times, murmured Beryl, her first genuine enquiry all trip. She was trying to imagine herself really old, to prepare herself for the shock as she was seldom in such a group where the average age was so much older than hers.

— Some do, said Mrs. R-W, but you can always bring them with you. No, we have group therapy tonight and we're anxious for our twenty minutes each.

— A progressive occupational therapist, thought Beryl, at least Australia looks after its old people.

As they left the desert, Lex turned the loud speaker on again to explain the state of the roads.

— You will notice this road isn't tarred and the drive is very bumpy. Well, you'll be interested to learn that there are no plans to resurface it. We had an American with us on one trip who told us they'd closed Yellow Stone Park because so many people carved up the trees. Well, they've decided here that anyone wanting to visit will have to show their good faith by enduring its bad roads.

Beryl noted the lack of dates and tonnage and found this little anecdote so unlike the driver's previous style, that she wondered at the change in her. She could almost believe that Lex had a genuine feeling for the desert and had not learnt this tale in a guide book. By the time the coach dropped her off again at the end of her road, she was glad she had not stayed overnight as she was dying to talk to John about

Marble Bar. She was well pleased with her first day off, and intended to take many more, and if any of her daughters should laugh as she unpacked her packet of flour, they would surely forgive her first obvious caprice for years.

Chapter 11
In Which Nothing Happens

Although she had blurted out her guilty secret to her mother only that morning, Minnie still felt misunderstood. Beryl's reaction was to go away for a long walk and not come back until suppertime. It must have been quite a shock for her; Minnie understood that, but surely they could discuss it like adults? She was prompted to repeat her declaration so that her mother could not pretend to have misheard. Minnie was sure she had heard, otherwise why would she have rushed off like that?

During her walk back along the road Beryl became more and more convinced that of course her family were worried about her and she had been very good not to stay out all night without warning them. She could see them sitting, white-faced, round the kitchen table, wondering when to phone the police.

— It's alright, Mummy's home, she almost shouted as she walked in.

— Hi, Mum, wanna cup of tea? Minnie asked.

— Love one if you're making one darling, I've had rather a long walk.

— I'm just taking one to Laura.

— Oh, where is she?

— In bed.

— Hmm, where's Ingrid?

— In her room painting her nails.

— Hadn't they even noticed she'd been away? Beryl wondered, vaguely hurt.

Hadn't her mother heard what she'd said that morning? Min thought. Perhaps Pious and Plod's altercation had blocked it out. If only Erica was still around. Beryl would have come home, seen the two of them together and just known. Then her reaction would be her own business. Why did her mother have to take such long walks?

149

Ingrid wandered in from her room and looked in the fridge for something to punctuate her reading matter. Now where was that cold chicken she had noticed earlier on? She bent down to look behind the salad bowl, then caught sight of her mother and sister looking at her. They were thinking she was quite fat enough already, and Minnie was staring at the pleats of her stomach as she knelt. If they knew all about last night, why couldn't they just say so and have done with it?

— What's wrong with Laura? asked Beryl.

Ingrid grunted a reply; she couldn't give Laura away.

— Did you have a nice time, Minnie? Beryl continued. Were her daughters being deliberately offhand to punish her for being out all day?

Minnie smiled weakly and said,

— Yes, the people were very nice but I felt a bit out of it not knowing anyone.

The evening wore on. Conversation was scanty. Ingrid watched the teeve and ate peanuts; Minnie curled in an armchair and read Monique Wittig; Beryl finished the ironing. It was a very masculine silence. There was no phone to interrupt them, no catastrophe to unite them and no one relished frontal attack. When John came home, Beryl went to bed.

Laura lay in the dark, wishing one of them would come and talk to her, but imagined that Beryl was angry with her and the other two bound up in their own lives. She remembered very little of the accident, though sometimes when she closed her eyes, she saw headlights on a high beam. She fell asleep, and awoke fitfully wondering where she was. The seven hour drive, however, she recalled with perfect clarity: the little troop of sisters, all dressed alike, driven into Perth and deposited into the arms of women they learnt to call "aunty", as before they had called men "uncle". Only now she could see the younger Laura, and shrug at the child's ingratiating smile, and when Donna cut herself climbing in at the window after Moira, Laura junior coped with it, oblivious of Laura senior looking on. Laura wished that if Beryl was going to yell at her, she would get it over with, but she could hear her talking to John with all the bubbling enthusiasm that had first persuaded him to leave London for Perth.

— I've had the most lovely day.

— Have you, darling?

Beryl could not explain about the knitting and being allowed to help push a coach.

— I met a woman from Marble Bar who says land's dirt cheap up there as it were, because there simply isn't any demand.

— I can imagine.

— Now, darling, you know how cross you get with the taxis, when you're pipped to the post by another chap doing a U turn, or a call goes out and you can't find the passenger.

— Or going to the back of woop woop and you don't know where the house is. Had one like that tonight, actually. Do you know, I went all the way over to Two Rocks to pick someone up at the marina and spent half an hour cruising round for them.

— Yes, dear, that sort of thing. Well, out there you'd be your own boss and set your own pace.

— Steady on, I doubt if they even have taxis, they'd all have their own cars.

— Oh, I suppose you're right . . .

— Still, could do a roaring trade fixing them.

— And you're very good at things like that.

— Yes, but you wouldn't like the heat.

— I've got skin like a rhino and the stomach of a camel.

— Don't tell me you want to go and live up there?

— Yes, I do, John, very much.

— But what do Ingrid and Laura say?

— Well, of course, I thought I should ask you first.

Minnie wondered whether Erica had given her her number because she wanted to be phoned or because it was the done thing. In this situation Milly always advised Minnie to write her address and stuff on a very small, easily lost piece of paper if she didn't really want to be called, and very clearly on a large sheet if she did. Minnie smoothed out the slip of paper Erica had given her. It was torn from a cigarette packet; average size, could have meant anything. Minnie couldn't bring herself to risk it and even Milly did not welcome the awkward pause which tells you that your correspondent does actually have other things to do and could you please make your message brief. She had finished Le Corps Lesbien, and was at a loose end. She decided to go and see how Laura was.

Laura was musing about Moira and how long she would

stick the catholics without going on the game, but she had no wish to live her sister's life for her. Nausea coupled with being bedridden made her feel helpless and depressed. She had entertained the idea that if she went to see John, he might do something for Moira. This avenue was now closed. Surely they had learnt enough not to start making their mother's mistakes? It was now quite clear to her what sort of help John would have given them. When the door opened, Laura jumped.

— Oh Laura, it's only me.

— Good, I was getting lonely. Everyone else in bed?

— All except Ingrid who's watching some crap on the box. Don't know how she can sit through it. She's just got no idea. (Pause).

— Laura, if you like someone um quite a lot and you know they like you too, well, where do you go from there?

— To bed?

— Don't be so glib.

— Tell your best friend to tell their best friend that you want to sit next to them in maths?

— But how do you know they wouldn't rather sit next to their best friend?

Laura pondered the problem and it occurred to her to ask herself why Minnie was hiding behind "they". Surely she knew it was safe to say "she". At first Laura assumed that Minnie was talking about Erica, but she was being so guarded about it that Laura began to wonder, not realising that Minnie was afraid she would blush if she said Erica's name out loud, so often had she whispered it to herself. So perhaps, went Laura's train of thought, it wasn't "she" that Minnie meant, but "you".

— Well, you could go out with them somewhere and see how it goes.

Minnie wondered how she could arrange a coincidental encounter with Erica, without ringing her up to fix it beforehand. She could hardly get Milly to go round there, dressed in a veil to make an anonymous rendez-vous.

There was a noise outside the door as of someone sniffing.

— Ingrid's gone to bed, Minnie remarked.

As Ingrid undressed, she thought about work the next day. There was always breakfast to look forward to; the one

152

meal of the day you could earn by simply sleeping for eight hours beforehand. Then it would be uniform, bus, smile, sign in, smile, rubber gloves, idle chatter, smile. Even if Mrs Bovis came, it wouldn't brighten up the day. She had done her duty and gone to church. Or rather Fran had, but Mrs Bovis would surely have noticed she had not been her usual self. And if she hadn't noticed, what did that say about Ingrid? The polite answers, intelligent questions, obedient kneelings and prayings had obviously been so devoid of any spark of herself that even the devoutest church-goer would have thought her a lifeless parody. That Mrs Bovis got pleasure out of blue straw hats and white gloves was beyond Ingrid. How did you talk to someone whose idea of a fun time is so different from your own? Oh why couldn't life be easy and amusing like before? She began to cry. Experimentally at first, little tears of self pity to see if it made the pain less. Minnie was not yet in bed so there was no one to witness the collapse of the round and romping, fat and friendly, plump and perky, Ingrid. Had she been long thin and wasted there might have been some pathos to her tears, but given her excess mounds, she was sure she looked like a stranded whale doing a belly flop. Water everywhere and no dignity. As long as church-going was an unavoidable evil, Ingrid could send Fran, just as Minnie sent Milly to settle Barbara, but Ingrid liked Mrs Bovis and would feel she had failed as long as she could not share her ruling passion or refuse it honourably. And Mrs Bovis was passionate about church; Ingrid could not dismiss it as a covert invitation to lunch, even though they had eaten together afterwards. That was what made it so awful: one moment her beloved Mrs B. was adoring an inert deity and feeling superior to other people who worshipped the wrong one or none at all, or with too much ceremony or with not enough (no one but our good Mrs B. seemed to have hit on quite the right mix — they could all go on dialling wrong numbers, it was she who had the hotline). The next, they were out of that nasty airless sepulchre and having a picnic on the beach.

— Pull the wish-bone with me, Ingrid, Mrs Bovis cried in strident tones. No, not like that, for heavens sake; didn't anyone ever teach you to cheat? And Mrs Bovis had shown her how to split the bone so that both partners got their wish.

153

Fran was shocked that cheating should be made light of, but Ingrid realised Mrs B. was her old self again. She jostled Fran out the way. Mrs Bovis asked what she had wished for, and Fran, sulky at being pushed out, answered priggishly,

— You're not supposed to say.

Mrs Bovis turned away with an audible huff and Ingrid was afraid she would resort again to piety. Ingrid reached for a cream bun. Mrs B. looked up with an evil glint and asked,

— Do you know why they call a custard pie fight a custard pie fight?

— No, said Ingrid encouragingly, expecting a verbal witticism.

Mrs Bovis looked very wicked, picked up another cream bun, removed the top layer and propelled the bottom half into Ingrid's nose.

— Because you get egg on your face, she chuckled.

Ingrid blinked. Her eyebrows, fringe, cheeks and mouth were covered with cream. The respectable company looked the other way.

— Dearie me, said that morning's chauffeur, what a nonsequitur, and she dabbed harshly at Ingrid's face with a dry tea-towel which she wet with the corner of her mouth, just as if she had been her mother.

— Spit, she demanded, holding the tea-towel out for Ingrid to moisten. You must be more careful, Elizabeth.

Ingrid began to wonder whether Mrs Bovis had in fact just slipped but the twinkle in her eye was unmistakeable.

Her tears had halted while she mused over this incongruous scene, but they now redoubled and she sobbed because Elizabeth Bovis was a hypocrite, because she had work tomorrow morning and because she could not stop eating.

— I'm so lonely, she cried piteously to herself in the dark. Mum didn't even listen when I said I was going to church and Fran was so pissed off by the service that she was rude to Erica and Minnie will never forgive me. Mum's got her John and Laura's getting off with Minnie and my John was lost at sea. At the pathetic picture of herself as a naval widow, Ingrid renewed her howls. John didn't mind her being fat, he used to say it made her boobs bigger, like force feeding a goose.

— You've got a very naughty body, he used to say, and she would feel mature and provocative.

154

Laura was watching Minnie in the darkness. What years there were between sitting companionably in separate silences and sitting together sharing the same thought.

— You're deep in thought, Minnie, think it makes you look mature?

— I was just thinking about going out tomorrow.

— Ok, where'll we go?

Minnie smiled. A sister was as good as a best friend. She could bring Laura with her to see Erica.

— Dunno yet. Meet you in town at 7, after you finish work.

Beryl returned to her favourite theme. She must have a definite answer before she fell asleep.

— Perhaps I'll phone the woman tomorrow and ask about the motel.

— Is it for sale?

— Don't know, but it doesn't do to let the grass grow.

— When are you going to tell the girls?

As before she had told her husband she was divorcing him only when the new flat was confirmed, she would tell her daughters once all the arrangements were made. No point saying you're leaving someone and going on living with them in the meantime. They only get silent and reproachful.

— What if they don't want to come?

— Good god, of course they won't want to come.

The idea of Laura melting in the heat, Ingrid whining that she was hungry, and Minnie's plaintive sarcasm! She would be delighted to have them visit her but she was not clearing up anyone else's mess or sleeping on one ear so as to hear them come in.

Minnie was sitting on Laura's bed; there was not enough room for an armchair. These new units were built especially to encourage the growing family to move out and buy one of its own. Laura wondered what it would be like to sleep with a woman.

— If uncle John had been a woman, I wonder if things would have been different.

— What? Minnie gaped.

— Well, while I was driving to Kalgoorlie, I kept trying to work out why mum put us in a Home.

— Didn't she say?

— Only to joke about what a wicked mother she was and

155

how we were better off without her.

— Perhaps she couldn't afford to keep you. Did she have a job?

— She was a cabaret artiste, overtures and beginners please, you know . . .

— ?

— I think she was a prostitute.

— How do you know? Minnie assumed this was old knowledge and Laura had but to repeat old phrases.

— Well, I don't really, that's the problem. I just think about it and get frightened, and there's Moira, she's so like mum.

— Can't you just ask Irene? But the hippy trippy honesty sounded stale as soon as it left Minnie's mouth.

Laura shook her head; herself in smart clothes from the depths of respectabilia: mother, father, job, car, saying gravely to Irene,

— Mother, dear, are you on the game?

— No, said Minnie, I know you can't ask. It was like that with my father. Mum never told us why she divorced him, so I always used to wonder. She wouldn't tell me what day she was going to court, but I phoned the Clerk and found out anyway. It was like finding out what happened was more important than not making her angry. But on the actual day I had an exam.

— What were the grounds?

— Mental cruelty.

— What's that mean?

— I really don't know. Humiliation or something. But I never found out why exactly she left him.

— Is there an "exactly", though?

— Well, at least you know that your mother sent you away to keep you from uncle John.

— I'm not sure, Minnie. You see for me it's as though I always knew my mother got money from men but I was angry with her for getting rid of me and I couldn't be angry with her if I had to see it her way.

— Mmm, no sudden revelation in the bush? (Minnie thought for a while). But I don't think I do know what it is about my father, and that's the problem; I've inherited my mother's fear without her explanation. My aunt Alice's house was only round the corner from my dad's; I'd see him

156

sometimes shuffling along the street after my mother left, but I'd duck down behind the cars till he passed and my heart would be racing lest he turned round and saw me.

— Maybe my mother's fear of uncle John wasn't reasonable either, she just wasn't taking any chances. But then, women are frightened of men, aren't they, and it isn't always based on anything real.

— Yeah, wonderful, it's called patriarchy, Laura.

— Patronising.

— No, patriar . . . oh, sorry.

— I wished I didn't know about my ma, I can't hate her any more.

— I wish I did know about my dad.

— It's your fault for coming here and making me think.

— It's your fault for making me talk. I never talk about my father.

— What happened to him?

— He died.

— Straightaway?

— No, . . . he used to phone me up some times, and we'd have dinner in Italian restaurants.

— Did he talk about mum, I mean, your mum?

— No, but he always mentioned the cat. He said if ever I couldn't look after her, he'd be happy to have her back. She was a lovely sleek little thing except that one eye had been blown out by a firework. We called her Cyclops. Mum never mentioned Dad either, and if I wrote about him she'd ignore it, but she kept asking after Cyclo.

— Weird.

— Yeah.

— So what did your dad die of?

— Cancer of the jaw in the long term, but bronchitis actually carried him off. Same as Cyclo.

— Heavy.

— S'pose so, but I wouldn't go near him. I was afraid of taking over from my mother and looking after him instead of her. Then I'd have these dreams where she'd come back to London, hear that I'd been seeing him, and just leave again calling me "scab". They were awful. I'd wake up crying, I mean actually crying, and go downstairs and beg someone to cuddle me.

— Dear Minnie, said Laura, I would have cuddled you. And

she put her arm round Minnie then and there in case it wasn't too late.

— Is that why you changed your name? Laura wondered what she should call herself, now she could no longer use John's name.

— Well, actually, . . . Minnie thought back to the scene at Lloyds Bank. Her father was wheeled in by his private nurse and companion (at least he pays her, Minnie had thought brutally). He had leaned on the counter, paralysed down one side of his body from a stroke Minnie had not been told about, and signed over his money to her.

— No death duties, he had croaked, in that awful clock-work voice, on legacies before I snuff it.

Minnie had suspected this might be his intention when the nurse had phoned her that morning. Her father, who had refused Beryl half the family home on the grounds that she had not put any money into it, was now leaving everything to his daughter.

— I can't possibly accept.

— Then I'll give it all to the government to pay off the national debt.

He meant it, the bastard, he had her whichever way she looked. Beryl had slipped through his fingers by adamantly refusing either compromise or communication, but Minnie was still in the palm of his hand, and he had thought of a way to keep her there, even after his death.

— The only proviso I'll make on my will, is that you keep your own name.

They were now sitting in the solicitors' office. Minnie marvelled at his gall in calling Débar her own name.

— I don't mind if you get married, he crackled, I'm a very liberal sort of chap.

The joviality of "liberal" had a sour taste. Mr Débar could move only the right side of his mouth and the liquid "l's" slurred embarrassingly together. Physically closer to her than her mother, he knew there was no chance of her getting married.

Mr Débar might be lonely and bed-ridden, but he still had a television and Minnie had been very easy to spot on the Gay Pride March as she took over the Lesbian Line banner from a fellow Sapphite.

— Quite enough excitement for one day, said the nurse

158

briskly, as she wheeled Mr Débar out again.

Minnie realised from the pool on the floor that her father was now incontinent. The smart flannel suit, the camel hair coat and the royal blue tie with the phoenix, yet he couldn't control his own bladder. Minnie looked around to see if the pinstriped lawyers had noticed the quiet, inoffensive puddle, now sinking into the thick pile carpet. Doubtless they would have the secretary clean it up as soon as Minnie left, and send the bill to the nurse. Minnie wondered if her father even knew he had disgraced himself. For the first time she could remember, Minnie felt sorry for this big, impressive man, who thundered out opinions like nine pins and now pissed himself in a wheel chair. She wanted to run after him, for everything to be over, not to have to feel angry any more and for them to be able to be fond of each other; and she wanted him to die, so that Beryl would come back and she could take up her life again where it had left off.

—Actually, Laura, it's my friends who call me "Jay", but officially I'm still Débar.

— Oh, Laura nodded comprehendingly, relieved to learn that Min did not have everything under control. I don't have a middle name, and besides, I want to have the same name as my sisters.

Minnie was beginning to feel that every second of this conversation was precious and she wanted to go on having it, even if it meant talking all night. It wasn't so much what she actually said to Laura, which must, she supposed, sound rather banal, but the things Laura's simple questions forced her to remember. However, she didn't want to hog the floor.

— Yeah, you're quite worried about Moira, aren't you?

— She must just seem really gawky to you, but I remember when she was my closest friend and it seemed like no one in the world would ever understand me like she did. We used to plan how we would live together when we grew up and bring up our kids in the same house. I'm not sure how we imagined we'd have them. (Laura giggled). (Ingrid sobbed).

— What was that? said Minnie.

— I was just sniggering at how naive me and Moi were. Laura snorted as she thought of her and her sister planning to go to Coober Pedy, pick up a fortune in opals and make themselves a dugout to sleep in.

Ingrid sniffed as she heard a peal of laughter from Laura's

room, wishing she could pad over in her nightie but sure they were giggling about her.

— Mum says she couldn't cope with having Moira to live here.

— I know but now I've got a job I was thinking of trying to get a flat or something. I can't live off your mother forever.

It sounded so reasonable, but Minnie didn't want the little family in Australia to split up. She wanted Laura to go on talking, however, so that she could work out what it was she had invested in an institution so radically unsound as the family.

Ingrid's head appeared round the door,

— Can't you keep it down a bit? Some of us have work in the morning, she said, hoping to be invited in.

— Laura was saying she was thinking of getting a flat with Moira.

— Oh, said Ingrid, nestling on the end of the bed not knowing whether to be pleased or upset. Was this certain enough for her fantasies or was Laura just talking?

Ingrid's arrival made the conversation less personal as each tried to envisage how they would be living next year and none could believe that anything was going to change. Finally they went to their separate beds, Minnie to think about Erica, Laura about Minnie, and Ingrid about cream buns, though the shadows of Mr Débar, Moira and Elizabeth Bovis still hovered relentlessly in the air.

* * *

As the lights went out at 64 Sterling Crescent, they came up briefly to accompany the nightly insomnia of deaf Mrs. O., whom we will finally call Dorothy. She sat on the edge of her bed and pondered the day's happenings. In her mind's eye she could see the bright sunlight and the group of women sitting on camp-stools by the coach, but the action replay went into slow motion as it watched Dorrie's agony at not being able to clean her fingers and it froze as Blanche gently leaned forward and passed her a tea towel. She was so used to it being Betsey who anticipated her needs.

Dorrie slipped to the floor and, with careful step, visited the assorted objects in her room; her nightly custom of the last ten years. She rearranged photographs, combed her hair

160

with a battered silver brush, folded clothes neatly into a drawer, and then silently paid her respects to the glass horses on the window sill, her first rush cross, a crystal powder compact and finally, the drawer containing Betsey Bovis' sky blue bathers with their surf board insignia from 1925 when she had won the ladies' free style championship. Betsey had given it to Dorrie one day at Mundaring Weir eight years ago on a Nags outing. It had been very romantic.

— Oh, Betsey, she had cried, while the others went off to see how the dam was filling up. Your blue bathers!

She held them up to show she appreciated the sacrifice.

— The two most important days of my life, declared Betsey, the day I won the championship, and the first time I slept with you.

They were tempted to stare into each others' eyes and sigh, when Betsey suddenly clasped the bathers to her now flat chest and announced her wicked intention of trying them on just one more time, and swimming in the dam.

— You can't, Dorrie breathed, more shocked at the idea of her lover's parchment thighs being exposed to the air and the common eye than the sacrosanct reaches of the Water Authority being desecrated by Betsey's body. Fortunately, the bathers no longer fitted. Betsey had shrunk and now stooped a little, but her stomach had grown.

— Too many candle-lit dinners, she smiled benignly down at herself.

As she tried to stretch the cotton across her girth she burst out into fiendish cackles and Dorrie smiled at her friend's unselfconscious gaiety. That night Dorrie had wrapped the bathers in some crinkly paper which had previously been used for bread, but still wonderfully pink and appropriate. Now she looked at the small parcel and wished she had Betsey's spontaneity, a trait she had called "sheer self-indulgence" in the past.

Chapter 12
The Markets

Beryl was luxuriating in bed, congratulating herself on her day off, when Laura knocked.

— Mum, said her voice through the door, I'm taking a sickie. Can you ring Cole's for me?

Beryl lumbered to her feet and heaved her objecting body across the road to Sandra's. Sandra was in the middle of her weeties but perfectly good-natured.

— Didn't last long, did it, she smiled.

Beryl's eyes refused to open more than a centimetre and her throat felt like a dried up river bed, she was in no mood for neighbours.

— What? she rasped, her hair alternately tousled and flattened according to its previous relation to the pillow, greasy reservoirs of mascara smeared in the corners of her eyes.

Sandra recognised the symptoms and did not insist.

— Morning after the early night?

For a moment Beryl envied Sandra's ordered home, the luxury of arriving at places on time and the space to clean her teeth between meals. She conceded a watery grin and asked to use the phone.

— Is your Laura alright?

— Oh she's never felt better in her life, it's the car I'm worried about.

— That's always the way, I knew it wouldn't last. I felt lost without it sitting in the middle of the drive, didn't know which of these concrete blocks was mine. Still, I suppose they have to go their own way in the end.

Beryl nodded sympathetically. You could always have more children, but you had to buy a car. When she slipped her bare bunioned feet back into bed the warm patch had disappeared and the sheets were anybody's. She would have to work at retaming them to achieve the soft loving

162

relationship they had so recently enjoyed. The other thing they didn't tell you about growing older (oh that mild comparison, bloody euphemism, that's what) was that you would be constitutionally unable to sleep beyond seven o'clock in the morning, a victim to the whim of any mere paper boy who picked that moment to call out his delivery, little guessing that his innocently informative cry had nefariously wrested you from the bosom of the manchester for another sixteen hours. Beryl savoured the word "manchester", one of her more recent acquirements. Soon she would be speaking Strine with the best of them without sounding like she was recording a dying language. But her thoughts were no longer comfortable in the supine position, her toes were encountering crumbs at the bottom of the bed, and whichever way she chose to lie, she always seemed to have one arm over. Through the window lace she could see the warratah calling for attention and she wandered out to the garden to see if any frogs had grown from the black darting objects Laura had brought home in a plastic bag from the Helena.

Minnie wandered up Wellington Street towards East Perth without a thought in her head; her eyes scanned the road for any sign of Erica. If only they were both involved in an ongoing struggle situation — so good for getting to know people, but there was only Nookinbah and 54b. They could have laid on something a bit more interesting for Minnie's first trip to Australia. She was mildly interested in the Aboriginal pastoralist deprived of his land by the mining company, but she wasn't going to occupy the company offices. Even Beryl was infuriated by the ban on meetings in Forrest Place, and if three people constituted a conspiracy, then what were mothers of six to do? Beryl's lawyers were busy defending both causes célèbres but as Erica hadn't been arrested, this provided scant opportunity for Minnie. Besides, she was beginning to feel oppressed by the passing of time: six days left, and she had still not really come to grips with the feminist scene. She was sure that behind the calm exterior of the cleanest city in Australia, simmered a whole cauldron of activity waiting to bubble up and besmirch the smug sterility of the State of Excitement.

While Minnie brooded, a cyclist swept down a side street, derailleur working overtime as she clicked smoothly from ninth to third gear. She stopped at the lights, applying safety brakes only.

— Wow, thought Minnie, either that bike's new or she keeps it finely tuned.

As the lights changed, the bike spun across the road, its spokes glinting in the sunlight like twin moons. Minnie walked on. Something had caught her attention but she couldn't pinpoint what. Absently her eyes came to rest on the number plate of a car driving along the road: "WA State of Excitement" it said, same as all the others. Hang about. No it didn't. In exactly the same lettering and just the right colour someone, the owner?, had changed it to "WA State of Excrement".

— Dumb insolence, thought Minnie and hoped a woman had done it. And already the capital of a third of Australia, nestling betwixt the Swan River's blue expanse and the clean white sands of the many ocean beaches, seemed to be facing a subtle challenge which it didn't even recognise.

From her vantage point on the saddle, Erica had easily spotted Minnie, but wanted to be sure the latter was really going towards Updike Street. She sped across the traffic lights, but swung back again into the main road when Minnie walked on up the street. As Minnie raised her glance from the number plate to the road, she heard the faint screech of new rubbers on bike tyres. Erica threw her right leg over the saddle, neatly extricating her left foot from the toe clip, and jumped sprily onto the pavement. In her sandals even the hair on her toes was bleached blonde by the sun. Minnie felt the air knocked out of her as Erica landed at her side.

— She's beautiful, she thought, but it was more a comment on her own stocky build and square frame and their undoubted ugliness. Perfectly objective.

— You can't view other women as solely objects of desire, Milly tut tutted.

— Erotisation of same sex attributes, said her father's psychiatric voice.

— Lesbianism is not just about sex, Milly rebuked him severely as he turned in his grave to hear better, it's an emotional and mental commitment. Even virgins can be lesbians.

Minnie left them to it.

— Bought yourself a new toy? she grinned, wondering how

much delight it was permissible to show on her face.

— How d'you guess?

— You keep changing gear.

— Had to, I can't start off in ninth. Erica abandoned explanation, what are you doing around here? Come to see me?

It did seem easier to agree.

— Well come on round the corner, Updike Street's just before the railway line.

Minnie picked up the new bike with two fingers to see how light it was and sounded suitably impressed. She was glad to see that if all else failed, she and Erica could always talk bike.

— How's Sky?

— Oh, alright. She went back to Applecross last night swearing not to touch another drop, till the next time.

Minnie smiled, obscurely relieved.

— There's a women's tea party in the street. Why don't you come?

Before, it had been too dark to see and then Sky had been ill, but the houses in the street were amazing. In London they would have been high quality squats. No garden out front, just a tiny veranda where the front door and meters were kept, the paint was giving up and the walls had gaping cracks in them. Then came a long thin corridor with two bedrooms off, a larger room and the cavernous kitchen with burrows of pantries, larders and sculleries complete with dingy yellow paint. The toilet was at the other end of the garden next to the chooks.

— Cor, a dunny, said Minnie in delighted discovery, "May all your chicks turn to emus and kick your dunny down."

Erica groaned, sensing impending fireworks.

— Thanks for the friendly thought, said Lilith, the woman of the house. Were you at that party in Guildford? You're not the woman from England I accused of slumming in the colonies?

— Well, I am English, said Minnie in her London accent . . .

— Oh good, then the accusation still stands, and when you feel a quotation coming on, try and get it right.

— We say chooks not chicks, Minnie, said Erica to relax the tension, but Minnie felt she was being told off.

Linda appeared and Erica was thankful for the interruption.

165

— Francine wants to come, she said, I told her it was only for Updike women, but . . .

— Never mind, said Lilith, this one's not even from Australia, let alone boring old Updike Street.

Minnie felt cut and wondered what Erica thought of her now. She hadn't meant to sound gloating, but come to think of it, exclaiming over dunnies was like Australians in Brixton exclaiming over riot shields. How could she prove conclusively she wasn't an ethnic snob? In Manchester when the motordikes had gone for a ride she had gazed at the line up of bikes and chuckled at the small one on the end. It was yellow, and there was a dip in front of the saddle for you to put your feet on, instead of a stirrup either side.

— Whose is the scooter? she had asked.

— It's a Honda fifty, Gerry said sourly, don't make fun of my bike, it's oppressive.

— I'm sorry, it's just that my bike . . .

— Oh yeah, what have you got then? A one thousand cc?

Minnie had not had the courage to explain that far from smart-arsing about Gerry's bike, she didn't know enough to realise she had insulted it. Fortunately the long suffering Milly saved the day.

— Minnie thinks her push bike beats your Honda, cos it's got 10 speeds not three.

Gerry had been forced to laugh, but Milly did not know how to disarm Lilith's irritation. They sat around the table where an enormous cake lay in state, the shape of a double women's symbol, surrounded by mounds of sandwiches. Nobody said anything. Minnie exchanged glances with Erica, then looked down at her finger nails.

— We've heard a lot about squatting in London, said Linda, and Minnie, agonising over the silence, had no choice but let Milly rise to the bait. Milly's slick well-informed lecture was far worse than Min's blundering ineptitude. She started off with the housing acts, continued with the GLC hard-to-lets, the proliferation of short life and co-ops. Again the silence descended and instead of realising she was causing it, Milly struggled to disperse it. She described Christiania, drew in the Berlin occupations, waxed lyrical over Amsterdam and culminated in "defenderem lo Larzac". The other women sat tight, stunned by the gush of information pouring out of Minnie's mouth. Erica watched in embarrassment,

166

fidgeting with a cigarette packet.

— Is this a non-smoking house? she butted in, finally.

Was Erica sharing her embarrassment, or Lilith's? Minnie wanted to know so much she almost asked. Someone shoved over an ash tray. Still no one else spoke.

— What did you think of the party? whispered one woman to her neighbour.

Linda caught the question, and as this was what she had come for she exclaimed,

— What about those Eastern Staters in the lurex tights and sequins?

Erica was sure Minnie was not naturally pompous, but did not know her well enough to help her out of it. She welcomed the opportunity to get Minnie out of the grime light. Minnie noted the change of subject and felt dejected and doomed. Why wouldn't they give her a chance?

— Dressed for rape, I call it, said Lilith soberly.

Milly was about to launch into a polemic about how at a woman's party you should be able to walk around stark naked and who, one might ask, was expected to do the raping? Erica, however choked on a crumb of coconut, and said:

— I'm sorry but I'll really have to be going. This sounded a little lame so she wracked her brain for an excuse.

— I'm hungry and I'll have to put some dinner on.

Minnie gazed at the table still spread with cucumber sandwiches and the practically uncut cake. Of all the excuses to come up with. Even Milly would have done better, but at least it got them out of there and established that Erica was right with her.

— Pull up a beer crate, said Erica, solidest chair in the house.

— They're so puritan, Minnie shuddered.

— Purist, they'd say. Lilith bangs on the wall if she hears her neighbour brush his teeth.

— You'd think it was a competition as to who could last longest without saying a word to a man.

— Well, that's understandable. They don't like men. Neither do I, come to that.

— No, thought Minnie, but don't some men get credit for being less sexist than others? Otherwise what's the point of being a socialist?

— But it's the way they slag off other women that gets me, she said out loud. All these jokes about rape, I can't handle it.

— They're still working it out, Erica shrugged liberally.

— With a sledge hammer, Minnie snarled.

— Actually, I really like Lilith; she doesn't take shit from anyone. Erica's comment reeked of reproof.

— N'arf give it out, though, Minnie could not resist, and Erica chuckled. They rewrote the tea party and the New Year's Eve party and giggled vociferously at various comments that had been made with which they didn't agree but feared to counter at the time, and Minnie got the chance to explain about Milly. Erica said she sounded very useful if you could keep her in hand and she wouldn't mind borrowing her some time. By the time Minnie had to meet Laura, they had discussed nursing and the Eastern States, which Minnie must visit, when they became lesbians and how Minnie managed to travel to Australia on the dole. Minnie's parting shot was an invitation to dinner the following night.

— They've taken it into the garage and they'll have it ready by next Friday, were Laura's triumphant first words.

Minnie assumed "it" was the Kingswood.

— Fine, she said, wondering at Laura's triumph. This seemed to be the sort of thing you paid insurance for, still, far be it for her to understand.

— They said it was a write off, but it's not true, and I shamed them into admitting it. They don't know fuck all about engines.

Minnie nodded abstractedly. She was suffering that awkward agony where you go over everything you said and everything she said across a crowded tea table and come to the conclusion that you're a pretty worthless individual and if she doesn't wash her hands of you completely, then you'll never be able to trust her judgement.

— Come on, Min, let's go, said Laura, still bubbling with her own cleverness.

— Where? In what? I thought it wasn't ready?

— I've hired one for the next two weeks.

— But it costs the earth. At last Minnie was listening. Could Laura really afford to spend all that money? The crash wasn't her fault.

— I've been saving from my wages at Cole's.

— But you were going to buy your own car.

Laura shrugged, pleased that she had thought of this way to undo the damage she had done. Minnie felt awful, knowing that she had enough money to pay for a new car, let alone hire one, but she could not wade in with her foreign money. Passively she slid into the suicide seat, she would enjoy Laura's treat like a gift.

— Where to, Modom?

— Oh, the sea, the sea.

Actually it was an ocean, but Laura did not correct her as they gulped down the kilometers, high on the speed and the wind through the open windows.

— Traffic lights, Minnie sang out, not quite relaxed enough to forget she was an elder sister.

— Yes, sweetie, smiled Laura pleasantly, crashing through an amber.

They parked on the sand dunes, grabbed hands, and raced down to the water. The moon and stars were obligingly visible as they played chase the waves, one rolled up her trouser legs, the other hitched up her skirt, and they felt the wet sand between their toes. Laura found it difficult to dissociate an appreciation of Min's bouncy gaiety and the feeling that she ought to think her pretty. When they had done all the falling over in the sand, running along the seashore and collapsing in panting heaps that two women can stomach given a starlit evening, balmy atmosphere, and mutual ease in each other's presence, Laura decided to give Minnie a tour of the sites. They drove to Freo Mall and parked on the groyne. There was a line of panel vans swaying gently from side to side.

— Feel a bit out of place, said Minnie.

— Yeah, I used to come here with John, but I guess it's different with two chicks.

Laura decided to simply comply with anything Minnie might suggest. They began to clamber along the boulders, but Laura's high heels impeded her, a car flashed its headlights and another sounded its horn. Soon the whole row was honking and flashing and the light was as dazzling as a police raid.

— I don't think they want us to start feeling welcome or anything.

— No, (pause), I used to think two chicks cruising was

pretty weird, but now I think it's real fun.

Laura slipped her arm through Minnie's as they walked back to the car.

— I'm hungry, said Minnie, prosaically.

Laura postponed a thought on Min's hair in the moonlight, and a wish that there was more of it to muse on, and concentrated on the problem at hand.

— Let's go to The Markets, she suggested, it's this big indoor hall with chairs and tables in the middle and all these exotic stalls round the edge. They compete with each other to get you to buy their stuff: Japanese, Taiwanese, Burmese and blah blah.

Minnie stopped going over, "so I said, so she said, so they said", and joked with Laura about the other people in the room. It seemed like everyone she had met since arriving in Australia was sitting in that restaurant. At the Taiwanese counter, a man in a suit stood very still, right arm raised and held away from his body at an angle of 45 degrees. It was bent at the elbow and the forefinger was outstretched as if for pointing. If you followed the line of the finger, you came upon a tray of prawn crackers about fifteen centimetres further on. The man's mouth was open,

— And some of those, he was saying.

At the table nearest the counter was a group of four rowdy youths, swilling their sorrows in their beer. One had already laid his head on the table and his snores filled the room. It was still early. Further over in the Lebanese corner was the doctor from the hospital in earnest conversation with the skipper from the ferry. About to buy some hummus, hard-earned dollars in hot little hand, were Moira and Pam from the Home. Quite a few people were eating, plates piled high with bean sprouts and prawn balls, onion bhajis or falaffel. Near Hong Kong was a family group of John, Grazyna and Simone, who was still wearing her "purple senior" uniform. With them were a woman with bruises under her glasses and a younger who might have been her daughter. An acute observer might have recognised them as Mrs Bolt and Alexandra, known affectionately as Lex. Diagonally opposite Rangoon were two groups of women, at two definitely separate tables. There was a gap of perhaps 30 years between them and a whole generation between their manners. One was noisy and flamboyant, talking loud and fast, fists banging on the table, bright colours flashing, bits of paste jewellery picking up the light in sparks; the other was quiet and intense, colours sombre, varying from grey to navy blue, nowhere overstepping a staid green. Among the former, raucous bunch, Mrs Bovis stood out with her contagious giggle, and deaf Mrs O. with her uncontrollable pitch; the latter was composed mainly of Sky, struggling personfully not to overdrink, Linda and Lilith bickering quietly over smoking and the Woman's Movement (wherever did the Liberation go?), and Erica worrying about her bicycle. She'd thought of leaving it chained to a lamp post, but the citadel lock would only go through one wheel and anyway, the post was too thick. She would have to take off the front wheel and she wasn't sure she'd be able to slot it back into position in the state of inebriation that normally followed an evening at The Markets. In the end she slung it over her shoulder and marched up the steps with it.

-- You can't bring a bicycle in here, Sandra protested feebly.

Erica twisted her head sideways as if to look at what was perched on her shoulder and quipped,

— It isn't a bicycle, it's a parrot. She had left it by the Ladies.

The earnest young men from the coach, having completed their pre-survey of the Pinnacles, were discussing gay self-abuse with Johnny François. A young man in white knee socks was explaining to a woman around forty that if Charlie Court got his way he'd dig up the whole of Australia and sell it to the Japanese.

— Then they'll sell it all back to us as Toyotas.

Irene wondered if "this was the one" and feigned interest in uranium as before she had done in rock melons. A harassed looking Sandra was washing endless chop sticks for Hong Kong, trying to work out her hours that week without losing count. Yes, this was definitely overtime, she must get a record of it 'cos no one else would remember. She was over the worst now, and Beryl's cash payment had been a great help. Over in another corner of the hall, somewhere in the Malaccan Straits, were a young girl eating on her own, and a couple with eyes only for each other.

The young girl had ordered a mixture from the Indian counter and a plateful of Taiwanese. Both to run concurrently.

171

She spurned chopsticks as too slow and shovelled the food up with a fork. I have never seen anyone eat so fast. She was plump, it is true, but if she ate like that every night, she ought to have doubled her surface area every 35 days. I suspect some girlish trick to cheat the laws of calory, and in her hand bag I am sure you would have found a half empty bottle of ex-lax and a metal container of salt pills. At first she looked round warily, but then she began to gobble as if in fear of some celestial hand which would take her food from under her nose and slip her a lettuce leaf instead. She swallowed great gulps of water to help with the peristalsis. As she looked up, pausing only to drink, a sight met her eyes which the tangy smell of sweet 'n sour could not entice back down again.

She stared at the two sisters, sitting in conspiratorial closeness, Laura's arm on the back of Min's chair. And, for a moment, she experienced not guilt, as her eating was sure to be found out, or jealousy at this bond of affection which effectively shut her out, but a sense of excitement that such friendships were possible. Since Min's party in Guildford, she had had her suspicions and wondered if Laura had been at it too, as both had come back together. An acute longing stabbed through her and she winced. This brought the beckoning bean shoots into eye shot and she crammed her mouth full of them, making up for lost time.

The couple with eyes only for each other did not see the plump woman, or the sisters with their chairs so close together. Beryl was whispering that they should go as soon as the house was sold. Her mind's eye saw, not John, but banks of Geraldton wax, and the promise of more exotic flowers, weirder even than the kangaroo paws whose stalk was red and flowers green, in total contradiction to English common sense; plants with valves on their leaves to control their salt intake, trees which shed their bark as the temperature rose. It wasn't just the people she wanted to avoid, there was the traffic too. Her irritation with Laura had been somewhat abated coming to The Markets, as she realised quite how easy it was to have an accident. All those shiny metal wills, determined and autonomous as an unruly playgroup. She could control her own vehicle but she could not cope with feeling responsible for everyone on the road. As she had turned across the traffic she narrowly missed another car

172

and decided to pull in for a minute.

— What's up, doll? asked John, affectionate, if boozy.

— Oh, it's too silly, I'd forgotten to switch on the head-lights.

Laura was not really hungry, she rarely was, but the strain of working out Min's feeling made her peck away at food she never normally touched.

— I thought you didn't like banana, remarked Minnie as Laura gobbled distractedly at her banana smoothie.

Laura wondered if Minnie had seen through her, and was thinking her shallow and artificial. The smoothie was all gone and her tummy distended and fat, before she noticed what she was doing.

— If I go on like this, I'll end up like Ingrid, she thought uncharitably, and pushed the empty bowl away from her. Min's far away silence made her clean the bowl nervously with her fingers.

Minnie was beginning to realise that Laura expected something of her. Fancying someone seemed like wanting something you didn't deserve, coveting more than your share. She was aware of Laura's arm resting on the back of her chair, and of her own hand leaning lightly on Laura's. What messages was her sister getting? She liked Laura, but oh Jesus, sleeping with your foster sister, and her not yet eighteen! She moved her head away as if to gaze round the room, but in reality saw nothing. She felt she understood her mother's desire to get away, though for her beckoning safety was not the red desert but dense crowds in the close vicinity of Portobello Road on a Saturday morning.

Sandra finished putting away the chop-sticks and gave Ingrid her second helping.

— All the family here tonight, she said conversationally, wondering why they were all at separate tables; it made for more cleaning.

Ingrid gaped, and looked around.

Moira grinned at Beryl as she and Pam found a seat. Beryl's eyes followed her vaguely thinking,

— Thank Heavens I never have to be 15 again, when another couple caught her attention. The eye roved, overshot its mark slightly, came back, focused, then zoomed in. Two women were discovered in a tête-à-tête, one a little older than the other at the age when those things still matter.

The harsh electric light softened as the eye blinked and close-upped on the younger woman's smooth clear skin, blonde hair and sweet, round jaw. It lingered round the left eye, seen in profile, where no crow's foot lurked and fixed itself on the left hand lying gently in the fresh cotton lap. Did it or did it not conceal the merest hint of a nascent spare tyre? The eye desired to tear away the hand and the clothing to reveal the truth beneath it. The hand refused to budge, despite this spearhead of attention focused upon it from across the room. The eye was forced to observe its own hand and the neat pouch seated snugly beneath it — it seemed to Beryl that her missing womb caused a soft pocket to form beneath her skin.

From another table, another glance dissected Beryl's. Ingrid's eyes described a slow semi-circle as if surveying the scene, bumped into Beryl's and were diverted outwards until both women were gazing at Laura and Minnie. Laura was contemplating Minnie, who was biting her nails.

Lights flick on, then off to establish a change of scene, eye contact is dimmed as in slow motion Beryl, Ingrid and John get up and join the other two.

— Fancy meeting you here.

— What a coincidence.

— Can you give us a lift home?

Before the conversation could degenerate once again into a practical exchange of inanities, Beryl said firmly, by way of introduction to a weightier topic,

— I'm very glad we're all here together like this, especially as you have paid for your own meals.

Her three daughters shifted guiltily, each one thinking they were the only one to do this.

— Now, Beryl continued quickly, I have something to tell you.

Minnie was hindered in her desire to confess once again, now they were all together, by the unexpected hint that her mother might have something to say. Ingrid took the opportunity to nibble one of Min's untouched falaffels. Laura wriggled, convinced she was about to be formally forbidden to drive.

— For some time now we have not been happy together.

Minnie was sure Beryl was talking about John and sensed another separation in the air.

— Our entire domestic conversation hinges round the services I perform and you consume.

Ingrid blushed violently at the word "consume".

— I hope you won't take this to heart. As human beings I think you're very likeable, but as children you're a complete drag.

(An unusual turn of phrase for a middle-aged woman, but Beryl was a rampant individualist and what is more, she watched the telly).

Minnie welcomed these signs of maternal revolt; she herself had found her mother too subservient, and expected some form of collective housework such as they had in Brixton.

— The only solution I can see, continued this extraordinary woman . . .

— I'll make out a rota tonight . . .

— I could give you more from my wage packet . . .

— The insurance is paying for the damage . . .

— is for us to dissolve our relationship, Beryl finished implacably.

While Ingrid was wondering what she meant, Minnie burst out,

— You can't, you're our mother.

— Why not? I didn't marry you. There's no "till death us do part".

— But mum, you can't divorce your children.

— Please stop calling me that, it's oppressive.

— Mum, Beryl, why take it out on us?

— Kindly stop shouting, I'm not a public meeting.

It was an idle boast; every woman in the place had her ears tuned to the little domestic tiff, silently taking sides on the great parent, non-parent divide. Every woman who wasn't herself a mother was suddenly very conscious of being someone else's daughter. Beryl, sensing her audience, jumped up onto the table, and let go the invective.

— My first husband was a bastard, did you hear me there at the back? I said a bastard.

— We hear you, Beryl, we hear you, came from Mrs Bovis' table, like American hippies making a comeback.

All eyes were on Beryl, mouths joining in the speech they rehearsed sometimes to the mirror.

— I will spare you the details, but for those of you who

don't believe me (everyone believed her, but she continued anyway) let me say that I lived with him for eighteen years and all he ever gave me was three children. He kept us, yes, in dire poverty while he traipsed off across the world. I gave sea food lunches to his partners while my little girls ate Heinz beans. Yes, I admit it all; I am a guilty housewife who buys smashed mashed potatoes, Vesta savoury rice and instant whip chocolate mousse. I spent my married life "just adding water", heating pre-cooked packets and kneading ready-mix pastry. And just as I thought I was on the winning end, and his friends praised my gourmet cooking, my husband would sneak up behind me, put his hands over my eyes and load the table with empty boxes;

— Oh, she's a wonderful cook, is the missus, he'd say in his mock London accent, and she's a dab hand with the tin opener. He would raise my band-aided finger,

— A martyr to her art, he would say.

You can't bring that up in court, so you pile on the agony of solitude, "He's never home", you complain. The judge takes pity on your loneliness, and sets you free to try again.

Sandra thought about her John in Queensland: it would be nice if he sent her money, but she didn't really want him back. Not now, with the mortgage on the way to being paid off.

Mrs Bolt knew things had never been the same again, not since they left Marble Bar. John had not forgiven her for getting so ill every summer. Lex had got used to seeing her mother looking sick and did not realise some of it was due to her father's heavy handedness.

— And the children, Beryl's voice boomed through the hall. It isn't the coats in the lounge room, or cleaning sick off the floor, the three meals a day, every day, or the endless demands for more. It's being someone else's property: their's because they need you. Your thoughts are never your own. Your attention is grabbed and competed for and even your sleep is interrupted by little voices saying they're home.

Grazyna recognised the problem.

— Take long baths, she offered, wisely. They will not burst in on their mother naked, for fear they grow old the same way.

— And the feminists speak about sisterhood; I know, I heard them, when they thought I wasn't listening: "All

176

women suffer under patriarchy". But I tell you, feminism is for the under forties, the childless and the lesbian couples. It does not hear the voices of women who want to live with men and are prepared to take the consequences. When I pushed my daughter to the library, the feminists dropped contraceptive leaflets into the pram. Did they think I wasn't able to make my own choice? That I wouldn't take a leaflet because my hands were full? When I left my husband, they rallied round me, helped me to paint my new flat, but when I took up with my Johnny, they skidded off home to the cat. Did they think I was incapable of making up my own mind? I moved to Western Australia, and am itching to travel up North, but the Women's Movement (where did the Liberation go?) tells me my daughter's my sister, and you never leave a sister in need. Well, what about my needs? I could tell you a lot about them. There is more written about childbirth than the rest of our lives put together. Is there any wonder we turn against our own? I wanted my children when I was younger, but now I give them back to themselves.

Beryl was soaring into the air.

— Minnie fixes me with her honesty, and confesses like the Ancient Mariner at every opportunity: she's gay. I'm pleased for her, I'm happy for her, but when I went away the whole day, she didn't even notice I'd gone.

Beryl was zooming up to the ceiling.

— Laura crashes my car and doesn't give me the courtesy of an explanation. She makes me into some kind of ogre to forgive herself for her guilt.

Beryl was burning up the light.

— Ingrid, my youngest, my favourite, munches secretly in the night, but leaves dirty plates on the dresser and half eaten tins in the sink.

Beryl had reached a pinnacle from which it would be very difficult to descend.

—- Who but a mother would put up with all this? Well, I'm handing in my resignation, I'm nobody's mother any more.

There was a murmuring in the room as the women experienced recognition, compassion and revolt. While Beryl was slating her husband, not a woman there would disagree, but as to leaving her children, or slagging off the Movement (yet again!); a low rumbling began as of an unkempt volcano, and the talk, when it came, was thick and fast.

— It's true what she says, started Erica, why do we always blame our mothers? Why did she make me wear such tight shoes? Why did she bring me up a girl? Why didn't she stand up to my father?

— The worse my father behaved, the closer I was to my mother, but when he left, it was just me against her, Sky continued.

— Even when they don't live with us, they still manage to divide us, said Linda.

— I don't think she ought to leave her children, said the soft spoken Grazyna, in her deferential Polish accent, not that they aren't big girls now, but they need someone to see them right. (Her Simone was her pride and joy).

— And the language! said Mrs Bovis, I think we can do without that. Mrs O. shook her head wisely.

— She can't blame all that on feminism, we're struggling too, and we don't always agree.

Meanwhile, back among the patriarchs, the ranger, blissfully unaware that anything momentous had happened, was expounding enthusiastically to Irene,

— and they're brutalising miles of native Karri forest to provide wood chips which they'll glue together again to make boards . . .

Irene listened to him with half an ear as though for the small cries which would tell her the youngest had woken. She had of course recognised Beryl and was not gloating over "I told you so" but hoping that the other woman would be able to fulfil her declaration without guilt making her turn back.

— A little more wine my loves? smarmed Johnny François to his following, and snapped his fingers for the waitress. Yes, he continued, when we ape the old stereotypes, when one has the car, the other the apron, we do indeed oppress ourselves. Take this nasty mess away, dear, and give us some more wine.

Sandra moved slowly, wishing she could divorce her customers. She could not listen to what the women were saying while still servicing the men.

The doctor and the captain were getting on splendidly. She was explaining how state government were giving with one hand and taking away with the other by raising nurses' salaries but closing their quarters. She was flattered to find a man who took her seriously as a political thinker. The captain was adding up her clothing bill and wondering if there was a direct ratio between that and the time necessary to get a woman to bed. It was one of those little mathematical games he liked to amuse himself with. When she paused for confirmation that he was interested in her opinion, he changed the subject. She could have killed herself for boring him. When he started off on boats he had sailed, was sailing or nearly sailed (not to mention the one that sailed away), she set her face and tuned into what Beryl was saying. Having specialised in obstetrics, she took an interest in these family matters. Childless herself, and with both parents dead, she could not realistically feel personally involved. She would be thirty seven next month, so if she was going to have a baby at all, it would have to be soon, and to have this woman go on about the trials and tribulations, was quite frankly irritating.

— I put my finger in the woodpecker's hole, and the woodpecker said "God bless my soul" . . .

The Byronic youths had reached that stage of their meal where one normally has a little sing-song.

Chapter 13
Later That Night

While the men at The Markets were continuing as if nothing was happening, which, in their terms, it was not, and the women were discussing their relation to the means of reproduction and discovering new class alliances, a solemn leave taking was in progress in their midst. Beryl, fired with enthusiasm, and high on her own energy, was not going to come back to earth ever again. Below her were the upturned faces of her daughters as well as other fainter outlines; the women who came in to see the lawyers and ended up talking to her for hours; the neighbours who depended on her to water their plants and feed the gold fish, and, even more faded, somewhere in the background but getting smaller and smaller as Beryl soared higher and higher, stared the haggard, half-eaten face of John Debar, his magnificent beard shaved off to accommodate the surgeon's knife as it played cat and mouse with the malignant tumour threatening to mar his looks.

— I miss you, darling, don't you ever miss me?
— How can I miss you, when you never go away?
It was the final showdown.
— You can't leave me, Beryl, I can't live without you.
— Die then, said his ex-wife, twenty feet above him.
Through the open window, way up in the roof, beckoned the shimmering heat of Marble Bar. It was silent, a promise of silence and long moments of nothing on earth. One short swift glance at the ground, and Beryl cut her last tie with the common weal.

On Monday, 2nd January, 198-, Beryl and John T. melted into a West Australian heat haze. The three girls felt the air become oppressively hot, and the sun's glare as bright as day. They blinked to accustom themselves to the light and when they looked up again, their mother, sorry, Beryl, was gone.

Ingrid sat open mouthed; how could your mother just

float out of the window without you having a say in it?

Minnie realised now that her mother would never come back. It wasn't fair; other feminists had mums to go home to.

Laura thought gloomily "plus ça change", or might have done had she spoken French. The vague attempts to find a flat for herself and Moira would have to become concrete efforts.

— Beryl, said Minnie to the air which had once contained her mother, I think you're quite right to go off and do what you want to do. She was conscious of sounding stilted, but this was a speech which she refused to let Milly write. She would never know if her mother heard it.

From now on, Ingrid was her own person, free to eat when and whatever she liked, make friends with whomsoever pleased her, and leave her bedroom unswept for the next fifty years if she chose.

Silently, as silently as Beryl's departure, the three of them left The Markets and made their way down to Barrack Street to watch the ferries taking off. It gave them something to wave good bye to. It was dark on the whole, and the water was sloppy, but the view across the harbour, over King's Park and along the bank to Crawley, was sort of peaceful and unchanging. The Swan Brewery, soon to be sold off as a historic monument, was lit up in the shape of HMASS Swan.

Ingrid stared across the gloom at the wake of a departing boat.

— Come back, take me with you, she screamed suddenly. She felt tired of being brave, looking the other way and murmuring "Queen Victoria" while other people jabbed live injections into her. She wanted to be someone else's problem. She dropped down onto the wooden boards of the jetty and let out a yell of anger and pain that these enormous changes could take place in her life without her say so. It phrased itself in the single scream,

— Mum, I want my mum, like a lost child in Boan's store, like a soldier on a battlefield. I don't want to be grown up, I don't want to be Miss Débar, I want to be Mummy's little Thingy forever and ever.

Minnie and Laura recognised the feeling.

— It's alright, Ingy, you can do what you want now, you know.

—What I want, said Ingrid firmly, is my mother back.

— But Beryl doesn't want to come back, said Laura, she doesn't love us. And the pain over her heart hurt so much that her eyes prickled.

— Of course she loves us, Minnie snapped, impatient at their weakness, come on, we'd better go home or your wage packets will suffer.

— Aaagh, said Laura, I've got a pain in my wage packet.

— Money, Minnie, money, it's all you think about.

Minnie sat down and examined her nails, feeling ratshit. Too much had been happening for more than a night's growth to have appeared. In despair she thought of her toe nails, but her feet were really too dirty.

— If mothers don't love their children, they should tell them so from the beginning, Laura protested, but in a breaking voice.

— Simone's mother loves her, Ingrid blurted out angrily.

— It's too much, one person shouldn't have to be that important to another, said Minnie, eyes purposefully focused hard on the road sign in front of them. "No Standing", it read.

— That John's important enough, she lets him go with her.

— But you choose your husband, you don't choose your kids, they're dependent on you.

— He can't even boil himself an egg, talk about dependent.

— Mmm, said Minnie meditatively, I asked mum once, what it was about her John, and she said, Min, dear, what does "refractory" mean? Camels, I said, without thinking, and she said, exactly; when I asked John he said, oh, an unmalleable metal, you know, difficult of fusion or reduction. Then she said, you see, I've spent my life with people who know that camels are refractory, John is the first person I've met who says it means metals.

— I expect there's a point to that, snivelled Laura.

— Yes, but I'm not sure what it is: either that John isn't petty bourgeois, doesn't know his Eliot, genre working class hero, or that mum only respects what she doesn't understand herself.

— But I don't know what refractory means, or whatever the stupid word is, and she doesn't think I'm wonderful.

— Thought it had something to do with glass, murmured Laura.

— Well yes, you see, she thinks that John can complement the gaps in her.

— I think she just wants his protection because she doesn't fancy travelling alone, Laura commented, and even my Moira could think her way round that one.

They had reached the nose blowing, deep breathing stage, but the shuddering had stopped and the old slatted wooden boat house looked as peaceful as it always did.

— Want a toffee? said Ingrid, producing a packet from her pocket.

They sat and sucked gloomily till Minnie looked at her digital watch and said,

— 11.33, we'll have to be going.

Back home, they all sat in Ingrid's room. Family conclave time. Fearing a long sitting, Ingrid got out a bowl of peanuts.

— Don't mind me, she said, I do this when I'm nervous.

— I'd noticed, said Laura, not unkindly. I curl up into a ball like a cat and won't move, and she (pointing at Minnie) bites her nails as if she was scared to let go.

Minnie pulled her thumb out of her mouth crossly, then grinned and sucked her little finger.

— I get migraines too, she said.

They laughed, and talk broadened into a discussion of their own personal worries. When Minnie mentioned Erica, Laura felt a twinge of jealousy, after all they'd been through, how could Min go for this outsider?

— She's coming to dinner tomorrow night, Min added.

— Who's going to cook for her, then? said Laura.

— I am, who do you think cooks for me at home?

It was true, Min's home was in London.

— I'll make the custard, offered Ingrid, thoughtfully, you only had to follow the packet. Privately Ingrid was sure that if she was very good and helped Min do everything while Beryl was away, and never threw her dirty knickers on the floor, then her mother would come back. Poor little thing, I only wish it was true.

* * *

While the political is personal was hitting the three sisters in a big way, the clientele of the Markets was experiencing a different kind of struggle. Beryl's impassioned speech had affected all of them to varying degrees but it seems it was Laura's sister, Moira, who really started it off.

Throughout Beryl's tirade Moira had sat watchfully, calm and immobile. She had listened to the other women's comments with an air of detached interest. Waiting. Patient. But when Beryl disappeared the women clapped and Moira felt her power to speak had been taken from her. If this was something they could discuss reasonably, with only measured cries of 'steady on' and 'how irresponsible', then she could not begin to show them what it meant to her. She would need to be convinced and confident to counter Beryl but she doubted her ability to find words at all, let alone the right ones.

Dorrie watched as Moira's face clammed shut with the resounding ring of a portcullis. With no sign of distress, her face smooth as a sheet, eyes wary as usual, Moira sank slowly through a bottomless ocean. She turned her head away and stared at the blank wall behind. Dorrie saw her hand on the back of the chair was clenched and her knuckles were white.

— Have you left us too? Dorrie asked, coming over to Moira's table.

The words took a long time to reach her and sounded a long way off. Moira shifted in her chair and scratched at the table with her nails. Her face remained cold and impassive.

— Was she your mother? Dorrie ventured, fearing to stir Moira's pain but knowing no other way.

This time Moira turned, but still she said nothing.

— I can't hear you, said Dorrie, I'm deaf. I have to see your lips move.

— No, said Moira, the muscles in her throat hurt.

— But she might as well have been, said Dorrie.

— Alright, said Moira with sullen anger, You tell me.

She had come back to the surface and it seemed as though the waves she'd been avoiding in the calm so far below were now breaking over her head. A scream echoed round her brain and threatened to rush out as soon as her mouth was open.

The other women were locked in conversation.

— Other women's cigarettes give me cancer, Lilith bristled at Linda, waving away a wall of smoke.

— Perhaps I should just lock my bike up, murmured

184

Erica, who hadn't once taken her eye off it. The table in front of her was piled high with equipment she deemed it safer to keep with her: pump, lights, panier.

Sky was still pondering the mother problem.

— I don't think we do patronise women with children, we just don't have much in common.

— Rubbish, a lot of women are very supportive of other women's kids.

— There's something horribly normal about having a baby, like you can compensate for being a lesbian if only you knuckle down under childcare.

Grazyna glanced across at Moira and shook her head.

— Poor little duck, she clucked.

Betsey followed her glance.

— It's all very well, this freedom of choice business but nothing replaces a granny.

The Nags Women's Group was off on its favourite subject.

— Now we've grown out of child rearing we think we're experts on younger women's problems. We should let them tell us what they want.

— But they're too busy with kids to come to meetings and we can't do it for them.

— Perhaps we should run a creche at Nags.

The conversation was circular. Some women missed having children around; others were glad it was all over.

— But if we don't do something, other women will go off like her, Sky pointed to the ceiling to indicate Beryl.

At some point the two tables realised they were covering the same ground and blended their flow together. It is to be hoped that the good example of the younger taught the elder to moderate their voices and that the elder showed the younger pessimism was radically nowhere.

— Mum, did you ever regret having me? Simone asked Grazyna hesitantly.

— Mum, did you really hate it at Marble Bar? But Lex was interrupted by Grazyna who leant over to point towards Moira.

— When you go, she said, you always leave something behind you.

Simone was astonished that her mother, who normally dropped everything at her daughter's imperious request, should blankly ignore her question. It seemed an answer in itself. Lex realised as Eva stared across at Moira that her mother's face had also masked silent misery, almost all the time they'd been up north.

Moira breathed out and the scream which had been building up inside her behind clenched muscles and closed eyes seemed to burst forth into the air taking with it Eva's years of patient isolation and Grazyna's brave-faced, painful motherhood. The room rocked purple and yellow, red and green, but no sound came out.

The men seemed not to hear, whether through feint or design, and continued eating as before. As they never listen to each other anyway, I fail to see what difference it could have made. But the women were united in deafness, refugees from a bomb warning. It could have been any one of them.

— Moira, said Dorrie firmly, taking her by the shoulders, You must try and say what you want.

Words were racing round Moira's head, angry and unbidden. It's not fair, you shouldn't have let her go, mothers have to look after their children. Anyone could go anywhere; just not like it here and go away. But what about us? What about me? What about me? I can't bear it, I won't bear it; I'm not going back.

— I'm not going back, she said.

— Back? asked Dorrie.

— To the Home, whispered Moira.

— Is that all, thought Dorrie, and said without thinking, it's alright, sweetie, you don't have to.

As the doors at the back of the room opened, she realised her mistake. In walked a man of about forty with the awkward affability and corduroy trousers of a child welfare officer. Like a grey shadow the message passed around the room from face to face, eyebrow to eyebrow. When Erica heard it, she knew what she had to do. Slowly she got to her feet and walked towards her bicycle. To her credit it took no more than a backward look at the roomful of women all nodding encouragement for her to wheel the bike over to Moira and show her how to slip into the toe clips. Mrs Bovis handed over the key to Nags and explained how to get in the back way. Sandra told her where the fire escape was and how to get there from the Ladies. Simone passed the bike through after her.

— It's so light, she whispered in amazement.

186

— Reynolds 531 frame, Erica hissed, almost appeased for having to lend it.

But how was this marvel of modern transport to reach the ground so Moira could effect a getaway?

The welfare officer did not notice this flurry of activity. He was busy questioning the Captain as the most respectable man in the room.

— We're looking for a young girl, he began.

— Aren't we all? said the Captain jovially.

The officer smiled.

— Fraid this one's under age, he said, she . . .

The Captain instantly looked serious.

— She may have got in with a bad crowd. We've had to bring the police in on this one.

And, dead on cue, with an accompaniment of screeching brakes and smelly rubber which would not have disgraced peak hour viewing, the cops appeared on the scene. Positive discrimination in favour of the thick and the brutal had evolved a species highly adapted to life in the modern movie.

— Out with the ammunition, said Blanche R-W.

Women carry handbags everywhere and as a woman grows older, so her bag grows to anchor her in the world and contains all the hankies, quickies and cardies that protect the fair sex from the patently biased. A man carrying a slimline portfolio might excite suspicion, but no one would think to frisk an old lady with the most cumbersome portmanteau, let alone a younger whose reticule might easily contain those nameless female objects somehow connected with 'understains'.

Large balls of wool and knitting needles were passed out among the crowd and when the first cop hit the scene the room was full of the utterly unaggressive click of forty needles and the low hum of female voices. The wool was not used as a projectile nor the needles to pierce or skewer, thus in his later report the cop failed to mention the woolly activity in which most of the room was engaged. Like Johnny and the Lads, the drunken Shelleys and Coleridges, the Captain and the Ranger or Grazyna's likeable husband, Plod simply failed to notice that anything was going on at all. Knitting, like the colour white, denotes an absence of all activity: its perpetrators do not exist.

A roomful of invisible women sat knitting their way into

an invisible we(b) which wove around the hall in glorious twists of colour growing centimetres per second in long woolly tentacles. The police swarmed in thick as flies and were immediately enmeshed in the fine strands which wound their way from table to table. Poor little insects, they never knew what held them back. While they stopped short in confusion, Lex was lowering Erica's bike with tow ropes (a must for every professional driver) and Moira was creeping down the fire escape.

— She's about fifteen years old and wears a metal tooth brace, the welfare officer was saying.

— We'll look out for her, sir, said one of the lads, adding under his breath to his mates, fancy a steel blow job?

— Would you give the description again, asked the man in the smart suit.

— Think you've seen her?

— Not half an hour ago.

Dorrie got slowly to her feet and hobbled towards the stairs. The young officers of the law shifted aside to let her pass. Every one a gentleman, every one a brick. There was no sign of Moira. Dorrie let out a sigh of relief. She wondered where it would all end and whether an old people's home would ever be allowed to adopt a fifteen year old girl. She rather suspected not but if there was a way, she was sure Betsey Bovis would find it.

— Well, that about wraps it up then, said the welfare officer to his cortege of policemen, after the well-dressed man had given a painstaking description of everything Moira had been wearing, adding that he was sorry but he had no idea of her present whereabouts.

— Well, Betsey Bovis said, the time for fence sitting is over.

Erica wished Minnie was there to hear it.

— Yeah, said the voice of dissent, we're landed with baby-sitting instead.

— You can opt out if you want to . . .

— Cop out, more likely . . .

It wrangled and twisted round the room till there was a clear majority in favour of leaving all decisions till the morning.

— All those for the motion? cried Betsey imperiously.

— Betsey, whispered Blanche R-W, there isn't a motion. But Betsey was well away.

— Against?

— Procrastinations?

— Right, she stated, the procrastinators have it. Meeting adjourned till tomorrow.

— Is she for real? said Sky, with a mixture of awe and contempt.

— 10am Cottesloe Pier, said Betsey, who was enjoying herself.

— Are any of you waiting for a grey green coach with Nedlands written down the side?

— Yes, chorused half a dozen sleepy voices.

— Well it's driven off.

The voice of dissent was about to grow raucous in its abuse of Betsey whom it saw as the chief cause of them missing their lift when Lex realised there was a way to make good her humiliation at the Pinnacles.

— I'll take you, she offered.

And the women departed variously, all promising to meet again on the morrow to thrash this thing out once and for all.

Chapter 14
Life, Be In It, Norma

Ingrid had not seen Mrs Bovis since Sunday, and was still dreading the encounter, but today she had other problems. Where was she supposed to live now? Would she and Laura get on well enough if they shared a flat together? The new flat made it seem vaguely exciting, but she knew before they started that Laura would climb into a cupboard with her cat and leave all the work to her. She could paint her room green, and if they got a flat in town she wouldn't have to worry about buses. Still, she wasn't sure if she was ready to be reconciled to the idea just yet. That day she had a lot of time to reflect, custom was very low.

— Not a grey hair in sight, she remarked to Johnny François, knowing this was the sort of remark he liked, but feeling bad about saying it.

— Definitely down on last year.

— If I'd known, I'd of taken the day off like Simone. Ingrid didn't mean to dob her friend in, the words just spilled out, and it was true, hardly anyone came into the salon all day. As though Simone had known that this was the day to take off.

— Just slacking off after the festivities, Johnny dismissed the phenomenon. He was in a foul mood. The young men from the East had been a very receptive audience to his thoughts on sexism among the gay left, and had made him feel like John Socrates, though not of course as ugly. One of them, whom he'd secretly renamed John Alcibiades, even showed signs of liking him. The youth in question had the bronzed, flawless physique of the surfie, the shoulder-length bleached hair, but none of the stupidity.

— Surfing's enough to put you off wet suits for life.

— ?

— Because you piss in them to keep your legs warm. Johnny found him gentle and amusing, but just as he was about to make a romantic suggestion, the bloody welfare officer had interrupted him with his stupid questions.

— Doesn't mean we can afford to be slack, though, he continued. You didn't clean the basins out yesterday.

Ingrid was livid. How the hell did he know? He'd left early to look after his sick mother or something, leaving the girls to lock up. Someone must have told on her. She was about to suspect Simone, when it occurred to her that Johnny was quite capable of making the whole thing up. She smiled pleasantly, and lied.

— We left the cleaning agent in over night for that extra special shine.

And she went back to thinking about Beryl, and Johnny to his J. Adonis.

Laura fared no better. Coles was boring at the best of times and today there weren't any customers. No little old ladies looking longingly at pot plants, counting their pensions and saving up till next week. No grannies at check-out admitting shamefaced that they could not afford all that cat food. After you'd rung up the till, naturally. Not even mothers with school kids knocking over lolly racks and apologising profusely. When she'd watered all the plants, slipped a fresh banana in the fern, and run a damp cloth over the leaves, there was not a lot left to do.

— Laura dear, called the Varieties Manager. He had not been in the job very long and had no idea how to go about it. The only piece of wisdom to glimmer in his otherwise cloudy brain, was to defer to Laura in everything. She always knew what was selling and where was a good place to display new stock. She also had a knack of guessing what the housewife would go for. He used to joke that the only thing she couldn't do was wear the trousers, and plunged his hands into his pockets to look streamlined and efficient.

— Laura, when I bend down I can see your skirt peeping out below your uniform.

Laura refrained from the obvious comment and tried instead,

— But it's the same green as the overalls.

— That makes it look like a petticoat. In future don't wear any thing underneath. You're so slim, it's a pity to pad yourself out, you know. You look far more attractive with your skinny legs under a Coles lightweight overall.

Laura felt half way between pleased and pissed off. She gathered a few fallen leaves to look busy.

— Where are all the customers? she wondered, do they know something I don't?

As the day wore on, Minnie felt less and less eager at the prospect of her dinner guest. Laura was jealous, she knew that, but although this irritated her, she didn't want to make things more difficult. She, after all, would be flitting back to England in another three days where the sunburn, disappearing mothers and lost opportunities would fade into nostalgic memories beside living on the dole in Brixton. It had all been very emotional, Minnie thought, as she vacuumed the house for the evening. Erica would be a strain, and Milly would put her off. Laura would make catty remarks and Ingrid would pig herself.

Ingrid came in from work in a bad temper, muttering something about Johnny François, and dumped all her stuff on the table. Then she got some barley water and didn't refill the water jug.

— I've spent all day cleaning this place, Ingrid Débar, and you don't even bother to put the ice back in the freeze box.

— You sound just like your mother, Ingrid snapped.

Laura had come home wistful, and draped herself in a chair like a wet raincoat. Minnie rummaged around laying the table, her sister sighed meaningfully as if it was all Min's fault.

— When you've finished groaning, Minnie said unpleasantly, perhaps you'd like to rinse some glasses.

Mutely Laura rose to her feet and trickled a little languid water into the sink. Each step was too much effort and by the end of the operation she was exhausted. Ingrid seized one of the glasses and refilled it with barley water.

— Not those, Min yelled, they're for dinner.

— I'm thirsty, said Ingrid, and I'll be drinking out of it anyway, or are they all for your precious Erica?

Only a very insensitive or utterly preoccupied woman would have failed to sense the atmosphere in the room. Erica rocked in, unconcerned.

— The door was open, she said, sitting down in Laura's chair and emptying Ingrid's barley water.

— Scuse I, she added, I'm parched just driving up here.

Ingrid and Laura revelled in their hurt dignity and Milly slipped out to deliver a speech about the West Australian climate.

— You'll think me very boorish, Erica continued, allowing no pause for interruption, but I've got to tell you what's been happening.

She was still high on the day's excitement and as most of her friends had been at the meeting she was dying for someone to describe it to. So, ignoring Laura's groan, Ingrid's moan, and Minnie racking her cuticles, Erica began,

— Last night at The Markets Moira challenged us all to prove that support meant more than propping up rafters.

— Would you mind telling me what you're talking about? I mean, I know you're here to see Min, but if I have to sit in the same room with you, then I'd like you to talk plain English.

Seeing her audience was now sitting comfortably and no longer fidgeting about barley water, Erica detailed the Great Debate which had occupied Nags the whole day.

* * *

The first to reach the Home was Moira, with the speed of a finely tuned racing bike. Now that the fear was over and she knew the women were on her side, she began to enjoy herself. She whizzed past the police cars as remarkable as the pavement itself. Old women with handbags, knitters and lone cyclists have not yet hit the police manual. She could have been a man going about his business for all they cared. The Home was not difficult to find; nearer to Dalkeith than to Nedlands, it stood on the main river road from Crawley, shining out, an impressive two storey building with verandas top and bottom. It might once have been a private mansion with its cool view over the Swan to Applecross, but now the daylight spectacle of pensioners in deck chairs bore witness to its more plebian use. Moira could see it before her as the lights changed and the stagnant lines of traffic became liquid on the road and poured forward in rivulets of headlights. It had never occurred to her before that traffic could be beautiful.

Senior citizens or wards of court, both are at the mercy of the state, and Moira entered the building with no curiosity and little difficulty. She paused only to swing the bike onto her shoulder and make her way upstairs.

— Home from Home, she sniggered cynically. Bet we have

the same curtains.

Not only the curtains, but the rough blue carpet, made of rope for long life, and the statutory upright chair (1) and red bedspread (1) per person. Moira sat down on the bed which creaked at exactly the same moment, in the same way as her own did. She would be sharing with Dorothy whose room-mate had gone to Brisbane to die. Moira could not hide the bicycle, so she stacked it in a corner of the room and took a shower.

The second home was Dorrie, puffing and wheezing as she climbed the stairs and shouted a good night to the warden. She did not attempt to engage Moira in conversation, used as she was to the surliness of the young towards old people of whom they are not in a direct line of inheritance. Her age and disability should have placed her on the ground floor where there was a ramp and hand rails, but she had not been able to quite rid herself of the prejudice prevailing in the Home, that ground-floor dwellers were senile. Moira watched sullenly as the old woman paid silent homage to the chipped or torn objects around the room. Finally Dorrie shambled out, and Moira wondered what part of the ceremony this was. She found herself picking up her own bits and pieces, in response to the crowded orderliness of the room. Dorrie came back with cocoa; Moira gave her the wry, hesitant smile she gave strangers so they wouldn't see her brace.

— Thanks, she offered in a subdued voice.

— I am an orphan, a victim, a runaway, she thought, and now? I am asleep, she decided.

Absently Dorrie tucked her into bed and kissed her on the cheek. They would talk about it tomorrow when they were all together, and Betsey, of course, would take control. Just before she fell asleep she registered the glare of the minibus lights on the window, and knew that everyone was Home.

The flicker of the flame spread rapidly. Short shift was made of breakfast and there followed a slow wending down towards Cottesloe pier where years of frequentation had established the women's claim. The speedier amongst them fitted in a pre-reunional dip. The spot was perfect, providing shade for the pale and foot rests in natural rock for the hard of circulation. One group made their way down from the minibus in wheelchairs, the others arrived on a fleet of bicycles. The morning sun shone on their wheels and a thousand spokes sparkled as they turned. Erica had arrived before the others, having collected her bike from Nags and she now sat on the pier, her toes dabbled absently by the waves, and looked back as the two lines converged: backs looped over handle bars or upright against cushions; feet on pedals, hands on wheels. So much power, confidence that what they wanted to do they could do, and here they were doing it.

There were women sun-baking on beach towels while their toddlers covered each other with sand. A girls' school doing life-saving, holding their partners carefully under the chin and kicking their legs furiously to effect a rescue; both would end up under water and surface splashing and giggling, spitting salt and wiping their noses.

— Miss, if you were really drowning you wouldn't care if it was your chin or what they held.

— No, darling, don't eat the sand. Dirty, urgh, not nice.

Grazyna, Eva and Simone were off buying cups of tea but they would be down presently. Lex sat in the driver's seat, she was busy with the transmission but when all the women had assembled she rolled down the window to listen to what they might say.

Once Nags, Updikes and fellow travellers were settled either in the sand or out of it, Betsey rose to her feet and pulled a roll of paper from her pocket. There was a silence. Dorrie did not fidget with her hair; Linda put off asking for a fag; the toddlers looked up wide-eyed, fingers in belly buttons; and even the waves withdrew respectfully, though the tide would oblige them to return again soon.

Betsey unfolded her notes and looked about her. Several women found themselves counting pages as they dangled from her hand.

— We'll be here all day, whispered Simone.

Betsey furrowed her eyebrows and a godly look came into her eyes.

— Dearly beloved, muttered Sky.

But Betsey was off on a different tack.

— Four score and something years ago our foremothers brought forth on this continent a new nation conceived . . .

— Betsey, hissed Blanche, someone's already done that one.

— Always a bit of a show-girl, our Betsey, murmured Dorrie to herself.

— Conceived under patriarchy but dedicated to the proposition that all men . . .

Some women cheered at the mention of foremothers, others booed the word "men". It was rather confusing. As Betsey pulled herself up to put her person behind her words, a little silver chain swung out from her neck. It held a double-headed axe, symbol of matriarchy. It had been Minnie's present to Ingrid who, finding it a little warlike, had passed it on to Betsey with the words 'to my dear old battle-axe'. Dorrie saw it and was sure Betsey had another lover. So that was why she was always tied up on Sundays.

— Sly old genuflector, she whispered under her breath, only her voice carried more than she realised.

— Claudicator, Betsey rounded on her.

Were these petty jealousies to dog the whole proceedings?

— Get your act together, sisters, snarled Blanche from her wheelchair. We're not here to have our picture taken.

Betsey, an old campaigner, changed tack.

— There was a fire last night burning in our . . .

But Blanche, fearing a religious interlude, interrupted.

— We want a bloody conflagration.

— A holocaust.

— An inferno.

— We will mobilise the girls' schools, Betsey declared.

— They look quite mobile already, said Dorrie, gazing at the figures bobbing up and down on the waves.

— And the convents and the ante-natal clinics . . .

— Wherever women together produce contempt in men . . .

— Women's prisons and girls' homes, laundromats and supermarkets, changing rooms and nurses' quarters . . .

A throng of women sat on the beach singing out the names of places only women go.

— But we have those already, said Blanche, more patiently this time. We want the rest of the world and personally, she added, I'm tired of waiting.

— Alright, said Betsey.

— No, said Blanche quietly, it's not alright. You know how hard we've been working at Nags to get a better deal for older women and now the issue of child care has come up, you refuse to take it seriously. I have not reached the age of seventy-five to start taking on outwork for the nuclear family.

196

— But Blanche, said Betsey. A personal appeal was often best in these circumstances, however alienating it might be for those who did not know the right first names. Children are part of the struggle, we can't just cut ourselves off from them. We've had so many discussions about not seeing age as a disability . . .

— Or more of a disability than it need be, Dorrie corrected her.

— That I can't see why you don't apply that to kids.

— Because it is possible to ignore, or alleviate by massage, a few sharp twinges in the joints, but there is no way a four year old with a box of matches is not going to be a problem.

— Aunty, said Sandra's niece Julie, when you get stung by a blue bottle, um, does it kill you stone dead or does it have time to hurt?

— Why, sweetie, you haven't been stung, have you?

— No, but Leeanne has, on her leg. Right there and she can't walk.

A timely interruption.

— Oh, this is impossible, said Blanche as Leeanne's screams rang out.

— How can we discuss anything with these kids around?

— You never finish a single thing if you have a child, said Grazyna.

— Look, said Erica, working with kids is just as much part of reclaiming the world as mobilising behind a vanguard and storming . . . storming . . .

— Storming what? said Lilith.

— Oh, you know, said Erica vaguely.

And everyone did. Vaguely. It was hot and already women were disappearing to find ice lollies.

— I've got a feeling we all agreed to something just then, said Sky, I'm not quibbling, but I would like to know what it was.

— I think we just made childcare a life-sentence, said Blanche.

The others wrinkled their brows and shifted position in the sun. Betsey stood with her back to them all, staring out to sea. They followed her gaze.

— Look at the waves, she murmured dreamily, how they rise up even in this heat and rush towards the shore, then as their strength grows and they join together as if to invade the earth something happens, they roll over, turn white and break ignominiously on the sand. Time after time. Time after time.

The women watched as the waves towered fleetingly then sank, leaving only blue swirls and foam.

— It is irritating, she intoned as she turned to address her flock, to have to answer the same question a hundred times; it is irritating to have to respond to new women in the movement who arrogantly assume we owe them an explanation; it is irritating to have to go over the same ground again and again when we want to soar higher and higher dropping all accessories so we can travel light, but if we don't take them with us, we have nothing to fall back on but the sand under our feet.

Dorrie felt again the breathless mixture of admiration and embarrassment that Betsey could speak with such biblical intensity. Betsey's hands had been following the movement of her voice, but they now dropped clumsily as though she too felt the awkwardness of taking herself seriously. She shrugged her shoulders, shook her head with an apologetic grin and shambled off to play castles with the toddlers.

* * *

— So Nags are going to run a creche, are they? said Minnie, resentful at missing the excitement. What's so revolutionary?

— A kindy? Laura brightened up. Triffic. Can I work in it?

— I expect it'll be wonderfully non-sexist, but you haven't got any funding. Minnie regretted her note of triumph, but why this feminist energy hit just as she was leaving the country?

Erica felt irritated. There seemed no way of explaining the tremendous feeling of excitement which had come over her on the beach. Why hadn't these three been there? she thought angrily, instead of getting off on their own private tragedy. Forgetting that this was the very sparking point which had brought the women together.

— Well, do you have any money? Minnie persisted.

— As it happens, yes. We're applying for state funding from Life, Be in it, Norma.

That wasn't it, though. Surely that wasn't all that had happened. She'd had such a strong sense of the beginnings of a women's community. Perhaps no-one ever liked other

198

people's utopias.

— Not Norma, Norm, Ingrid couldn't resist correcting as she munched chick peas au gratin, the rest of the dinner having congealed hours ago.

— I don't believe it, Minnie scoffed. There isn't a campaign called Life Be In It, Norm. How ridiculous.

— It's a federal government campaign against the bloke who takes his dog for a walk with its lead tied to the car door handle and then proceeds to drive slowly along the side of the reserve.

— So he's s'posed to tie his wife to the handle instead?

— The government is worried about obese Australian women giving birth to obese Australian children, said Erica icily.

— Walk, don't drive, jog don't walk, run don't jog, Ingrid reeled off.

— One way to swing the vote, said Minnie.

— Anyway, we convince them that you can't actually go jogging with a baby on your back, and they cough up for child care.

— Easy.

— And we hope to supplement what they allow us by asking rich women to donate money.

— Makes a change from soup.

— No, not as charity, but in their own interests. Women are all classes of society, but as long as men see us as undifferentiated prey, then we have the same problems.

— Couldn't we eat now? suggested Ingrid anxiously.

Laura was grateful to her for bringing it up and was beginning to suspect that Ingrid's anxiety was not so much for food as to allay the tension in the air.

They sat up at the table to eat.

— Mmm, it's nice, chewed Erica over the re-heated rice, and the rest of the dinner was spent in similar phatic communion.

Minnie regretted her obstinate incomprehension, but Erica made it sound like mystical experience. Erica wondered if talking at women was quite the best way to resolve mutual antagonisms and resolved to do better next time. Laura set to watching Erica for signs of interest in Min, which led to a lot of eye contact as she and Min intersected glances. Erica wondered why Laura was looking at her. Ingrid, who from her lookout point behind the risotto was recording the proceedings, felt that possibly lesbianism had a less direct

199

relation to feminism than she had thought.

Minnie twisted the handle of her fork guiltily. With her father's money she was certainly in the wealthy woman category, and inherited wealth was the dirtiest of all. But money seemed like the only asset she could really depend on. She had adopted the tactics of the long-term unemployed as had her friends, but whereas they squatted, cycled and delivered their own mail through economic necessity, she sometimes worried that for her it was little more than an interesting game. She clung to her bank account to save her from the men who terrified her on the tube.

After dinner, when Erica and Minnie were chatting about Ova and the Ovarian Sisters, Erica bent forward, struggled and said,

— You know, I really like you, Minnie, but you'll be going back to England in a few days.

— Friday, Minnie nodded.

It was true, what Erica was saying. Were they really into one night stands, exotic adventures in foreign parts? What would it mean if they slept together? Hell, what did she want? Marriage? At times she preferred bicycles; they squeal when they need oiling and rattle if there's a bolt loose.

— Can you type? asked Erica.

— Yes, said Minnie, but not as well as Laura.

— Good, come to my place tomorrow, we're putting out the newsletter.

Minnie avoided asking where the money came from and pointing out that overthrowing oppression did not rest solely in the dissemination of ideas, and the three of them agreed to go, though Ingrid wondered what on earth they expected her to do, seeing as she couldn't type.

— I'll be off, then, said Erica, not looking at Minnie

Chapter 15
W.O.W.

The alarm rang at 7.30 next morning. Ingrid's first conces-
sion to accepting her mother had gone. It felt strange not to
see Beryl's puffy face round the door, saying,

— Come on, pudding, 7 o'clock, time to get up.

Minnie sat up in bed.

— I'm sorry, Min, did the alarm wake you?

— No, I've been awake for hours, mulling things over.

Ingrid left, but Minnie found it impossible to get back to
sleep. She wanted to see Erica and persuade her she was
wrong, secretly thinking that if they slept together, something concrete would have happened and they would be
more likely to see each other again. What were her chances
of meeting someone in London who shared her passion for
bikes and her interest in Australia and who grinned the way
Erica did? At 9 Min went into town, not knowing what else
to do. The questions she had come all this way to answer
had turned into other questions. She did not know who she
was and she still let Milly answer for who she wasn't. In
the end it seemed a political choice, but a lot of the choices
were blocked. She had gone to university to keep her options
open, and now it seemed they never had been open at all.
It was still too early to see Erica. She milled around for a
while, awaiting a more decent hour, and gravitated towards
the Down-To-Earth book shop where she forced herself to
read all the notices on the board: lifts to Melbourne via the
Karri forests, Ananda Marga study groups and close encounter weekends. Then she bought a copy of *Cactus* and determined to read it on the return flight and not tilt it to one side
for fear of someone reading it over her shoulder. It was
9.47 by her watch. A quick dabble with a Dinky Di to crown
a Down Under holiday.

Erica answered the door (which was open, only Minnie
had not mastered the Australian habit of entering without

knocking) in a shirt and hugged her a sleepy good morning.

— There's coffee in the kitchen, I'm just going to get dressed.

Min made coffee for both of them and took Erica's into her bedroom. She sat on the bed where Erica joined her, put a drowsy arm on Min's shoulder and let her head fall on Min's neck.

— I'm so sleepy, she yawned.

Why? thought Min instantly, had she been staying up late with someone else? It was pleasant sitting on the bed with Erica's head on her shoulder, Erica's hair brushing her cheek, but Minnie wanted some sign that it meant more than that. She had summoned up courage to say something, when Erica got up.

— Best be at it, she said, blocking what Minnie was about to say because she didn't think she could cope with it. You type, I'll write envelopes. Look at these names we collected yesterday, that's 50 more on the list.

Erica looked enthusiastic and flitted around finding pens, picking up envelopes, checking spellings and leaning over the typewriter, her hand playing with Min's hair. Min tried to work out what was going on.

— W-i-m-i-n's l i b e r a t i o n   l i b r a r y, L E S P A R, she tapped out, moodily.

— She does fancy me, I know she does, Minnie pounded the double spacer.

— Or do I just want her to?

— Minnie, you can't use words like "fancy" about another woman, Milly shrugged her shoulders at her alter ego's unrightonness.

— Pound, pound said the typewriter.

— A m a z o n   A c h e s, damn, got any Snopake?

— ? Oh, yes, it's called Whiteout.

Minnie tried not to search Erica's face as the latter handed her the bottle.

— Erica, it burst out of her, what's going on?

Erica took her hand,

— I like you a lot, Minnie, but I'm just not into it. If you were staying it would be different, you'd be part of what's going on . . .

Minnie extracted her hand to apply the Whiteout and bent over the machine to blow on the page. They both heard the

202

front door open and waited unmoving till the person appeared. It was Sky.

— Amazon Acres, she said, looking at the typewriter, that's where I was given my name. It's a lesbian commune, I went there to escape male reality. One night, I went out into the bush and all I could see was these stars twinkling down at me and this vast open ceiling.

— When we saw her next morning she said she'd had this beautiful, mystic experience and the goddess had told her to call herself Sky, Erica finished the story.

So Erica had been there too? Did that mean they used to be lovers? Minnie was just trying to work things out.

Thus it continued all afternoon as more women arrived to help, chat or drink coffee. Laura and Ingrid arrived together, neither quite sure what to expect.

— Hello, sisters, Minnie greeted them cursorily. Put these in alphabetic order.

Ingrid settled down to it, glad of something to do; Laura wandered round the house. The posters, books and magazines all reminded her of Min. But the three bedroomed house was quickly exhausted and she went out into the garden. She passed through an animated group of women, all older than her, and all apparently on the Women's Studies course at Murdoch.

Laura wondered how Ingrid was coping. Erica was obviously right into it, yet she'd seemed almost human at dinner. A cat brushed past Laura's leg. It was an ordinary cat, not a kitten, or Persian or maimed. Laura picked it up and sat in the sun out the back.

Erica, the flapping hostess, could see Laura was bored, so, summoning her social skills, she went out to say a few kind words.

— How're yer going there?

— Orright.

— Wanna take over the typing?

— Not really. Laura went right on stroking the cat.

— She's called Sappho, said Erica, wondering why she bothered; Min's little sister would never have heard of the Greek poetess.

- - They all are, Laura mumbled.

Erica didn't think she could have heard right.

— Nice, isn't she.

— Most boring cat I ever stroked, said Laura with a glimmer of enjoyment.

This time Erica was paying attention.

— World weary, tired, or just resentful? she asked.

— None of the above, said Laura, I'm jealous.

— What of? came the obvious question.

— You, said Laura directly, enjoying the effect she produced.

— Because I'm such a charming hostess? Erica rebounded quickly.

— That sort of thing.

Minnie was watching this interchange from the privacy of her typewriter, hoping Erica wasn't too bored. At last the stencils were finished and given to Francine to duplicate at WAIT.*

— It needs a name, she said as she tucked it into her bag.

— Perth Women's Newsletter, Milly suggested prosaically.

— Iskra, said Minnie. Flame of the revolution.

— Woemen, said Lilith.

— Wow, said Ingrid from the floor, wondering how long this would take.

— Women of the West, said Laura quickly, and Minnie typed it onto a stencil.

— You're the woman from London, aren't you? said Lilith to Minnie.

Minnie, seeing trouble, redoubled her efforts to put the typewriter into its case.

— Would you take some stuff back for us?

— Okey doke, what?

— Latest edition of Rouge and Sybil?

How long could this new spirit of co-operation go on for?

Sky rolled a joint as Lilith went off to get her parcel of subversive literature. Linda lit a cigarette and the others stared at the sky, trying to find the Southern Cross.

— It's getting late, said Erica, why don't you three stay here? We've got a spare room, and there's the sleep-out.

— Or there's my place, offered Lilith.

So Lilith had accepted her as a bona fide, despite her accent and her attitudes. Minnie felt pleased. Ingrid took out her tatty wad of bus maps.

— The last bus is in 10 minutes, someone will have to drive us.

* Western Australian Institute of Technology. (Ed.)

— Look, why don't you stay, it'll be much easier for you and Laura to get to work.

— Oh, but . . . mum will be waiting up, she was going to say, when she realised this was no longer a problem. She was glad that Erica had bothered to ask her, instead of leaving the decision to Minnie, but she felt tired and lonely and longed for her own little bed.

— Would you rather go home? Erica asked quietly, realising Ingrid had hardly said a thing all evening. In a way she wanted them to stay, to see that life in a woman's house might be chaotic, but it was warm and supportive. However, she didn't feel like crusading.

By their silence, Ingrid knew her sisters wanted to stay but were letting her decide. She felt overawed by Erica's friends and wondered what Simone would make of them. But she also wanted to know if all feminists were vegetarian and did they all eat their dinner on their knees? Furthermore she was intrigued by the house in Updike Street with its book cases made of floor board on brick, and it would give her something to think about back at Balga. Finally she decided the experience might be worth continuing and accepted it in the same light as she had church.

— I'll take the sleep-out, she said.

Minnie glanced, or tried to glance, but knew she was staring intently, over at Erica, to glean some information on why they had been invited to stay. Minnie was not a thighs and sighs person, but she still thought that if Erica was going to change her mind, she too could be persuaded.

Laura, playing it cool, remained hunched up on the back step, teasing the cat. She knew she was going to have to move some time, and here seemed as good a place as any. The first week-end she'd spent at Ingrid's she'd already been thinking about moving in (scheming, Moira had said), and trying to ingratiate herself with Beryl. Of course she completely misread Beryl's character and very nearly blew the whole thing. Now she had everything worked out. She and Ingrid would move into Updike Street, after all they had a spare room.

— I'll sleep in the spare room, she said, leaving Minnie the problem of which sister to share with.

Minnie, in her effort not to look at Erica, came to glance at her sister. Ingrid looked miserable, and fidgeted as though waiting for permission to go to bed.

— Poor little thing, thought Minnie, she doesn't know where she is.

Ingrid pressed her lips together. She wished she could either go to bed or cut herself a slice of bread.

— Let's have a cup of tea, said Erica, though Leeanne and the others were drinking beer.

Laura offered to make it, and Erica followed her into the kitchen.

— Only the back rings work, she said handing Laura a packet of nettle tea.

— Oh, hippy shit? said Laura nonchalantly. You don't scare me with your witch concoctions, I was brought up on lemon grass.

— Minnie, said Ingrid, as the other two fussed in the kitchen, I don't like sleeping in a strange bed.

To Minnie, Ingrid was nine years old again and frightened.

— It's alright, darling, I'll sleep with you and we don't have to turn off the light in case you wake up and forget where you are.

— I wish you weren't going, said Ingrid.

— Me too, said Laura, coming back in.

— And me, chimed in Erica.

Minnie cupped her hands round the mug to warm them, despite the hot summer evening.

— You must really like London to be going back after five weeks.

Minnie shook her head and gazed at the steam marks on the palms of her hands from the hot mug. Leaving made no more sense than coming. She wondered how it would all turn out: Beryl's life in the Heat; Life, Be In It, Norma, and Laura and Ingrid's part in it. There was this feeling in the air of something important happening that was lacking on the London scene where even the graffitti was dusty: "We won the Vote", "Women were angry", "We're voting Labour again this year". Ingrid cocked her head on one side, hands on hips and darted her eyes towards the door, as if to say,

— Come on, Minnie, bedtime.

The expression was peculiarly familiar.

— I never saw her growing up, thought Minnie, I was deprived of my own sister's childhood.

She looked around the room. It was Australian from the fly screens on the windows to the cement floor at her feet.

Even the ants on the wall told her she was not at home.

— Come on, Minnie, bedtime, called Ingrid, this time setting her gesture to words.

Minnie gave up the struggle, and as Laura said to Erica, she was already back in London two days before she left.

— Umm, Minnie, said a hesitant voice in her ear next morning, I think you and I should have a talk.

Minnie was preoccupied with wandering aimlessly from one room to the next, the only woman in the world with no obvious place to go. For a while she had thought there was something for her to do here, but now she was a passenger in a transit lounge watching a left-wing coup from the window; she could be pleased, but there was no reason for her to stick around. She tried to ignore the insistent little voice, but it started nudging her elbow,

— Listen Minnie, I'm not going to go away and leave you pitying yourself like this.

Sullenly Minnie turned round.

— Alright, what do you want?

— Well, said Milly, you're behaving as if you were about to throw yourself under a bus.

Minnie warmed to the idea.

— But it's no good, Milly continued relentlessly, I, for one, am not convinced. You chose to come here, and now you're choosing to go back because there are things for you in London that you don't have here. I don't know how you can talk like a feminist, and speechify about the personal, if you don't apply it to yourself.

Minnie wasn't listening. Her wanderings had led her to the spare room where she dropped down on the bed. On the floor beside her was an ash tray full of d.i.y. fag ends and an empty packet of Drum. Minnie stared at it. Laura didn't smoke. Either they belonged to a previous occupant or Erica spent the night there. Minnie picked up one of the butts and squeezed it between her fingers: it disintegrated obligingly. Methodically she picked up one after the other and threw them at the wall. They fell with a dull thud and waited quietly to be picked up and thrown away. Minnie tugged the pillow towards her and flung it away, together with the various books left lying within arms' reach. The cover of the Scum manifesto fluttered softly to the ground. Damage was minimal and easily rectified. Minnie looked around wildly for a more effective object. At the head of the bed was a full cup of stone cold coffee.

— Laura doesn't drink coffee, Minnie broke out, Erica should do her homework.

The cup hit the wall with a resounding crash and its contents trickled down, leaving a damp stain. The dark liquid collected in a pool at the bottom, obediently awaiting a cloth. Fury mounted in Minnie as it had in London, faced with the travel agent's cool impassivity.

— I'm not clearing you up, she screamed at the spilt coffee. Balls, she added, balls to the lot of you, and stormed out to the kitchen in search of Erica's bike. As she made for the street door, her way was blocked by the same irritating voice as before.

— I'm still here, Minnie, it said. Now, what are you doing with that bicycle?

— I'm going to throw it in the sea, said Minnie, panting with rage.

— That is the most ridiculous, puerile, vindictive thing I ever heard of.

— Don't care.

— Oh yes you do, and you know perfectly well that Erica isn't the point. You want to see this whole episode as a story of sibling rivalry and unrequited love because you can't cope with things on a wider scale.

— Stop pretending to know me better than I know myself.

— But I do.

— Well, if Erica prefers Laura to me, it's all your fault. You won't let me be spontaneous.

— I fail to see the relevance of that bourgeois individualist notion.

— And you didn't let me have a proper talk with mum.

— I didn't let you? She didn't let you. She didn't want to hear it.

— Oh Milly, what'll I do?

— Minnie, I don't know. Write to her.

* * *

The Rottnest Islander dipped and upped over the smooth sea.

— I wonder if the fish recognise me, thought Erica, I pass

208

the same waves ten times a day. On the first crossing there were only hardy fishers so she had time to herself. That talk with Laura last night had been good; she was glad she had had it, even though it meant she hadn't gone to bed till really late. Laura had been so cool, coming straight out with it; the way she put it, it would have been difficult to refuse. They did have a room in the house, and there'd been talk of getting more women in ever since she arrived. Would it work, though? having two straight women there? But then Laura wasn't really all that straight and Ingrid seemed very young. Erica paused to reflect before she went back down to rinse glasses. She had never met a family with such a strong sisterly identity: all so bristly and fierce and joking all the time so you were never quite sure what they were laughing at. She would like to have known Beryl. As Erica lurched round the deck, her face was sprayed by foam and Minnie flashed into her mind: Minnie at the party bopping away on her own; Minnie at the Infirmary, looking after Sky; Minnie at the women's tea, raving on about housing; Minnie conscientiously typing the newsletter with two fingers; and finally, Minnie sitting on her bed, fingers gently stroking her hair. If only she were staying; Erica could have worked with her, forced her out from behind her cryptic barrier into saying what she was thinking. Only when they were mending a puncture together did Minnie seem capable of putting one word in front of the other without agonising over what it all meant.

* * *

Minnie and Milly seemed to have reached some agreement, they had their arms round each other and Minnie was saying,

— At least they said they'd miss me, I couldn't bear to go and not be missed, it would have felt like I'd never come.

Milly nodded, thinking she didn't go a bomb on leaving Fran just as they were getting to know each other, but instead she said,

— Now, be a good girl and put Erica's bike back, and Minnie grinned in docile agreement that maybe it would be nice to see Kate again and catch up on what had been happening in Brixton.

Chapter 16
Four Letters

Min,

This came a week after you left but I've only just got round to sending it. Me and Laura have moved to Updike Street, so please write to us there. Oh, and Erica says "me too, me too", so you've got to write to her as well.

Byeeeeeee, Ingrid. + love x 1,000,000 (is that a million?)

Ayers Rock,
16th January 198-
My darling girls,

I do hope this reaches you before Min leaves. I felt very miserable leaving you all, you looked so forlorn sitting in the middle of The Markets, waving, like three itty bitty orphans. Anyway, pets, mustn't dwell on that. I do miss you, but I expect you're much better off without me.

(Well, thought Ingrid, not quite ready to concede this point entirely, at least there's no-one to say, milk coffee counts as eating, it's very fattening, you know).

We set out for Marble Bar as planned, to take a look at this garage and passed through places with the most gorgeous names: Yarra Yarra, Walkaway, Day Dawn and the Opthalmia Ranges. The roads were so bad (and this is the dry season) that we couldn't have done it without a four wheel drive and John being so clever with engines.

We were driving up a little hill, when John stopped the car and insisted we go on foot. I wanted to get to Meekatharra before night fall, but men like to have their little secrets. He led me up a ridge and told me to close my eyes. When I opened them again I was so surprised. Stretching for miles and miles was an enormous expanse of water, almost 400 kms inland, in that dry, dusty place. What was really unbelievable was that from where we stood, you could see the road going straight across the water, like Christ (or whoever) dividing the Red Sea. I imagined it must be built on a dam or something, but do you know, I was quite wrong. We walked down a ravine full of scrubby uprooted bushes washed there by the last rains, until we came to the water's edge. And there, well, my dear girls, the ripples I had clearly seen from the hill were none other than crystalline salt formations. 50 miles of dry salt, an inch thick, like ice on an English pond. It was like seeing the sea for the first time (I think). John stood there and laughed at me.

    — And yonder all before us lye
      Desarts of vast Salinity.

(Minnie mumbled the mis-quotation as she read).

Marble Bar was incredible, like standing in liquid heat. You let the air in through your nose and it seems like you're drowning, it has such a strong presence. You can feel the lining of your nostrils and the insides of your lungs — or perhaps that's just because I don't smoke. It would cure anyone of hiccups. I loved it, but then it took us a week to get here so we acclimatised as we went. John kept warning me about nervous lassitude and heat stroke and insisting I take salt pills as if I was a colonial wife in India, but I never felt better in my life.

The garage was rather a damp squib, I'm afraid. Mr Bolt's tenants were very sweet to us but horrified at the suggestion that they might wish to leave. I wouldn't have missed it for the world, but John started talking about lawyers. We had such a marvellous drive up here that it seemed ungrateful to complain.

(— What's she on about? said Ingrid.

    — Oh, you know Mum, said Laura, she's wandered off to think about something else. She means she had such a lovely time getting there, that buying the garage hardly seems the point.

    — Oh.)

Anyway, words were exchanged and there was a coolness, but somehow I persuaded John that we should make this the grand tour we'd been promising ourselves as we'd come so far already. We flew out in a tiny little plane which only had seats for 20 or so. John loved it, kept trying to work out speed, wind direction and height above sea level. Drove the pilot potty. Then he insisted on doing all the right things; hiring a car and going out to the Olgas, Ross Rover and the

211

Namatjira ghost gums, but it got a bit fervent and I was tired of boiled eggs. It felt like a job of work, getting up early, making a picnic (me) and poring over maps (him). I sat out the Standley Chasm and spent my day pottering about town. Low hills and a dried out river bed where they have an annual regatta rather like Henley only without the water, and lots of Aborigines sitting in gulleys in despair. Very touristy, every second shop sells plastic tribesmen with spears, second-rate paintings by son of Namatjira and water colours by budding Sydney artists. It gets rather depressing. There's the most grisly art gallery with a panorama of the area round Alice, all exact and measured, and so dull and lifeless. The women's contribution is by no means forgotten, however, there is even a statue to the Pioneer women.

(Minnie grimaced when she read this,

— That woman needs her consciousness examined.)

There was some interesting stuff about Aboriginal customs, but it's all so voyeuristic. They had the grass shoes worn by a tribesman who is chosen by the elders to follow a condemned man, till on the third day the man drops dead from fear. To impress upon the follower the importance of his pursuit, his little toe is dislocated. But they make it sound like a perfectly fascinating native oddity, as if people in England didn't throw themselves out of top floor windows on receipt of hundred pound gas bills.

(— Oh, all the time, muttered Minnie, cynically, daren't look out the window some days, lest someone falls on top of you.)

We saw some caves on the way up to Marble Bar with Aboriginal paintings on them: geometric animals in symmetric patterns; nothing like the paper bark rubbish with inky black boys and bounding roos the Europeans have them make. You can take a coach tour out from Alice round an Aboriginal township and gasp at the broken windows and gaping doors and the children sitting in the sand with the flies swarming over their faces, not bothering to brush them off.

— It's a waste of government money, these people don't appreciate the comforts of civilised living and look at the way they treat their children.

Oh, it's so ghastly, really, I don't know why I make light of it, I know I shouldn't. But there does seem to be more of

212

a mix here. We went to a rodeo the other day, and all the top prize money went to Aboriginals or half bloods. They mostly work on the cattle stations round here, which is at least a job, though I'm sure there's no union. It's funny to think I've lived in Australia five years and never really thought much about Aborigines, I mean you just don't see them in town; here whole lorry loads come swinging past with people clinging to the sides.

Well, I showed some of my embroidery pictures to one of the tourist shops and they think they'll sell, so I must try and persuade John to stay here a while. I already have quite a collection of bitties to make things with: paper bark and emu feathers and some nice pearl buttons for water, (doesn't look like I'll be using a lot of them).

(— But she doesn't say how she's feeling, said Ingrid as Laura read the letter.)

Sorry this is such a travelogue, I know Min hates what she calls my apolitical geography trip, but we all have different priorities. At the moment mine are never to work for another boss or wear another pair of shoes. I shall let the soles of my feet grow hard, and my bunions can grow old gracefully. I intend to be known as the mad, barefooted woman so people will leave me alone and when John tires of my way of life, he will move on without regret.

For the moment I'm at Ayers Rock, John thinks it fascinating. He's right about the rock itself, it's quite beautiful; throughout the day it goes from grey to yellow to brown, orange, red and pink. Yesterday I climbed it; the wind on top is something fierce, it caught hold of my raincoat and I thought it would blow me over the side. I was absolutely terrified, but I reached the top. The way up is littered with plaques to various people who fell off to a nasty death below. John stayed at the bottom and walked round the edge. The place is crawling with police, reporters and Aboriginal trackers at the moment as some unfortunate woman lost her baby to a dingo. One is very sorry for her of course, John even joined in the hunt, but goodness me all those people.

(— No sense of feminist solidarity, Minnie tutted, to think she managed to divorce my father and start again in Australia without gaining any inkling of feminism.

— Oh, come off it, Minnie, said Kate, as she looked up from the Guardian Women's page, only part of the paper she bothered to read,

— Those are amazing things for her to have done.

— But so simplistic.

— You're just jealous because she went off with John.)

So we're going back to Alice tomorrow. Write to me at poste restante, Alice Springs, NT. I would so hate us to lose contact.

All my love,

Beryl.

Brixton,

12th February 198-

Dearest Laura and Ingrid,

Thanks for sending Ma's letter, I hope she knows what she's doing. I'm sure she won't make enough money sewing samplers or whatever, but she does sound excited. I read bits of her letter to Kate, and she says it sounds like a wide-eyed school girl. It shocked me a bit too, the way she calls us "itty bitty orphans" and says "but I mustn't dwell on it", as though it was nothing to do with her and far be it for her to comment. Then I got embarrassed because I know my letters are often distant and tell lots of funny anecdotes as if I was writing for a newspaper. I wish she could say how she feels about us without thinking that means she's weak-willed. And the way she says "I would so hate us to lose contact", like we were people she met on holiday or something. I got very sarcastic when I read that part.

Well, actually, I burst into tears. Come to think of it, I've been doing that a lot recently. When I left you in the departure lounge, my eyes were too smeared with tears to read, but the last thing I saw before we boarded was an enormous poster for Prisoner, with Nora in her boiler suit in the background as though even government bill boards were slowly being perverted. I slept most of the flight because this bloke kept trying to peer over my shoulder at what I was reading. Not very liberated, me. Every time I put my hand in my pocket, my bag or my purse, I found a dotty note from one of you two. My favourite was "Don't despair, at least you won't meet your future husband on the plane". Whenever did you sneak them in?

(Laura and Ingrid chuckled over this,

— See, she didn't think we were silly.)

At Heathrow I hung around a while to see if Kate'd come to meet me, but I was quite glad that she hadn't because it gave me that bit longer to pretend I wasn't really in London. The tube journey was awful, everyone looked so pasty-faced, all going to work with grey skin, red noses and mounds of clothes. I kept thinking of the Stirling Bridge and the sunlight playing on the water by the jetty. When I got off at Brixton there was this plane flying low overhead and I burst into tears all over again. Everything felt so cold and awful, and I stood out because I was tanned. The sky seemed lower and darker than in Perth, like there was no escape.

I didn't go home straight away. Instead I wandered around with my pack on my back as if I was still a tourist, and stared at the Ritzy and the Tate Library and the enormous tree outside. Then I crossed over by the Phoenix and went back through the arcades, thinking the reggae would cheer me up and make me think of somewhere hot. You know, or at least Ingrid may remember, how on a Saturday you get the Evangelical singers and the whole gamut of WRP, SWP and SOLWAR touting their wares on the street corner? Well that day there was no-one, only rows of pig's heads dyed an awful pink and the tobacconist next to the record shop told me he hates reggae and doesn't smoke.

I trudged home via the dole office thinking of all the hassles I'd go through getting signed on again. The squats in Canterbury Crescent really hit me, they were so run down: those three storey houses with the cardboard tacked to the windows, the gutters coming away from the roofs and those great patches of green slime that tell you the walls are dripping with damp. And the wind was incredible; this icy draught seemed to pierce its way inside you and stab at your throat on the way down. Everyone was shuffling around in donkey jackets with scarves pulled up over their noses.

There must have been a blizzard earlier in the week because the wind had blown open the window in my room and there was unmelted snow on the lino. We'd run out of tea and coffee and the kitchen window had been smashed by kids on the estate. Oh yes, there wasn't any bog paper either.

(— She's revelling in it, said Laura.

— Leave off, said Ingrid, how would you like to live in

England?)

Then Kate turned up; she'd gone to Gatwick not Heathrow and seemed quite pissed off to have missed me. We stood there staring at each other and being awkward and polite until Kate noticed the torn up Guardian in my hand and said,

— I see you're coping admirably with the crisis.

We burst out laughing and clung to each other until I had to rush to the bog or I would have wet myself. Next day, though, I woke up with this splitting headache. I went downstairs for some tea and got as far as boiling the water and washing out the teapot before I remembered there wasn't any and no-one had got it together to go and buy some. I really wanted that cup of tea. It was crazy. I just felt that if I didn't get a cup of tea, I'd die. I clung onto the side of the sink and my head dropped into my arms. When I raised it again, I couldn't see. Well, not properly, anyway; sort of tunnel vision, and when I picked up the paper to calm my nerves, I couldn't read it. I tried to remember if I'd eaten any dope, because it sometimes has that effect, but my head just got worse and worse, and by the time I got upstairs to bed, there were bright lights flashing in front of my eyes. I kept hearing Mum saying "Now, Minnie, you'll feel quite different in the morning." But I didn't, I was really scared, like, was I going to have to spend the rest of my life in a darkened room? I felt like John Usher who could only stand the sound "of certain stringed instruments". I think someone was building a bed base and every time they banged the hammer, it went right through my head. When they had the brainwave of trying the electric drill, a thousand broken marbles sliced through the pink soft bits of my brain. I wished I could chop my head off. I kept remembering all these things I had to do, and that made it worse. After a while I was sick.

It lasted about 36 hours. Then the others got worried about me and walked me down the street to the doctor. I must have looked a sight. My hair was all over the place, because I couldn't bear to brush it, and I was holding my head on so that my steps didn't wrench it off. I think I looked like a druggy. The receptionist glared at me.

— What's wrong with her?

— Migraine.

— She registered with us?

— No.

— Squatter isn't she? Can't see her here. Take her down the hospital. That's right, put her on the bus.

It took another half hour to get to Kings. I couldn't believe it. At the hospital they fussed around me; put me on a stretcher, thought I had meningitis. Kept asking me had I been worried recently. Well I mean, I couldn't tell them about leaving Australia and mum going off and how cold it is here.

But I'm not just writing to tell you how awful everything is. I mean, I knew when I went to Perth that I wasn't going to stay there, and it was worth going just to have made friends with you two. Besides even though I won't admit it, I'm actually quite pleased to be back. Me and Kate are as thick as thieves again and there's a lot happening here in Brixton. Oh you know: setting up a South London Women's Centre, the People's March for Jobs, and we've just had a landslide victory on the GLC. Nothing you two would get high on, but I'm pleased. Or is that me being patronising again?

(— Yes, said Laura.

— But she is your older sister, said Erica.

— It isn't only older sisters that get patronising, said Ingrid.)

Newtown, 3rd April 198-
Dear Minnie-ha-ha,

Whoopeeeee! Made it to Sydney. And I've got a job, and I'm all in one piece. So Coles can take their varieties section and shove it up their remnants, every last variegated leaf. I'm working in a kindy in Leichardt Street, and there's as many pooey nappies as a chick could want. Erica winces every time I say "chick", but she daren't say anything in case it's patronising. I get away with murder.

Latest witticism: Erica, A woman without a man is like a fish without a bicycle. (yawn). Me, (a.k.a. Laura), Yes, if it's a red herring.

The house we're living in is a bit dilappidated (does that mean the hinges are wonky and there's no hot water?) Your squat reminded me of it, especially the bit about the snow coming in, only what we get is rain. Even the plastic

217

buckets are going rusty. But me and Erica use it to wash our hair in. We must have the most unpolluted hair in the whole of Newtown. Erica says I romanticise, and life is hard at the lower depths so I say after lemon grass, anything else is up and she feels guilty because she isn't of working class origin, like what I am.

(Minnie grinned, and thought of the shocking pink triangle they would have made if she'd stayed.)

Thanks for your letter, Ingrid sent it on to me, and I'm very sorry about your migraine. Perhaps you should move out — look how well I am on it. I haven't so much as curled in a corner for a month.

We (that's Erica and me) quite agree with what you say about mum, but Erica reckons mum can't talk to you because she taught you to speak. She and John are going to tour the north coast in about 3 months so me and E. will go and meet them somewhere.

In case you're worrying your hedgehog head about Ingrid, I had better tell you she's not only perfectly alright, she also happens to be one of Perth's foremost manicurists.

Anyway, see you soon, sweetie,

luv, Laura.

PS Erica wants to add a few well-chosen words.

Dear Minnie,

Just a note at the end of Laura's letter. I thought I'd let you know that the Australian Women's Underground is branching out in all directions. The Norma money came through and we were surprised to get as much as we did. I rather suspect Betsey B of possessing a tame senator, old family connection through the Presbyterian church. (Do you remember her? Amazing woman — went with the Australian delegation to the Copenhagen Conference, says she's only going so she can swim in the Baltic). Before we heard from Norma we started approaching wealthy women for money and of course that meant Blanche R-W. She said children weren't her priority and what about transport? So we challenged her to put her money where her mouth was and she and Lex have started a safe transport system for women. Sandra's signed up as a driver, says she misses the Kingswood and can't run one on what they pay her at the Markets.

That's about all really, only there's a move afoot to go

round Australia (Lilith says you made her feel parochial).
Meanwhile Laura and I are in Sydney; she said she wanted to
get away and I, well I spose it must seem very romantic to
you but I found Perth a bit difficult after you left. I kept
seeing you around the place and hoped it wasn't too late.
Sorry to sound excessive,
Love and Sisterhood,
Erica.
(Gosh, was Minnie's only comment.)

Perth, 12th May 198-
Dear Betsey,
  Sorry, can't get used to calling you that. Denmark sounds
exciting. I can just imagine you asking all your questions in
Scottish in support of minority languages. To answer your
letter first. No, I haven't taken up squash yet and yes, I still
eat as much as ever. Only I'm very busy so I have to gobble
things down or sit through meetings with a packet of lollies
in my pocket. All the girls at the salon went work-to-rule.
I couldn't image that lot taking strike action, but the cus-
tomers (led by your friend, Dorrie, of course) put their
foot down. If it said ten minutes for a perm, they wouldn't
budge till the time was up. You know Johnny used to have
copies of Dolly, Clio and Woman's World for you to read
under the driers? Well, Dorrie said it was a load of sexist
rubbish and refused to hear any of Johnny's arguments. So
he's subscribed to Rouge now, and the girls sneak a read of it
in their lunch breaks. Now let me tell you about the meet-
ings. In a way I started them, only it isn't fair really, because
I hate going to them. What happened was, when I moved
into Updike Street I couldn't put my uniform in the washing
machine, because there wasn't one, plus I didn't have the
money to buy a second uniform so I used to go to the salon
with a uniform that was two days old. I couldn't help it, it
wouldn't of dried and I didn't want to wear it wet. So one
day Johnny called me out in front of the whole salon and
said,
  — My dear Fran (he won't call me Ingrid because he says
the customers don't like it) a lusciously beautiful woman
with a model figure, long lingering thighs and the complex-
ion of a milk maid, might possibly get away with sweat
stains round her cuffs. (At this he grabbed hold of my wrists

and paraded them in the air). You, however, oh adolescent sack, are as lissom as a bucket and your skin would rival a moonshot for craters per square inch. Nobody said anything, but Simone came out and found me crying in the toilets and asked did I want to go down the pub with her and she'd buy me a drink. So I did and she said it was disgusting, picking on me like that and next day all the girls were talking about it. Which is when the meetings started and the work-to-rule and everything. I don't know what will happen in the end, but I said I didn't want to work with Johnny so I'm doing day release at college and they've started me on manicure.

Do go and visit Minnie while you're in London. I wrote to her and she says she does remember you and she'd be happy to see you again. Only phone after 11 o'clock on weekdays because that's the only time you're sure to catch her in.

Love From
Ingrid.

CACTUS by Anna Wilson £2.25

CACTUS is Anna Wilson's first novel. She writes with un-sentimental freshness about a subject not often described in fiction — illuminating an area of women's lives without pandering to old attitudes or propagandizing.

" . . . about two lesbian couples, one modern and managing to live in a society still fundamentally alien to them, one which broke up some twenty years before, mostly through social pressures. It is the least pretentious of books in terms of its subject matter (the women live in a small town, one keeps a greengrocer's shop) or of the statement it makes. This absence of artificial drama and the clear perceptions and skill of the author carry their own dignity."
The Guardian

" . . . at the end of it one feels as if one has just had a diffi-cult, tiring, sometimes argumentative conversation with a friend . . . CACTUS has an honest emotional power which makes you take seriously the unfamiliar experience of others."
The New Statesman

KINDLING: poems by Mary Dorcey £1.95

Irish lesbian feminist, Mary Dorcey gives us poems that are intense, accurate and witty. With characteristic clarity she describes both emotional and physical landscapes as well as political actions. Her passionate words about life in Ireland and about her experience of living in other cultures make this short volume an eloquent journal. This is Mary Dorcey's first published collection, though her work has appeared in feminist journals in Ireland, America and the UK.

" . . . this is a lesbian voice, adding to a contemporary lesbian culture which can know more, see further and feel more finely than the cultures which surround it . . ."
Gay News

BRAINCHILD by Eve Croft   £2.95

BRAINCHILD is a novel about breaking loose, about working class Ginny and the women she lives alongside and loves. Rejecting the security of existing roles — working class girl made good, wife and mother, hippy, career-woman — Ginny chooses the dole and drifting; failure for most, but freedom for Ginny.

Lively and humorous, the book follows Ginny's life from a rebellious childhood amid the extended family of run-down city back-to-backs, through the liberated era of sixties rock 'n roll, early marriage and motherhood to the joys and pains of single parenthood and living on the dole.

" . . . should on no account be missed. Stylistically adventurous (yet in such a way as to make the writing more, not less, accessible) it describes the life of its bloody-minded, working class anti-heroine with so much aggression, honesty and wit that one ends up, not merely liking her, but taking on board her eternally defiant, remorseless view of the world."
City Limits

" . . . an East End version of *The Women's Room* . . . enjoyably scathing about middle-class radicals."
The Observer

" . . . lean, elliptical prose, brazen humour, crackling dialogue and clear consistent regard of her characters . . . gleeful fury and self-assertion."
Gay News